ALSO BY D. J. BERSHAW

SISTERS IN ARMS SERIES

Other Blood

Blood's A Rover

Blood Tide

Blood Sisters

OTHER NOVELS

Saving Sophie Scholl

Guardian Angel

Oral Wars

Seen the Elephant, Heard the Owl

Damsel

2

ECO-FREAK

By

D. J. BERSHAW

Published by Sucker's Junk Press
P.O. Box 85
Lafayette, OR 97127

Second Printing, March 2020

ISBN: 978-0-9986796-5-5

Cover design by J. Kathleen Cheney
(jkathleencheney@gmail.com

This book is a work of fiction. The characters,
events and dialog are the product of the author's
imagination. Any resemblance to actual events or
persons, living or deceased, is purely coincidental.

ONE

Day death found Reckon in a shallow cave near the borders of the Mount Jefferson Wilderness. Awake, she sat in lotus position near the cave's entrance, sucking on a water bottle, her ears tilted toward the outside world. Through the screening brush, the last rays of sunlight fanned orange over a western ridge covered in young Douglas fir. The smells of resin and pollen saturated the cooling air.

Save for sleep-bound day life going to shelter for the night, the forest lay nearly silent. Soon the bats roosting on the cave ceiling behind Reckon would begin to chirr and fly for prey, to be joined later by other creatures of the night ghosting through the darkening forest.

All hunting.

Including Reckon. Hours earlier, the sound of chainsaws had penetrated her rest. From a direction where no chainsaws should be. Now a faint trace of bar-oil and two-stroke mix rode the light breeze passing in front of the cave entrance.

Something would have to be done about that.

She rose to her feet and stretched, her knuckles nearly touching the cave roof. Sticking the bottle into its holder on her hip, Reckon slipped out of the cave and moved smoothly downslope over the broken scree. A small stream burbled and purled in the shadows below.

First she would drink more, and fill her bottles.

Then she would hunt.

The Black Voice called, and she must answer.

TWO

Alexander Carson's adam's apple bounced in amazement against the neat knot of his black tie as he watched the video monitor screen. On it, a young, dark woman ran on a speeding treadmill, her gaze fixed in the middle-distance. She wore running shoes, black running shorts, and a black sport bra. A water tube dangled in front of her mouth. From time to time, without breaking stride or seeming to notice, she drank.

Carson swallowed to moisten his own throat. "How long can she do this, Doctor?" he asked Maureen Sims, who headed the Reckoning Project.

"We ran her for five hours once, at the treadmill's top speed, until a bearing over-heated in the bogey mechanism." Sims paused, blanking the screen, and wiped her wire-rimmed glasses on her white lab coat. "This run we made just for the video, so you could see her face better. Usually she had oxygen-exchange tubes in her mouth, and function patches taped all over her. Don't get me wrong, she can -- and *does* -- fatigue. As long as she has water, though, that wolverine-like metabolism will work. Helluva food bill, however."

Carson nodded. "Why a woman? And why *this* woman?"

"A woman blends in better. Men aren't inclined to be suspicious of women, except when the reproductive apparatus is involved. And we chose her for three reasons. First, she was a street kid, strung out on amphetamines and worse, half brain-fried, with no one to look for her and no one to care. Second, she's tall. We needed shoulder width and arm and leg length for leverage points. And third, she has black hair and brown eyes. I wanted her to be as dark and monochromatic as possible. Easy enough to adjust skin tone for a vaguely Native American look that doesn't show up at night, but even I can't change hair and eye color."

Carson laughed. "So there are rules for playing God?"

"I won't have the luxury of starting from scratch like the biblical creator for a few more years, Mister Carson," Sims replied, her smile sardonic. "My team did, however, make a six-foot, one hundred and twenty-five pound drug-slut into exactly what you ordered. And then some."

"She certainly doesn't weigh a hundred twenty-five now," Carson said, recalling the video.

"One-seventy at maximum hydration. But let me show you what she looked like in the beginning." Sims keyed the video again, and a second screen lit up. A pasty emaciated skull stared out at Carson, eyes fever-bright and sunken, pupils constricted. The huddled scarecrow body and limbs beneath were wrapped in filthy too-large clothes.

"Migod," Carson gasped, his voice barely audible.

"A little dose of reality, Counselor," Sims chuckled. "I know lawyers like you enjoy that on occasion, even though it doesn't pay as well as massaging files and orchestrating courtroom antics and protests involving endangered species."

"May I remind you, Doctor," Carson said, an edge to his voice, "that those 'antics' have enriched you and your firm by several million dollars."

"Well, *vielen Dank*, Herr Carson," Sims replied, smiling down at the seated lawyer from where she leaned against a conference table. "And please understand that I have some sympathy for what you're trying to do with Reckon. I voted for Citizen Ralph and Big Al, I don't want any trees cut or roads built in Wilderness Areas, and I definitely think humanity could reduce their numbers by two-thirds or more. But that's it. Most of what your people do to further your causes sort of turns my stomach. All those little old blue- haired ladies writing letters and sending their stock dividend checks..."

The seated lawyer gave her his most indulgent smile. "So you'll frown all the way to the bank, eh, Doctor Sims?"

Sims' pale green eyes glinted behind her glasses. "Let's not get too smarmy and self-righteous, Alex. I've seen what the tree-hugger bigshots make. You serve on a lot of boards and committees, plus you're first up in the batting order when the wood products people mount an objection to your efforts. Large dollars, my friend."

This was not an avenue of conversation Alexander Carson wished to explore. He changed the subject. "Perhaps we should see the remainder of the development video."

A fleeting expression of amusement crossed Sims' round features. "Fair enough," she said, and pushed the button.

Carson spent the next fifteen minutes watching the subject of the Reckoning Project in a workout room or running through a forest, leaping streams and chasms, and climbing trees like a squirrel with its tail on fire. Image after image of incredible physical feats, one following another in rapid succession. Through it all, whenever Reckon's face was on the screen, Carson kept seeing that earlier skeletal ruin superimposed over the healthy young features.

How was such a thing possible? A total physical resurrection.

At the tape's conclusion, the lawyer looked at Sims, trying to think of something to say that didn't show how impressed he was. He coughed, stalling, and saw Sims' amused look surface again. "What exactly did you do to her?" he asked finally, ignoring Sims' smirk.

"Not to put too fine a point on it," Sims replied, "but we rebuilt her from the inside out. Some of the new nanotech stuff -- carbon fiber bone reinforcement, strengthened muscle attachments, super-induced lungs. Trick cells that promote oxygen transfer, accelerated healing mechanisms, other things you see only in movie special effects -- not in the real world. She can bench-press close to a ton, and dead-lift well over. You've seen her run and jump." Sims sat back down on top of the table, crossed her arms over her chest, and regarded Carson levelly. "Now ask me how her head works."

He hadn't thought of that, though he should have. To realize that things he thought of as in the realm of science fiction were at least possible at the experimental level had been bad enough. "*Could* you modify her attitudes? And how much of her old life is still in place?"

"Good questions," Sims replied. "She'd blown most of her old life right out of her head. We backgrounded her before we brought her in. Eighteen years old, a dropout, originally from Kelso, Washington. Parents divorced, mother works in a convenience store, dad an ex-jock druggie. We let her keep what basic memories she had left -- school and stuff like that -- made up some other things to fill in the gaps. Then we established an ecological moral code to your specifications. Programming, I'd guess you'd call it."

"Will she do what she's told?"

"Oh, sure, depending on how you mean that. She will do as her conditioning dictates. She will take some risks, but won't expose herself foolishly. And you should know that she *will* evolve. For the first time in her life, she is a stable and well-

9

adjusted individual, largely able to think for herself to arrive at the ends she must. She will mature *very* rapidly, I suspect. Past that point, she is beyond predictability. Like a new-born child, in a way. What we have now may not be even close to what we see in six months."

Carson frowned. "I'd hoped for more certainty, Doctor," he said. "She *will* protect the environment, won't she?"

"Yes, but we aren't talking Smokey Bear here, Counselor." The tall biologist laughed. "Unless, of course, Smokey were to start hitting people with his shovel. Do you read *Outside* magazine at all?"

"On occasion. I'm a busy man."

"Did you ever happen to see Tim Cahill's column on the successor to Smokey -- when the Forest Service decided to replace him with some other spokescreature?"

"No, I don't believe so," Carson replied, searching his memory.

"A pity. Cahill suggested replacing Smokey with Rodan, the giant Pterodactyl from Japanese horror films. He even worked up a projected public service ad, where Rodan swoops down on a camper who doesn't put out his fire properly. The closing scene has Rodan perched on a rocky peak, picking at something held under his claws. A tad less user-friendly than Smokey."

"What's your point, Ms. Sims?"

"Just this, Mr. Carson." Sims' eyes flashed again. "Reckon is a lot closer to Rodan than she is to Smokey."

"That's quite all right, Doctor." Carson rose to his feet. "I believe I've seen to it that you and I and our associates are standing well outside the hot zone on this, whatever may happen. But you should destroy that video disc, just as a precaution."

Sims nodded. "My thought. Only makes sense. We have funding in place for her maintenance. It's early May. The fan should start feeling the impact of the shit very soon."

Blood rushed unbidden to Carson's face. "Please don't tell me she's there already, Doctor." Damn Sims! She was entirely too independent. He forced his voice to remain steady. "Why didn't you clear that with me?"

"You were 'unavailable,' Counselor, and I couldn't exactly leave a message, could I? If you have any concerns, save them for the good folks in the little town of North Cedar, on the North Cedar River. They're going to need it."

THREE

The long bar in the Green Chain Bar and Grill had developed some clear places in the last hour or so. Harley Dilts looked at his watch and rubbed his eyes with a grimy knuckle, trying to clear his vision. North Cedar on a Monday night might not be the best action spot in eastern Ross County. The two or three women who'd been in the place tonight had been your basic 'closing time' girls, all workers from the day shift in the little peeler-pole mill the Schirmer family ran on the river side of town.

Harley felt a pang of envy that the Schirmers had managed to stay financially afloat when the loss of government trees had taken down most of the little family timber operations locally. Junior Schirmer and his old man had sold off all but the bare bones of their woods equipment, and set up the peeler mill to provide evergreen and hardwood veneers. Their good fortune still pissed Harley off.

The little mill ran three shifts year-round, though, and that and a couple of other woodlots and gyppo operations were all that stood between the townspeople and poverty. And the tourists. Harley raised his half-empty mug at the thought of the tourists, bitter though he was at the way the yuppies, motorhome snowbirds, and flatlanders looked down their noses at the Cedarites.

Some of those mountain biker bitches surely had nice-looking butts, though, he had to admit that. Harley licked the stubble on his upper lip in appreciation. Legs as smooth and hard as polished maple, yesirree. You had to wonder what it'd be like with those wrapped around your head.

That pleasant but unlikely fantasy sustained Harley through the rest of his mug of Henry's. Then he remembered his watch, the probable time, and the self-loader full of logs waiting on a skidroad up in the National Forest. Pushing his empty mug away, Harley spun on his barstool, slid off, and went over to the pool tables to find his brother. From the look on Lamar Dilts' long face, he'd lost a sizeable portion of the money he and Harley had boosted out of hikers' cars the past weekend. The trailhead on the end of Peckerpole Creek Road had been a bonanza for the past few summers. A man with a lockpunch and a brass mallet could make a good living popping Volvos and sport-utes.

"I *suppose* you done lost all your beer money?" Harley asked, grinning as he sidled up beside his taller brother.

A pool cue in his right hand, Lamar grinned back. He still had most of his front teeth, unusual for the Dilts clan. "Yeah," he replied, "but I made it last so's I could ad-mire the tits on that one ugly girl while she bent over the table."

"Jesus," Harley said, shaking his head. "We gotta find somethin' better to do with our lives."

His brother regarded him with pity. "Well, it's a sight better'n makin' foam animals in your beer, bro."

Harley knew Lamar had a point. "I 'spose," he said, grudgingly, holding his watch up under Lamar's nose. "Time to be gettin' that load of logs down to Three Forks. Uncle Ed's expectin' us around midnight. He said he'd stay up 'til after Letterman."

Without responding, Lamar racked his cue and resettled his current favorite baseball cap over his crewcut. After years of long hippie-style hair, Lamar had recently gotten it all cut off. In a town that had spiritually never left the fifties, the youngest of the Dilts brothers had rejoined the flock.

The two men sauntered out of the tavern, and climbed into Lamar's green 1955 Chevy pickup. Harley reluctantly let his brother adjust the bath towels he kept draped over the seats. "You been at this thing again?" he asked, once they were in the truck with the doors shut.

Lamar nodded vigorous assent. "Sure looks nice, don't she?"

For a moment, Harley could only look at him. "For God's sakes, Lamar, it's a goddamn *truck*. Your *room* ain't this clean!"

"A man's gotta have some pride in somethin'," Lamar said stubbornly, setting his jaws. "It ain't like I can take my tallywhacker out and wave it at people, ya know."

On that point, Harley subsided into his corner of the seat and shut up. He didn't want to re-open the tallywhacker issue. It had been bad enough when they were small, and their folks had made all the boys line up out by the three-holer for inspection.

Except for going through a couple of flat saddles, the road wound uphill on a steady grade, passing a few recent clearcuts that had been re-planted just this year. A half-hour found them driving between two stands of large second-growth fir, about three miles from the west edge of the Wilderness. They'd dropped a dozen good-sized dougies along the margin of a month-old cut, snaked them up onto their dad's old Reo log truck with the self-loader, then stashed the rig. This soon after a cut, chances were good nobody'd notice that a few extra trees just outside the cut boundary had disappeared, and, if they did, they'd go after the timber company who'd bid the sale. The brothers nabbed about a truckload a month during the nicer weather. Even after a fifty-fifty split with their uncle, it came to about seven hundred apiece per load for Harley and Lamar.

14

Nice money for maybe four hours work, including gas and travel time.

Lights off, Lamar eased the Chevy along a moonlit two-track, trying to avoid scratching the gleaming paint. Harley kept hoping that Lamar would drag a dry branch over the hood or down the sides, but no such luck.

Eventually, the narrow road opened into a small clearing. The Reo stood in the moonlight, its blunt hood pointed toward them.

A woman sat on top of the truck cab, grinning at them, long bare legs dangling down on the windshield.

"What the *hell*?" Lamar said, which pretty well eliminated this being someone he knew.

The brothers slowly got out of the Chevy. Lamar kept darting looks into the black forest depths around them, but Harley couldn't see this being any sort of Forest Service entrapment, something his brother always feared. Maybe pot growers, armed to the frigging teeth, ready to blow them away while they were distracted by this girl. Nothing else made any sense.

Both of them had small-caliber automatics strapped to their ankles, just in case, but had never had to use them. Watching the woman, uneasiness crawled down Harley's spine and settled in his gut, and his fingers itched for his pistol. She didn't exactly seem to pose any overt threat. Something about her just made him jumpy.

"This your truck, boys?" she asked, her voice low and husky. Her T-shirt, shorts, and boots were all black, and she was so dark that only her eyes and teeth were truly visible against the brown Reo.

"What if it is?" Lamar responded. The two men stopped about fifteen feet from the Reo's grill.

"Yes or no," the girl said teasingly, grinning even wider, her boot heels thumping lightly against the windshield's glass.

"Yeah, it's ours," Lamar admitted, with an 'aw, shucks,' tone in his voice.

Her smile *changed*. Harley knew for certain Lamar had given the wrong answer, and a brief shaft of regret lanced through him.

That regret lasted the rest of his life.

FOUR

In deference to local habits, the Dew Drop Inn served breakfast only on weekday mornings, except during hunting season and the Opening Weekend of fishing. Things had thinned out considerably by eleven o'clock, when Sheriff Virgil Merrill levered his long body out of his patrol car and slumped into his favorite booth in the corner next to the john. A short ton of paperwork needed to be done at his office, but that could wait for breakfast and coffee. He set his empty Thermos on the table, and watched the street outside without -- at first -- really seeing it.

A few heads had turned when Merrill entered the little restaurant-bar, but the sheriff wasn't known as a great talker, so the questions in the patrons' minds went unuttered. Voices subsided for a minute or two, then resumed as a low muttering.

Merrill ignored them.

Charlie Wamic, the Inn's owner, was nearly as taciturn as the sheriff. Patriarch of a Native American family which had somehow wandered off the Warm Springs Reservation a couple generations back, Charlie brought out a steaming cup of coffee and slid it in front of Merrill.

"Mornin', Virgil."

"Charlie."

"Omelette?"

"Sure."

Wamic vanished into the kitchen, the sheriff's Thermos in hand, and Merrill returned to contemplating the street.

As he watched, a full-sized black and white Chevy Blazer with the State Police Game Warden emblem pulled up behind the sheriff's brown Chevy Caprice patrol car. Behind the wheel, he recognized Greg Dickson, one of two local game wardens, and definitely the one Merrill would prefer to deal with this particular morning.

Merrill's tofu omelette and traditional green tea appeared before Dickson made it to the sheriff's booth. In fact, Merrill was halfway through the omelette when Greg finished answering all the "where they bitin'?" questions from the table of local fishermen near the door. Then Dickson chatted with Charlie, who'd gone back to the cash register after bringing out the sheriff's food and Thermos.

The game warden even had a few words with Flathead, the Dew Drop's resident cat, sprawled next to the cashbox. Merrill considered that both brave and foolhardy. Flathead, a wide, long-haired brute of vaguely Siamese coloring, possessed paws the size of beer coasters and the disposition of a mean drunk. Most times, Charlie kept a small custom sign reading 'Don't Irritate the Cat' on the counter, but at some point Flathead had made the connection between the sign and the dearth of victims. The sign had disappeared over the side regularly since then.

The sheriff heard the cat rumble threateningly, then Dickson's squawk of pain, then Charlie picking the sign off the floor and slapping it back onto the countertop.

A nice healthy dose of normalcy.

Merrill needed that today.

"Damned cat," the game warden said, sucking on a finger as he appeared beside Merrill's booth.

The sheriff grinned up at him. "Interestingly enough, Greg, my memory just flagged the fact that Flathead nailed you a couple weeks ago. The statute of limitations on slow learning runs out at just about your age, doesn't it?" He gestured at the

18

opposite bench. "Sit. We need to talk, and you probably know about what."

Dickson sat. "Yeah. I went in overnight to Spire Rock, didn't get back to the rig until about nine this morning. Your office radioed and said you were here."

"So, how's the pot crop coming?" Merrill knew he intimidated the warden some, because of his size as much as anything, and tried to keep the conversation light before they got down to the real business.

"Not bad for May. Most of the smaller family plots are already planted. Rumor has it that we might have a big former Eastern Block operation going in just east of Skunk Meadow. Heavy foot traffic on the trail going by there, then suddenly next to none. Usually means something large."

Merrill nodded, and took a sip of tea. "Been what, three years since we had anything out that way?"

"Three or four. I've still got a shed full of infra-red detectors and trip-wire gadgets from the last one. None of the federal agencies ever came by and picked the junk up."

"The feds still have their uses, though. One of their ever-efficient pot planes spotted the Dilts' old Reo around six this morning. Blew the whistle. I hustled right out there, then called in the County Coroner." Merrill looked down at his plate. "You had breakfast yet?" he asked.

"Sort of. Some trail mix and energy bars after I broke camp this morning." Dickson looked uneasily at the sheriff's omelette. "I'll hold off 'til lunch."

"Charlie does a heck of a job with this tofu, Greg. You really oughta try one. 'Heartwise,' you know. Can't start 'bein careful too early."

"I'll pass -- this time, but you *do* look pretty healthy."

19

"A whole bunch better than the Dilts' boys, that's for sure."

Now the warden looked even more distressed. "How bad was it?" he asked, keeping his voice down.

"Grim. Ever hear somebody threaten to rip someone's head off and piss down their neck? That pretty well sums it up."

"Must have been a bear?" Dickson asked, his face paling.

"Nope. I suppose a bear *could* tear someone's head off, but I've never heard of it. No claw or teeth marks, either. Whatever it was just grabbed on and yanked." The sheriff began to mop up his omelette residue with a piece of dry toast, but kept his gaze on Dickson. The warden's performance record on gore tended toward the pukey side.

"What about tracks?"

"Sorry you asked," Merrill replied, leaning back in the booth. "The late Harley and Lamar, true to their bloodline, parked the Reo more-or-less right out in the open, in a small meadow. A herd of elk meandered through on their way up to higher ground before I got there. Pretty much nibbled and trod everything. Didn't do anything to the bodies. Their heads, maybe. Heads were seventy feet away."

As he expected, Dickson had begun to look a little green. But the kid rallied well, and asked, "You've had thirty years' experience in law enforcement in this area. What do you think killed them?"

Merrill thought in silence for a few seconds. He couldn't find a good reason to hold back on Greg. Finally he rested his elbows on the table, and attempted to look as serious as possible. "I don't ever want to read what I'm going to tell you in one of those supermarket tabloids, but I'll give you my off-the-record opinion, and I think the coroner will

20

say the same thing. Greg, whatever did this didn't have paws or claws. It had *hands*. When I say their heads were yanked off, I mean exactly that."

Now the warden looked truly distressed. Probably figured that whatever did in the Dilts brothers could cross his path almost as easily. Dickson might be kind of a New Age granola, with his tidy beard and all, but he did a good and considerate job. He had a wife and two well-behaved kids. In a movie, Merrill reflected, Greg'd be about number three to get killed.

"Could they have been knocked out," Dickson asked, "then some kind of machine used to...do it?"

"You mean some kind of lever-operated gizmo with clamps?" Despite the context, the sheriff found that amusing. He grinned at Dickson's hopeful expression, wondering briefly if the warden read too many horror novels. "Sorry on that one, too, Greg. Both Dilts had finger bruises on their shoulders, and the flesh of Harley's neck was indented. I think Doctor Cameron'll make the same conclusion, and I hope to hell he couches it in medical terms and the press never gets ahold of it."

His eyes distant, the young warden said, "'The Sasquatch Murders.'"

Merrill grunted, shaking his head. "Christ, you had to go and say it."

"Sorry." Dickson managed a tentative smile.

"Don't be. If they exist, and I truly can't say one way or the other, probably you're looking at a gentle, reclusive creature. The Northern Spotted Owl of the primate world. As my son the engineer used to say, 'that doesn't compute.' Although I suppose Harley and Lamar -- or any other Dilts -- could piss off even the Pope." He looked at his watch, and put his hands flat on the table top. "I need to get the initial paperwork done on this, Greg. By the time that's taken care of, Doc Cameron

21

should have drawn some conclusions. I'll give you a call, okay?"

Leaving a ten dollar bill on the table, the Sheriff recovered his campaign hat, slid out of the booth, nodded to Charlie and Flathead, and headed for the door. Dickson trailed after him, speaking to people, but thankfully not stopping. As the door swung closed behind them, Merrill heard Flathead growl. He wasn't sure, but he thought it might have been a 'come again, sucker' growl.

Out on the quiet street, the sheriff adjusted his hat while scrutinizing the traffic. Two blocks away, to his left down the gradually sloping street, cars, trucks, and logging rigs flowed by on the state highway. Up the street, a dark green Peterbilt diesel tractor crawled slowly up into the forested hills, a John Deere loader chained securely on the lowboy trailer behind it.

Satisfied that no one was close enough to overhear, Merrill said quietly, "Make sure you keep your .357 handy, Greg, and maybe a speed-loader and a spare box of shells. Let's assume what we have isn't a Sasquatch, but it might be a speed-freak mountain loon who spends a bunch of time in some weight room. The Dilts both had weapons on 'em, with no indication that they tried to draw."

"Amphetamines can allow amazing feats of strength."

"True, but I put my hand on the bruises on Lamar's right shoulder. *My* hand was bigger than the killer's. Not much of this adds up, so when you're out there alone, keep your eyes open and your wits about you."

Dickson nodded absently, looking up the street, his attention caught by something beyond their conversation. The sheriff followed the younger man's gaze, took in the tall, dark woman striding toward them, wearing hiking boots, a black T-shirt, and six-pocket shorts.

"Will you *look* at that?" the warden said, quiet awe in his every syllable.

"Don't even give it a thought, boy," Merrill replied, as he glanced over the top of Dickson's head, trying to keep a straight face. "You're a married man."

She wasn't much, if any, over twenty, despite her height and relaxed manner. She grinned broadly at Dickson, displaying teeth brilliantly white in her tanned face, apparently finding his open-mouthed appreciation funny.

"Morning, Sheriff," she said, shifting her attention to Merrill. She slowed as she said the words, and toned her smile down a bit. Out of respect for his advanced age, the sheriff figured.

He tipped his hat, returning her smile. "Mornin', Ms. Rikka," he said.

"I enjoyed that book you recommended," she said, stopping. "In school, I didn't have much time to read fiction. Maybe you can point some others out to me next time we see each other at the library?" No trace of flirting sounded in her low voice. Her chocolate-brown gaze was totally sincere. But Greg Dickson didn't know that, and looked as though his blood pressure had suddenly doubled.

"Sure thing," the sheriff replied, tipping his hat again.

"See you then," the young woman said, and walked away. If you could call it a walk. That seemed a very inadequate term for what took place when she moved. Large cats moved like that, unhurried and unstressed, every muscle synchronized with every other.

"Nice young lady," Merrill observed dryly, watching Dickson out of the corner of his eye.

"Who is she?" the warden managed to stammer.

"Name's Rikka Thorsen. Graduated college end of winter term at OSU, biology major. Story is, she inherited a house up on 4th Street, plus a little money, and is kind of letting her wings settle in before she takes off for the rest of her life. Most evenings I'm at the library, so is she."

"What book did you recommend?" Dickson asked, running his right hand down over his face and pulling lightly on his beard.

"'Her Pilgrim Soul,' by Alan Brennert, a collection of short stories. Some very nice work."

"You have *time* to read?"

"Sure," Merrill said, nodding sadly, "since Deb's gone, I've got more time than I know what to do with. Oh, the kids call, and sometimes we get together, but basically I'm on my own."

His avid gaze still following Rikka Thorsen's progress down the sidewalk, the warden said, "I could think of something you might try."

The sheriff laughed. "No, I don't think so. Not only am I nearly three times Ms. Thorsen's age, old enough to be her grandpa, but inside I'm still married to Deb. We met in college, at Oregon. Married at the end of my junior year, in 1960. Forty years this year. She just died before our time together was up, is the way I look at it. *Five* years early at this point."

The expression on Dickson's face, visibly moved, reminded the sheriff of the man's basic decency, how that human touch made such a difference in Greg's line of work.

"Uh, I'm sorry," was all the warden said, but it was enough.

FIVE

After Dickson had driven off, on his way to his office upriver at Ross Forks, near the fish hatchery, Virgil Merrill sat quietly in his patrol car and shuffled the papers on his passenger seat, straightening things up a bit. He didn't want to look like he was going to the re-cycling center when he carried the armload of paperwork into his office.

He probably shouldn't have mentioned Deb to the warden. Greg would say something to Keely, his wife, and they'd have the sheriff over to dinner, or invite him to a New Age potluck, or somesuch. A tall, lean man with a very greying red crewcut and 'law enforcement' practically written all over him would be real out-of-place in such surroundings. Though Keely Schirmer-Dickson could cook up a vegan storm.

Merrill sighed and started the Caprice. Maybe he was more lonely and troubled than he thought, turning into a sensitive New-Age guy. That'll be the frigging day, he thought, chuckling out loud as he nosed the Chevy out into the street.

He glanced briefly at the windows of the Health Hovel, the local organic food co-op and health food emporium. Rikka Thorsen had gone into the little store while the sheriff talked to Greg Dickson. There was no sign of the tall girl inside the etched-glass windows, however, but Merrill guessed she might be bending over a soybean bin, buying in bulk. He'd seen Rikka eat a few times at the Dew Drop, and thought the kid must have the metabolism of a shrew. He also remembered that she'd rubbed Flathead's tummy and scratched behind his ears -- and gotten away without a mark on her. The big beige and cream monster had even purred.

Still, her cat skills aside, Rikka Thorsen was an enigma in a mutating populace of aging re-tread millworkers, shiftless hippies, Type A New-agers, conspiracy-theory nutcases, and yuppie entrepreneurs.

For one thing, she didn't exist. At least, not as Rikka Thorsen.

If his youngest daughter, Maryanne, hadn't been in the PE Department at Oregon State, he would never have discovered that fact. When Rikka began to turn up at the library, and her odd combination of direct innocence and street-smarts had manifested itself, the sheriff had questioned the librarian about her. Oregon State and Biology, the woman said. Seeing Rikka move, plus her size, Merrill had called his daughter, asked if a girl named Thorsen had played any ball.

Maryanne had checked. Not only had she never been in any of the sports programs, no one named Rikka Thorsen had attended the school in the past five years.   Then he'd snagged a teacup that Rikka had used in the tiny tea bar in the audio-visual section of the library, and run her fingerprints through the state and federal ID scans.

And discovered Ricky Jo Mullin, eighteen-year-old runaway and street child, booked for drugs, petty theft, and prostitution in Portland over a four-year period running from early 1995 until late 1998. Last arrested in December, 1998. First arrest -- age fourteen. Born 22 July, 1980.

The accompanying booking photographs had shown a horribly-altered, malnourished, and pale -- but recognizable, barely -- Rikka Thorsen. Her cheekbones looked as though they were about to split the skin over them, and her brown eyes were the flat color of mud. What intelligence lurked in those images was strictly animal, with no detectable soul.

Pleased that he'd uncovered a real mystery, the sheriff had next put the name Rikka Thorsen through the Department of Motor Vehicles. Another hit. A driver's license for Rikka Lynn Thorsen had been issued in January of this year. Tested in southwest Portland. Vehicle registration listed a white 1998 Jeep Cherokee -- the lower-priced squarish model, but 4WD -- purchased without financing from Bob Lanphere's in Beaverton one day after her driver's license test.

So he had started paying attention to Rikka's comings and goings, keeping track at a very low level. Mentally noting where he saw the Jeep or its long-legged owner. Not going out of his way, and never following her. Paying attention, too, to what she perused in the library -- she read more than he did, and she hiked and walked a lot, into the Wilderness, over the National Forest, and across Willamette-Cascade's private holdings.

To date, no discernable pattern had surfaced.

Rikka did own the house she lived in, though, a well-taken-care of bungalow that had -- he remembered -- been re-modeled last year after its owner died. And the taxes had been paid up through this tax year. He'd checked with the County. She spent a fair amount of time in her tidy yard, too. He generally tootled his horn at her if he saw her out weeding and planting.

That last thought sort of made Merrill think about just who he *did* honk at when he passed them in their yards, and the list his memory produced certainly contained no one in Rikka Thorsen's age group. He decided he was just being paternal -- though at some level he understood Greg Dickson's reaction to Rikka. Even five years after Deb's death, however, he was damned sure he wasn't ready to explore that level. Not that Rikka'd be interested in some old codger.

Which left him wondering again who had plopped the newly-minted Rikka Thorsen in their midst. Probably not the Department of Interior -- in this case the Forest Service or the Bureau of Land Management -- since those particular feds generally let the local law enforcement people know what was up. Generally, but not always, so they couldn't be ruled out entirely. He wished he had some decent contacts with their local or regional offices.

Maybe the DEA, who viewed much of the Pacific Northwest as a pot-head's playground, but they'd probably send one of their own home-grown agents, not some ex-streetie sweetie.

Maybe the Witness Protection Program, but her age argued against that likelihood, though it would explain the new name and identity.

Which left origin or origins unknown.

Merrill just couldn't imagine it wasn't the feds, though. It was the only thing that made sense.

During his musings, the sheriff had cruised slowly in the general direction of his office. He knew that Doc Cameron must be close to finishing his reports on the Dilts brothers. The old ghoul was likely unwrapping a sandwich from his lunch, setting it on Lamar's skinny dead chest, and taking notes on what appeared under his ultra-violet strobes. Cameron was a bruise-freak of the first order, and Virgil Merrill had a pretty good idea how the Dilts were going to stack up on that score.

Right near the top.

SIX

Rikka Thorsen sat on the toilet in the bathroom of the Health Hovel. Her arms were folded, resting on her knees. Shaking all over, she watched herself in the full-length mirror on the opposite wall. Her weak smile was tinged with triumph.

The Black Voice had risen when she approached the sheriff and little bearded officer wearing shorts. It had boiled through the bottom of her mind like blowing ashes, hating the sight of uniformed authority.

She had beaten it back, forced it to subside, and given the two men no idea of the battle taking place within her. In fact, Rikka thought, with a hint of smugness, she had carried it off rather well.

Doctor Sims had said this would happen, that she would change and learn in her new surroundings -- that she must, or the Black Voice would destroy her.

Rikka believed Sims. Sims had saved her.

Rikka had no illusions about what would have happened to her if Sims' recruiters had not taken her. Her memories, jumbled and fragmented though they were, were frighteningly clear on that. She had welcomed the needle Sims' people had offered, let the bliss well up through her body and carry her into the darkness. That was an escape she could understand.

Thinking about it now made her shudder.

Now the needle tracks had vanished with the rest of her scars. Her skin was smooth and unblemished. Even her navel had disappeared.

It had been winter then, before Christmas; Rikka was certain of that. She had truly come back to herself in the late winter, and much of what appeared in her mind as the seasons greened had been sharp-edged and new.

Like the seasons, Rikka had been reborn. The workouts started at that point. Doctor Sims laughingly told Rikka she'd been conceived in the weight room and delivered on the treadmill.

The Black Voice had urged her on. And kept pushing, ruling her existence, eager for completion, even more eager to begin its mission of protection and retribution. It had carried Rikka with it, street jetsam borne on the crest of an ebon wave.

Now she had beaten it, if only a little. The grip of its possession had loosened. The psychology books at the library had implied that such things were possible, though they didn't address anything as complete and pervasive as what had been done to Rikka. The rules and parameters of the Voice, the things she *must* do, those weren't in the books.

Of one thing Rikka was certain, however. The Black Voice wanted all of her, wanted her life totally, body and soul.

In the mirror, her smile strengthened. She brushed a drop of sweat off the end of her nose.

For the first time, she had won.

SEVEN

"Virgil, I *still* have to turn in paperwork on this," Doctor Fred Cameron said, exasperation and frustration filling every word, as he faced the sheriff across his well-ordered pressboard and maple veneer desk.

"I know, I know," the sheriff replied, popping the knuckles of his big freckled hands. He'd come in right at the end of the Dilts' autopsies, then helped the semi-retired physician tuck the corpses into body bags. The two men had rolled the wheeled gurneys away into the "mostly-cold room," as the doctor referred to the temperature-modified walk-in freezer he used for both decedents and perishable evidence.

Cameron practiced three days a week in a small clinic set on a hillside near the east end of the little town, and had been appointed Deputy County Coroner for the east county. The doc liked his work, the locals considered him a god-send, and the sheriff considered him a friend.

"It's the Sasquatch thing," Merrill continued. "What you've written is nice and non-commital, but both our reports have got more 'if-ands-or-buts' than a lawyers' convention."

"Can't be helped," the doctor replied, shrugging. "The Dilts boys were murdered by something or somethings unknown, and the absence of tooth or claw marks would seem to indicate an absence of teeth or claws in the assailant. There aren't many ways to disguise that fact, Virgil."

Scowling up at the slowly-rotating ceiling fan, Merrill sighed. "Oh, some jerkwad reporter will get a copy of your report from county records, then mine. Next day, they'll be on our doorstep, asking damnfool questions and speculating as to what supernatural critter did in a pair of ne'er-do-well timber rustlers."

"Let's have a drink," Cameron suggested, opening a side drawer and bringing out a bottle of Jack Daniels Black and two neatly-wrapped glasses. As he poured, he grinned at Merrill. "It had *hands*, Virgil. I know you noticed that."

The sheriff nodded. "Smaller than mine, but not much."

"But so strong as to defy the laws of bio-physics. I've got a forensic anatomy program on my computer, courtesy of the State of Oregon. I ran the thicknesses, muscle mass, soft tissue percentages, and spine densities through, fudging a little on the last, and the numbers came up about three times as powerful as even a very large male."

"They have examples?"

"Yes. No human on the planet could do what this -- 'person' -- accomplished."

"Even on drugs?"

"No way," Cameron said, the modern term sounding incongruous coming from a man older than Merrill, even one wearing a bright red-and-blue aloha shirt. "The limit is bone strength, Virgil. Human bone is stronger than many metals, but -- and this is the big item -- even with drug-fueled muscles, no human forearm bones could come anywhere near to taking the load necessary to rip someone's head off. Not even close."

"Oh, swell. Frigging space aliens, then."

"Malevolent space aliens, with small hands and large bodies." Cameron laughed. "And the really interesting part is that there were no significant torsional sheer forces. This was a direct pull, not a twist. The required effort may not have been anywhere near the limits of what strength was available."

"This just gets better and better, Fred," Merrill replied sourly. "Maybe I need to set a loaded shotgun by the front and back doors at home. And get a dog with the same disposition as Charlie Wamic's cat."

"There are damned few dogs as intelligent as Flathead, I'm afraid," the doctor said, "but that's a good direction. Perhaps a phone call to Roger Corman or Wes Craven, too."

"Who're they?"

"Horror movie directors. Either one of them could give you some suggestions, I'm sure. Or offer you the film rights."

"Don't get too cute and morbid with this, Mister Coroner. Just because the first feeding was at the bottom end of society's food chain doesn't mean that the next one will be. Not that it makes one damn bit of difference under the law. Harley and Lamar Dilts were citizens, after all."

"Not too many to mourn them, though," Cameron said, taking a healthy slug of his whisky.

"I called their Uncle Ed, gave him the news. He'll claim the bodies when the time comes."

"Now's as good as any. My work with the subjects is complete."

"What're you going to tell the press, Fred? And there *will* be press, you know."

Cameron slid his chair back and propped his feet on his desktop. "I think I'll just say that the boys had a falling-out during a speed session, and did each other in."

"Sort of the ultimate jerk-off?" the sheriff chuckled.

The coroner shook his head in mock disgust. "Don't you *ever* call *me* morbid again, Virgil Merrill," he said, smiling in appreciation.

33

EIGHT

A handful of dust, Reckon thought, as she scooped her cupped right palm into the trailside pumice. Evelyn Waugh had written that novel, she remembered. She'd worked her way through the North Cedar Library's small selection of English novels a few weeks ago, and fallen instantly in love with Waugh's dark humor. His characters were frequently as helpless in their situation as she was.

Then she corrected herself. As she had *been*. She would defeat the Black Voice and learn to control it, no matter how long it took. Her hand closed on the pumice, grinding it in on itself, pulverizing the fine granules even finer.

The high Cascade moon, four days short of full, shone down through the evergreen canopy, dappling the remaining patches of disintegrating winter snow lumped beside the narrow trail.

In the near distance, a sliver of moonlight sparked off a thin strand of wire strung between the brushy manzanita bordering the trail.

Bingo! thought Reckon. And now the nightwork begins. She removed a pair of lineman's pliers from the pocket of her pants, put on her gloves, and walked very slowly toward the gleaming wire strand. Her vision worked well on a wider-than-normal human spectrum, and Sims had given her a reflective *tapetum lucidum* layer similar to that of cats. Darkness slowed Reckon not at all. She could even pick out colors.

Gently bending back the manzanita at one end of the wirerevealed a foot-long black tube clamped onto a length of half-inch rebar driven into the soil. Reckon carefully gripped the short spring-loaded lever-arm that activated the firing pin, immobilizing it, then broke open the breach.

Nasty little thing, she thought, looking at the end of the enclosed shell as she released the lever. The firing pin struck empty air, and Reckon twisted the little homemade shotgun's barrel until the pivot broke. She stuck the shell in her pocket, cut the wire and put it with the shell after rolling it into a ball.

There were definitely too many military veterans in the pot trade, she decided, as she continued down the trail, moving north to south. How many deer got killed or badly crippled by these evil little devices? she wondered. Maybe not that many, maybe even none at all. The average deer was wary, traveled with all senses alert, and probably would see the trip-wire.

An hour later, nearly midnight, Reckon had disabled seventeen of the shotgun devices along the picketlines around the sprawling group of newly-planted pot patches. She had left the infra-red mechanisms in place and functioning. Now she checked the laces on her hiking boots. In her mind, a diagram of the trails and the locations of each infra-red device appeared. She intended to trigger as many of the things as possible in a five-minute period, then lie in wait somewhere in the middle of the perimeter and see who showed up.

There had been a camp of workers around the periphery of a creekside meadow on the northern edge of the growing area. Reckon had stood in the darkness a hundred yards from the little groups of cigarette-smoking men, where they sat around tiny fires playing cards and drinking. Whatever they were speaking, laughing softly in the night, it hadn't been English. In fact, it didn't sound like *any* language she'd ever heard.

Not that language mattered much with what Reckon had in mind. She fingered the hilts of her new knives hanging below each armpit, smiling to herself. Blood gurgling from a cut throat was a sort of universal language, she supposed.

The language of death.

Deep within her, Reckon felt the Black Voice begin to murmur in urgent anticipation.

That, she could deal with.

NINE

As he jogged through the night, AK-47 cradled in his arms, Ruslan Golubchik thought about how much he hated James Fenimore Cooper. Not the actual personage of the famous writer of frontier Americana, but his depiction of life in the wilderness.

As the big Ukrainian frequently told his compatriots, Cooper's writing was "total bullshit." His own childhood in the Carpathian foothills had taught him that much, and that part of the world was far less wild than this rough, lonely, lava-strewn land.

But their bosses had made the Ukrainian recruits read translations of most of Cooper's Leatherstocking Tales, to prepare them for the 'rigors of wilderness.'

Typical ex-Communists, Golubchik thought, as he slowed his pace to a more cautious walk, his gaze probing the moonlit forest with night-vision goggles. His bosses believed everything they read about America, or saw in the movies. He'd spent three years fighting in Afghanistan, and had found that most of the information they'd received there had been bullshit, too.

But when the perimeter warning screens had begun to flash in Major Berunius's tent ten minutes earlier, that had not been bullshit. Hard to decipher, yes, but real. The Major had been of the opinion that only one person or animal had touched off the alarms, and Golubchik reluctantly agreed with his assessment. Except that nothing human could move that rapidly in this terrain, covering a nearly a kilometer of periphery in less than four minutes. Logic then dictated that at least two or three people had to be involved. A quick check of the circuitry had revealed no malfunction, so Golubchik and several others had been sent out to check.

A pain in his ample ass, he felt, but necessary.

The perimeter lay just ahead, and Golubchik paused, swinging his lensed gaze very slowly from side-to-side, his rifle up and ready. Putting one foot in front of the other, he tried to keep his footfalls from crunching in the dry trail surface.

In Fenimore Cooper's world, he thought, glancing down at his feet, the deep forest was a minefield of twigs, and at least one waited for every moccasined foot, be it friend or foe, villain or hero. Sooner or later, the author's snapping dry twigs either alerted or betrayed everyone.

Total bullshit. He crouched down to examine the infra-red beam. A red light flashed dully on the receptor's surface. He reached into his jacket pocket for the key to restore the system to readiness.

Behind him, a twig snapped.

TEN

Body bags all in a row, Virgil Merril thought, looking at the row of silent encased corpses.

The scene in the small clearing, mist swirling up from the moist, sun-warmed earth was far too reminiscent of Vietnam for Merrill's comfort.

He scanned the pale blue sky, half-expecting to see a Chinook helicopter slipping over the tall old growth to make a pick up.

No such luck. The feds would take everything out by mule or burro, uprooting the young marijuana plants and placing them in bags not so very different from the ones occupied by their late caretakers.

More bags -- neatly-folded empty fertilizer bags -- lay stacked by what must have been the command tent, to judge by the amount of electronic gear inside. Merrill walked to the tent, sticking his head through the opened flaps.

"Aren't you done yet, Fred?"

The coroner didn't bother to look up. "Shouldn't you be helping with the pack animals, Virgil, or aren't the mules here yet?"

Cameron had forgone his usual bright clothing for a set of stagged-off denims, field boots, and a green wool shirt. A red-and-black-checked Filson jacket hung over the back of his collapsible chair. A man about the coroner's age sat to his right, dressed similarly except for a lighter weight wool shirt with a tie. He shuffled through a stack of Polaroids. Two cameras, one with an extensible ruler attached to its underside, lay on the table before him. The pictures were arranged by stacks. The close-ups seemed to be on the right.

"You ever meet Bill Alexander in your travels, Virgil?" Cameron asked, still not looking up.

"Bill's a dentist down to Eugene. Forensic Odontology's his hobby. Doesn't look like we're going to need him. These birds all had their Green Cards real legal and proper, the FBI says."

Alexander swung round in his chair and shook the sheriff's hand, smiling warmly, his eyes small behind thick glass lenses surrounded by wire frames. The dentist's grip was strong, his hands surprisingly large for a man his size.

"Nice, slick little operation they had here, Sheriff," Alexander remarked. "Very military."

"Sure was," Merrill agreed. He indicated the Polaroids. "Could I have a look at those?"

"Oh, I don't see why not." The dentist handed him the first stack. "Careful not to mix them up, though."

Each photograph had a label on the lower right corner, with the exact distance between physical landmarks noted, and the location of anything associated with the cause of death below that. Merrill whistled.

"I think I see why Fred asked you on board, Bill," he said. "You're one hell of a lot neater and more thorough than he is."

"Well, I'm used to working in a smaller area -- and I don't have those hideous shirts he favors to blind me."

Merrill poked Cameron on his right shoulder. "You should listen to your fellow health care professional, Fred."

Cameron waved him off. "Let me do my paperwork, Virgil. Just look at the pretty pictures. You can rag on me later, on the way back to town."

Alexander and the Sheriff exchanged glances and shrugged, and Merrill returned to the pictures of the bodies.

Greg Dickson had found the death scene during his duties, drawn by the circling vultures. When he'd quit barfing, he'd pulled out his cellular and called Merrill, his own office, and then the Forest Service. The Forest Service had phoned the FBI in Portland, who were extremely quick to respond to a situation involving foreign nationals.

In fact, the investigation proceeded rather smoothly, once the Forest Service had convinced the feebies that they couldn't chopper into the scene because it was located in a Wilderness Area. Now there were a whole lot of dark-suited guys and gals with thoroughly destroyed black shoes, excepting a couple of the female agents who'd had enough sense to wear Doc Martens. Lava was not kind to leather.

When Merrill and Cameron had arrived, slightly ahead of the feds, the bodies had still been in a pile, and Greg Dickson had been seated inside the command tent, unhappy and incredibly green, his head practically between his legs.

The local fauna, including apparently as many vultures as the game warden had seen at once, were happily feeding when Greg had first walked into the clearing. Probably that had set poor Greg off more than the bodies themselves.

Even with a certain amount of physical attrition, however, the cause of each and every death had been easy to ascertain.

Slit throat.

Some of the necks had been damn near cut through, O.J.-fashion. And the amount of automatic weapons fire had been high. Shredded brush and lines of ground pocks were everywhere. There looked to have been a lot of blind-firing into the darkness. The battle had to have been at night. Ten pairs of assorted night-vision equipment lay heaped by the bodies, right next to the stacked automatic weapons.

Like the camp, the killer had been orderly.

41

The fifth picture showed the first recognizable handprint, and, after a few more views of different corpses, it was obvious most of the bruises were made by a left hand. Every print looked virtually identical, and Merrill realized that there must only be one person involved.

How in the blackest and hottest hell a single person, with only a knife, could take out a dozen heavily-armed men confounded the Sheriff. Eventually, at least some of them had panicked, but that must have been near the end. Up to that point, they must have been picked off individually, from behind, in the darkness. Even in the sun-warmed tent, in broad daylight, Merrill felt the hairs on the back of his neck lift. A human being who killed so quickly and silently during a one-sided firefight -- with the losers overwhelmingly better armed -- seemed impossible.

But it wasn't. And, to make things even more mysterious, none of the bodies had been dragged to the pile. All had been carried, some of them were large men, and the ones near the top hadn't been the smallest.

After finishing the photographs, Merrill thanked Bill Alexander and went back outside. The feds, he had to admit, watching them go over the area, were amusing. The FBI people, familiar with crime scenes, were methodical and meticulous, setting up grids and searching carefully. The Forest Service personnel, accustomed to counting birds, fish, and maybe salamanders, spent most of the time being in the way. They would gather in little knots, twittering nervously, then, when some FBI person came close, bolt off to a safer spot.

The FBI agent in charge, a lean and laconic Indian named Paul Vizenor, seemed satisfied with the way things had proceeded thus far. Merrill admitted that reading the man was difficult, though.

Vizenor's face and eyes were narrow and inexpressive, kind of like Lee Van Cleef, the actor who'd appeared in so many spaghetti westerns.

"Any conclusions?" Merrill asked the agent, when he reached the man's side.

Vizenor gave the Sheriff a sidelong glance. One corner of his mouth quirked up in what might be interpreted as a reflex smile. "No more'n two people involved, even though the deaders had a lot of firepower. We'll bag the weapons, dust every smooth surface, but my guess is that we won't get any good prints. Anybody talented enough to whack this many people using just knives is gonna be smart enough to wear gloves."

"Any thought on motives?"

"No. These good folks were all Ukrainian, all single, been here about six months, worked in the Willamette Valley during the fall and winter, apparently came up here when spring arrived. All their equipment is ex-Russian Army, and I'll bet they are, too."

Merrill nodded. "Good money to be made selling dope. Might be they had a turf conflict with another group." As he spoke, the Sheriff tried to think of a good reason to mention the Dilts brothers and the extremely high probability that the same person that did them finished off these Ukrainians. He decided to let it go for now.

The FBI man mulled Merrill's words over for a few moments. "No reason to use knives here, out in the middle of nowhere." He gestured to the area around them. "This had to have been one hell of a firefight, and *nobody* noticed any of it. All due respect to my revered ancestors, but 'Native American Spirit Revenge' works about as well for me as anything else. Nobody I've ever seen could do what apparently took place here."

"What tribe are your people?" Merrill asked.

43

"Chippewa. And French-Canadien. Trappers and explorers. All of my great-great grandparents likely were pretty familiar with canoes. My folks have some amazing century-old family photographs."

"Nice to have that kind of record."

"Yeah, but I doubt it's going to do me much good today. Looks like it'll be 'person or persons unknown.'" Vizenor's mouth quirked again, and about a nano-second's amusement flickered in his brown eyes.

"You willin' to send me your findings when you get the lab work done?"

"Certainly. And if you hear anything, or come across a similar case...?"

"Oh, sure. No problem."

"Good." The agent's dark face slanted up to the late morning sun. He shielded his eyes from the glare with his right hand. "The DEA should be here before noon. I called their Portland office, but characteristically, they were a bit slow off the mark. They were involved in breaking a marijuana operation in here a few years ago, the warden said?"

"Well, mostly it was Greg Dickson -- the game warden -- who provided the information and set up the operation well enough so that the DEA couldn't screw it up."

Vizenor laughed, a tight, controlled, choppy sound. "I hear you, and that seems about right from my experience."

"Lots of eager young people in the DEA," Merrill observed.

"Lots of eager young people everywhere in the FBI, DEA, and ATF, and most of 'em seem to be Mormon."

"Hard to do undercover work when you look like you just got your knot-tying badge at Boy Scouts."

Vizenor shrugged and did his quick grin again. "Nice kids, take orders well, work like the very devil, just need some seasoning."

"If this business goes on," the Sheriff said, "they'll be making *me* take on another deputy or two, 'stead of relying on the little local police forces, and west county overlap from our main office in the county seat. Probably be nice young kids." He shot the agent a smile. "'Course, you seem like a nice kid, too."

"That's sure true," Vizenor agreed, not grinning this time, but still managing to look tickled. "You're pretty observant for an old guy, Sheriff."

"I've had plenty of that seasoning you mentioned."

"So what do you think went on here?"

"Well, I saw a disabled booby trap or two on the way in, and some infra-reds that had been triggered." Merrill took off his campaign hat and ran his right hand over his bristly scalp. "My guess is that one person foxed their tripwires, set off the infra-reds, then waited until someone came to investigate."

"Picked 'em off one-by-one?"

"Looks that way, 'til the last, when they began firing at random into the night. Then I have no idea what went on."

"*One* person?"

"Oh, yeah." Merrill nodded emphatically. "You seen the pictures Doctor Alexander took, yet?"

"Not yet."

"Every identifiable bruise that shows on any of the photographs is a portion of what appears to be the same left hand. From the size -- smaller than my left hand -- I'd say the individual is around six feet tall, medium build, and apparently possessed of supernatural powers."

Vizenor looked around the big meadow. "Four of them died here, two just inside the trees over there." He pointed to the northern edge of the clearing. "Another pair to the southwest, and the rest as singles, I suspect we'll discover."

"Sounds about right," the Sheriff agreed.

"The last four had to be almost back-to-back. Nobody I've ever seen could take down that many people in that short a time without getting pretty well shot up themselves. It just isn't possible."

"Apparently it is," Merrill said quietly.

Vizenor's brown gaze turned thoughtful. "That's what scares me."

ELEVEN

By mid-afternoon, the sheriff and the coroner were halfway back to the state highway, their end of the investigation finished. Bill Alexander had gone home via the Clear Lake Cutoff in his own rig. Alone now, Merrill and Cameron could talk freely.

As he drove, Merrill watched the fast-moving rapids of Whitewater Creek, visible to their left and below the road. Still swollen with run-off from the winter snow, and probably stay that way for another two-three weeks, the sheriff estimated.

He looked over at Doctor Cameron, who sat with his eyes closed and hands folded across his lapbelt. "You awake, you old fool?" he asked.

"Of course," Cameron replied, without opening his eyes. "Physicians never sleep. We learn that as interns. I was just thinking that if the murder scene had been another five miles south, somebody in Wynn County would have been responsible for the autopsies."

"I'm not certain we'd want that, Fred. Much as I hate the responsibility, we've lost fourteen people in the last ten days. Probably the lid just came off the situation, and, since that's the case, I'd just as soon you or me or Greg had the honors of dealing with the press."

"The feds'll have a press meeting in Portland, trying to explain how twelve oh-so-legal Ukrainian nationals just happened to get themselves killed during illegal agricultural activities."

"Then it'll be our turn, I imagine," the Sheriff replied, his gaze on the sun-drenched stretch of gravel in front of his Caprice.

"An *official* press meeting, you mean, Virgil. The kind you and I will have -- initially. The *other* kind will be held with Uncle Ed Dilts, Charlie Wamic,

Earl Pogue at the Shell station, or the man or woman on the street, whoever'll talk to the reporter from the *Star*, *National Enquirer*, or *People* magazine.

"Ed Dilts won't talk to anybody unless they pay him, but I get your meaning," Merrill replied.

Cameron sat up and moved his seatbelt into a more comfortable position, tugging his shirt down as he did so. He looked out the window at the passing foliage. "Maybe I could get enough for an exclusive interview to buy more modern equipment for the clinic."

"Naaah, then you'd just have to work harder. Wouldn't have time to fish with me."

"Virgil, your idea of fishing is to hike twenty miles through gawdawful terrain, and *occasionally* throw your line in the water."

"Okay, then donate the money to the paramedic unit down to Flint Lake."

They sat in silence for a few minutes. The gravel road widened, and Merrill knew that the highway was no more than a minute or two away.

"It was the same person, you know, Virgil," Cameron said.

Merrill nodded. "Yeah, only with knives, and right-handed apparently."

"Insanely fast, inhumanly strong, and maybe invulnerable to automatic weapons. I counted eight empty clips on the ground.

"Eleven altogether. The feds found three more up toward the north."

"Who's next? A Brownie troop?"

"No, I don't think so. Two incidents don't make a pattern, but the victims seem to be people who don't respect the forest, or who use it illegally. And, so far, it's been just federal lands, but I doubt that's a consideration."

"Only at night, too."

"Yeah, but the Dilts boys were in town until about ten that night, drinking and playing pool at the Green Chain, so they weren't up there until after dark. And these Ukrainians -- well, that was probably to allow the killer to move around freely, to have the advantage of darkness."

"Not a vampire, then?"

"No," Merrill replied, grinning, just as the highway came into view. He gently depressed the brake pedal, glad that police model Caprices had better suspension than the civilian models. He hated any sloppy unsteady feel in gravel. "Agent Vizenor did say that 'Native American Spirit Revenge' was as good an explanation for those twelve deaths as anything else," the sheriff continued, still smiling.

"There *is* something very awe-inspiring and spiritual about forests in general," Cameron said, as the Caprice halted by the highway, "and the Wilderness is even more so. It's not hard to believe that there might be some protective entity looking out for the welfare of the land."

"Well," Merrill said, pulling out into the westbound lane, heading back toward North Cedar, "if that's the case, let's hope nobody else pisses it off."

TWELVE

Though he told himself he wasn't nervous, Alexander Carson's fingers shook as he fumbled open the manila envelope from Doctor Maureen Sims. He'd recognized her printer font the moment he saw the front of the envelope.

Inside were two newspaper articles cut from *The Oregonian*. A post-it note stuck to them bore the simple message: 'That's our girl!' Carson smoothed the folded articles out on his desktop, and carefully read every word.

When he'd finished, he removed his glasses, laid them on his desk, and pinched the bridge of his nose between thumb and forefinger. He took a deep breath and held it. When the urge to shout his elation subsided, Carson fed the articles, Sims' note, and the envelope through his paper shredder, then leaned back in his chair, eyes closed, and considered what he'd just read.

Fourteen people! *Twelve* at one time. True to her word, Sims had created the ultimate human predator, but Carson still found it almost impossible to believe. If the article about the Ukrainian pot farmers was correct, hundreds of rounds of ammunition had been expended trying to stop Reckon, and she'd killed them all anyway.

How many Reckons would it take to save America's old-growth forests? Hundreds, Carson imagined. The cost per unit would go down, obviously. Reckon had been hideously expensive, but now the technology was in place. Each additional creature would cost less. If they could get the figure down to perhaps a quarter-million for each one, then their clandestine budget would easily handle two per year.

The larger problem was that this was a success that couldn't be used for fund-raising. No one could be told of the existence of something that killed to protect the environment. The funds would have to be quietly shifted and dispersed, coming together again only in Maureen Sims' lab and the bank accounts that kept Reckon fed and housed.

There were two additional considerations. Once the word got out that people who violated the forest eco-systems came to grim ends, probably fewer violations would occur. Perhaps only a few dozen Reckons would be enough. That would be a plus.

On the minus side, though, would be the finite supply of suitable candidates for Reckon-hood. It had taken weeks to find the lost child that became Reckon, and months more to finish the process.

Sims had also told him that she had limited resources for background creation, nothing like what the government could accomplish. Money could take one only so far. A truly thorough check of the new name Reckon had been given would find glaring omissions. Birth certificates, driver's license, and Social Security numbers were not difficult to fake, but the pre-Reckon street person had almost certainly had a police record, and Sims' people couldn't eliminate that.

Carson opened his eyes and regarded the telephone sitting on his desk. Perhaps he should set up a meeting with his opposite number with the Planet Prime! organization. That admittedly radical group of monkey-wrenchers had their fingers on a different part of society's pulse, and they knew and were willing to do things that the more moderate environmental groups he represented would not.

Of course, he mused as he reached for the phone, his funding of the Reckoning Project had, in one long step, completely gone beyond the worst things that Planet Prime! had ever done. Tree-spikings, booby-trapping recreational vehicle trails, and sabotaging road-building and logging equipment were small beer compared to wholesale murder.

And he was enjoying every minute of it.

THIRTEEN

There was a certain art to trail-building and trail maintenance, Walt Whitaker told himself, as he brushed sweat out of his eyes. He shoved his three-foot Johnson bar under an oblong boulder the size of three basketballs, and pried. The end of the rock slowly raised out of the lesser rocks and pumice in which it was embedded. Keeping the bar in place with his left hand, Walt stuck his gloved right hand into the crack alongside the rock, and rolled the boulder free.

Five minutes later, he'd positioned the rock, plus three others already laid in place, on the downhill end of a six-inch thick ten-foot section of a winterfall Lodgepole pine. The tree spanned the trail diagonally, half-buried in the soil, its upper end wedged tightly between a truly huge boulder and a still-standing Lodgepole.

Walt stood and surveyed his work, increasingly aware of the rising temperature. May could be warm in the high Cascades, even at nearly four thousand feet. He peeled off his Moose Gore-tex riding jacket and tossed it over the handlebars of his XR 250 Honda, parked at the base of the slight incline where he constructed his first water bar of the day.

Brushing the sweat away again, Walt began collecting fist-sized rocks, packing them against the uphill side of the fallen lodgepole. He started at the lower end and worked slowly and steadily toward the opposite side of the trail, crawling on hands and knees.

He didn't see the tall young woman standing by his motorcycle until he'd finished with the rocks and was getting up to unstrap his folding shovel from the bike.

She wore a black T-shirt, olive six-pocket shorts, and Nike hiking boots, the company's swoosh grey against the black boots. Twin water bottles hung from her hips, their strap around her waist, with a large folding knife inside a leather pouch attached to that.

Suddenly aware of his sweat, general grubbiness, and short stature, Walt still managed to smile up at the dark stranger. "Good morning," he said, running a hand through his white hair in an attempt to look more presentable.

She folded her arms across her chest, a faint frown on her features. Finally, after a short silence, she said, "Good morning," giving Walt a slow smile that gradually erased the frown. She still looked puzzled, though.

"My name's Walt Whitaker," Walt said, extending his hand.

"Rikka Thorsen," the woman replied. They shook hands. Walt felt calluses that matched his own.

"What are you doing?" Rikka asked, hooking her thumbs in her belt.

"Making a water bar. This's a fairly new Off-Road Vehicle trail, and a few water bars to deflect rain and snow run-off will keep the trail from rutting up. Mountain bikers and motorcyclists come in all sizes, shapes, and skill levels. The more experienced will go around the bar on the upper end, and not damage it at all, but some of the lesser lights will go directly over the top and eventually a slot'll be cut." He shrugged. "Usually those aren't too hard to repair. I try to catch them before winter."

"And *you* ride a motorcycle to do this?"

"Well, it gets me from town to here in a jiffy, I can carry my tools, and I don't have to hike between where the work is." He looked fondly at the little Honda. "I bought her five years ago, when I retired

54

from the post office. She gets me where I want to go."

The young woman -- Whitaker thought of her as a kid -- walked slowly around the bike, taking in the big muffler and all the trail tools, and briefly touching the little Homelite chain saw in its holder over the front fender. She looked at Walt, her grin much wider now. "I didn't know people did this sort of thing -- working on trails, I mean."

"Most motorcycle riders who've been around for a while are pretty conscientious. The young kids, well, we need to stick a two-by-four through their spokes once in a while. And the mountain bikers are a whole different breed, but even they're coming around -- gradually."

"I see," Rikka Thorsen replied. She gestured at the half-built water bar. "Do you need some help?"

In a lifetime spanning seventy years, Walt Whitaker had worked with dozens of people characterized as "hard workers," or maybe "good workers."

He had never run across the likes of Rikka Thorsen. She could out-work anyone he'd ever known.

While Walt sank eighteen-inch lengths of stabilizing rebar against the lodgepole, Rikka handled the grub-hoe and shovel. Ordinarily, a single water bar was a labor of three hours or more, but a half-hour later they were finished.

Walt lay on the hillside, propped against a stump, half-exhausted, drinking lemonade from his Thermos as he watched Rikka examine the result of their labors.

"Looks plenty good," he said, noticing how effortlessly she moved, even after shifting a thousand pounds of pebbly soil. He knew she wasn't the slightest fatigued. She *did* sweat, though, and she'd emptied a water bottle.

55

"Yeah, it does." Rikka flashed him one of her bright smiles, her teeth appearing whiter now, with her tanned features layered in sweat-runneled dust. Her black T-shirt, soaked, looked darker, too.

For as tall as she was, and basically slender despite being heavily-muscled, Rikka was well put together in every sense of the term. Walt decided he could still appreciate a good-looking woman, even if the end of his spine involved in that appreciation was the opposite from what it had been when he was a younger man.

"Did you say you had more of these to do?" Rikka asked.

Walt put a hand on top of the stump he'd been leaning against and lifted himself to his feet. "Well, I'd planned on doing another couple today," he said, capping off his Thermos. "The next one is three miles away, and I'll have the motorcycle. How'll you keep up?"

"I'll manage," Rikka answered, her smile turning smug.

Walt never doubted her for a second. And when she trotted alongside him as he rode down the trail, not breathing remotely hard, he wasn't the least surprised.

When they were done for the day, Rikka did agree to ride back into North Cedar seated behind him on the Honda, but Walt was almost too tired to enjoy the experience of a young woman's arms around his waist, his thoughts mostly being on the hot tub waiting at home. When he dropped her off, he was surprised to find out she lived in old Widow Murtchison's place, less than three blocks from his house.

And he hadn't known that the widow had a grand-niece, either, even after delivering the old woman's mail for close to thirty years.

As he eased his aching body into the warm healing waters of his hot tub, Walt felt certain that Rikka Thorsen was -- physically, at least -- the most truly unique individual he'd met in his long life.

Then he wondered if he could get her to help him again sometime.

FOURTEEN

After she showered, dried off, and belted on her bathrobe, Rikka went into the kitchen and prepared one of her famous -- to her, at least -- five thousand calorie meals, this one rice, vegetables, and chicken chunks. As she stirred and sauteed, she contemplated her day's activities with Walt Whitaker.

Walt hadn't sensed how close he was to death when he glanced up from his water bar and saw Rikka.

The Black Voice had wanted him. Rikka had shoved it away, down into the depths of her mind, waiting to determine what sort of person she'd found in her territory before she killed. In the end, her new inner strength had saved the retired postal worker. Doctor Sims' advice, all Rikka's reading about personality constructs, and her constant efforts to control the voice had borne fruit.

From what little she could remember of her life before Doctor Sims, Rikka knew she'd never done much inner examination, no searching for reasons and motives. She recalled being self-conscious at twelve for being so tall and geeky. She'd wondered then why the mythical creator had cursed her so.

But that was about it for adolescent angst. Her teen years had vanished into a drug-soaked and needle-poked limbo. She couldn't remember her own original name, and had no timeline linking a series of barely-remembered thens with the now in which she found herself.

She also found she didn't mind. Rikka Thorsen liked Rikka Thorsen just fine, particularly when she found out something new about her five-month-old persona. At least when it was something positive.

Her encounter with Walt Whitaker had been a case in point. Like most young people in America, in her old life she'd harbored a healthy disdain for older people. When Walt mentioned he was seventy, Rikka could only stop what she was doing and look at him in astonishment. She had towered over him by a good six inches. That had made him appear younger. But, despite his white hair and beard, Walt's movements and mannerisms were those of a much younger man. She'd assumed he was in his fifties, somewhere around the sheriff's age.

She smiled at her error.

The sheriff. An interesting man. That thousand-yard look he gave virtually everything and everyone which crossed his path could be very unnerving. The first few times she'd seen him at the library, reading a history book, his level of intense observation and quiet thoughtfulness almost alarmed her. Particularly after she found out who he was.

Later, when Rikka actually met him, Virgil Merrill proved to be a courtly, intelligent, and kind man. For the first time in Rikka's post-pubertal life, an adult male treated her as an equal, something besides a source of sex or drugs.

He missed little and thought a lot. He'd been first on the scene where she'd killed those two timber trash, and he and Doctor Cameron must have seen every square foot of the late Ukrainians' camp. Articles in *The Oregonian* had quoted both the FBI and the DEA as saying they had no substantial leads on the killer or killers, and the FBI had stated that the Sheriff's Department was aiding them.

As she transferred the cooked chunks of chicken into the rice and vegetables, and began to stir, Rikka wondered if the sheriff had mentioned the Dilts brothers to the federal officers.

She thought not, unless she'd misjudged Virgil Merrill, and that, she reminded herself, was something she could not safely do. Nor could anyone else, she suspected. Talking slow and walking slow in no way meant thinking slow. He might already have determined that one person, acting alone, was responsible for the deaths of fourteen men.

Rikka smiled again as she dished up her first helping. No one, though, not even the sheriff, would think to connect those fourteen bodies to a woman her age.

She wished she believed that completely.

But tomorrow she would drive down to Eugene and spend some time at the University of Oregon library, and see what else she could find out about Virgil Merrill.

This might not be one of Doctor Sims' "know thine enemy" situations.

But it might become one, somewhere down the line.

FIFTEEN

Dick Edmiston, the Pacific Northwest coordinator of Planet Prime!, could count on the fingers of one hand the number of disturbing phone calls he'd ever received from Alexander Carson. And have a finger or two left over. Ordinarily, Edmiston upset the conservationist lawyer, not the other way around.

This time, though, Carson had completely reversed their roles, and done it so well that Edmiston had even admitted it on the scrambled phone line he used for ultra-sensitive calls.

This one certainly qualified as ultra-sensitive, too. Carson hadn't been particularly forthcoming with hows and wherefores, but apparently there was someone in the National Forest on the North Cedar River drainage who was safeguarding the environment in a very deadly way.

There were always people on both sides of the environmental fence who *talked* about doing that sort of thing, but to Edmiston's knowledge, no one ever actually *had*. His organization had several younger members who expressed their desire to eliminate some of the timber industry's evildoers. Edmiston considered them unthinking loons, if potentially useful. It was one thing to damage property, render timber unsuitable for harvest, or booby-trap recreational trails, and quite another to deliberately take a human life.

How in hell someone had decided that the Willamette National Forest and the Mount Jefferson Wilderness were suitable for some kind of vigilante justice program puzzled Edmiston greatly. Carson preferred high-profile confrontations, having his day in front of the media and the courtroom.

And yet the stocky lawyer had intimated that he had something to do with the activity on the eastern reaches of the North Cedar River.

This should be happening closer to Portland and the centers of conservationist power and funding which were Carson's bailiwick. Carson liked high fee circumstances and high profile media attention.

Money and fame, that was Carson.

Quite unlike Edmiston, who courted only power, and disapproved of Carson and his methods. Dick Edmiston generally didn't care for lawyers and their less-than-direct ways, and he didn't like Carson, though he found him useful at times.

He would, however, meet with Carson and hear him out. There might be a role for Edmiston's followers in this. As the weather warmed, the spring tree-spiking season would begin, with forest sit-ins to follow later. This development could be very positive.

The Planet Prime! leader leaned back in his chair and laced his fingers behind his head as he looked thoughtfully up at the gigantic map of Oregon on the wall to his left. My battlezone, he thought. My kingdom.

Then his gaze moved to the framed saying some wag in the organization had come up with several years ago.

> If you think you understand
> Planet Prime!
> You don't know Dick.

Edmiston smiled and raised one fist in the air. Right on, brother!

SIXTEEN

The stack of cast-iron bars clanged against the weight machine's upper stops as Virgil Merrill straightened his legs. He paused for a few seconds, then bent his knees and eased the stack slowly back down. A hundred leg presses with two hundred pounds on the pin. Not bad for an old fart of fifty-nine, he thought, then amended that to sincere thanks for knees that still worked after so many years.

The bottom exercise-line for men his age were joints that functioned smoothly and freely, and he had those. For many younger men, basketball had proved to be the death knell of their mobility, leaving them hobbled and pain-ridden the rest of their lives. Not so for Virgil Merrill, old fart.

Lucky old fart. He climbed off the machine and headed for the shower. Still six-three and one-ninety, too, the same weight as college and only down a half-inch on height. North Cedar held dozens of men twenty years younger who moved like a daddy-longlegs with half its limbs missing.

Such was the reality of working in the deep, dark forests of the timber industry. A small mistake with a high-lead line, skidder, or setting a choker, or someone *else's* small mistake, and your life was changed forever -- if you still had a life.

Merrill had worked in the mills in high school and college. During the fifties and sixties in Oregon, almost everybody did. But that was before the influx of
out-of-staters had filled the northern Willamette Valley, and well before Portland urbanites began dictating land-use policies to the rural portions of the state.

Timber towns that *could* bounce back from having their job sources sharply reduced -- like North Cedar -- rebounded. The others, well, they became quasi-ghost towns, half their residents gone and the rest too old or too poor to leave.

The sheriff grabbed a bath towel and trudged up the stairs. He turned off the light and shut the door softly. Doors had been a problem for him these past five years, since Deb had died. Every time he shut one, the sound seemed to echo through the empty house, re-enforcing his aloneness, mocking him. Time to get out of the house, he thought, go down to the library.

He paused in the hallway by the bedroom, reaching around the edge of the doorframe and clicking on the light. Deb's picture hung on the wall opposite the bedroom door, his favorite of her, placed where he could see it easily and often. He'd taken it years before, when they were hiking over toward Mount Jefferson. Her knowing gaze and the half-smile on her freckled face perfectly captured the essence of her personality.

Merrill reached out and touched the framed photograph. He felt his lips relax into a wistful smile as he spoke to his dead wife. "Everything I wasn't, you were, Deb. Everything good I was, you were, too. Most of all, I was damned fortunate to be with you." Saying those words and seeing Deb's picture never depressed him, for some reason. Instead, he always experienced a pervasive calm warmth. It didn't exactly remove the aching sense of loss, but his mental focus shifted to their thirty-four years together, and away from the five years apart.

No time to dwell on the personal, however. Something was killing people out there in the woods, and it was just a matter of time before the tourists, fishermen, and hunters realized that they could be in danger. That would not bode well financially for North Cedar and the other little communities up and down the river. Right now, people were mostly interested in the odd deaths, not seeing themselves as future victims.

That could change overnight. They had three weeks, until the middle of June, to deal with the situation. Once school was out for the summer, and tourist season began, it could be too late.

He turned toward the bathroom, on the other side of the master bedroom, grinning wryly to himself. After Agent Vizenor's remark about Native American spirits, maybe he ought to check into that section of the library tonight.

That might be a stretch, though the killer was very low-tech and exceedingly up close and personal. It could, he supposed, be someone who fancied themselves a vengeful spirit, some incredibly skilled ex-military madman.

Merrill continued to examine the problem as he stripped off his workout gear and dropped it down the laundry chute. The Pentagon kept track of its former people fairly well. The person he'd be looking for wouldn't be retired, would have to be younger. Out on an honorable discharge after five or ten years of service and plenty of Special Forces, SERE, and Black Ops training. Maybe an odd psych profile, could be Native American.

Yet all those Ukrainians had been part of a special unit, had all served in Afghanistan, and, from what the authorities had been able to learn, were no mean shakes on the kill-skill chart.

And they were all dead, with no traces of anyone else's blood at the scene.

Then there was the problem of when the next killing would occur. They could be dealing with someone like the Green River Killer or the

65

Unabomber, who only struck at intervals, sometimes long intervals.

Not good, the Sheriff thought, as he stepped into the shower and reached for the shampoo.

In fact, no fucking good at all.

SEVENTEEN

The expression of faint distaste which briefly crossed Alexander Carson's face when he and Dick Edmiston walked into Esparza's Tex-Mex on Southeast Ankeny Street did a great deal for Edmiston's day.

When Carson had agreed to eat at a place where he was unlikely to be recognized, the great man had apparently not considered anything as mundane as Esparza's. Even in a Pendleton shirt and faded denims -- probably Carson's idea of a casual disguise -- the lawyer's self-importance and chilly disdain for his surroundings were obvious.

Hernan, the stocky Latino greeter who showed them to their corner table in the restaurant's darker regions, had seen Edmiston many times before. He sized up Carson immediately and accurately gauged Edmiston's opinion of his luncheon partner. Deliberately thickening his accent, bobbing his head repeatedly, and pulling Carson's chair out for him while winking at Edmiston, Hernan had as much fun with the situation as he could.

After producing their menus with a flourish and bow to Carson -- and a final wink to Edmiston -- Hernan left them alone.

His eyes narrowed, Carson watched the stumpy greeter return to his post by the restaurant's front entrance. The lawyer didn't say anything immediately, but the way his lips were pressed together, Edmiston knew Carson at least suspected that Hernan's fashion sense had allowed him to recognize a stuffed shirt when he saw one.

"Something bothering you, Alex?" Edmiston asked innocently. "Maybe the altitude?"

Carson frowned. "Altitude?"

"Well, I know you're used to eating at places in the upper levels of office buildings. Just walking in off the street must be a bit disconcerting. And nobody in suits, either."

"Very funny," Carson replied, looking around them at the faded posters, south of the border knick-knacks, mismatched furniture, and dried sea turtles, which -- along with the Mexican ballads from the sound system -- gave Esparza's its character. His expression of displeasure deepened.

"So tell me about your killer, counselor," the Planet Prime! chief said. "Don't worry. Hernan will see that we're served what I usually order, and any interruption will be brief. The lovely music'll mask our conversation."

"True, true," Carson answered absently, his gaze examining the empty tables around the alcove where they sat. A dented speaker hung from the ceiling just above their table, emitting a moaning Spanish love song.

Apparently satisfied that they could converse safely, Carson explained the Reckoning Project, its completion, and the resulting deaths. He kept his tone level and low, but Edmiston could see that the environmental lawyer was proud of what had been accomplished, even though Carson's budget had been enough to fund years of Planet Prime!'s activities.

As Carson finally wound down, Edmiston found himself even more impressed than during Carson's earlier call. Be damned if the arrogant putz hadn't come up with something useful that didn't involve words and paper! He searched for a weakness in Carson's scheme, and -- reluctantly -- failed. "Is her being on her own a potential problem, Alex?" he finally asked, just after a very non-Latino waitress brought their meals.

"Doctor Sims had a few caveats on that," Carson replied, his expression dubious as he poked at his salmon enchilada. "Most of her thoughts involved the creature's decision-making process, what guidelines she uses to determine her quarry. Thus far, however, all seems well."

"Maybe at some point she'll just kill everyone who ventures onto federal lands," Edmiston said cheerfully, taking a large bite of salmon and refried beans.

Carson nodded. "Sims considered that, but felt it unlikely. Her greater concern was that, as Reckon settles into the community and becomes acquainted with the locals, her judgement might become skewed. This is, after all, only a nineteen-year-old girl."

"She could fall in love," Edmiston suggested.

The lawyer's features clouded. "I brought that up. The doctor assured me Reckon's long estrangement from normal socicty should preclude any close relationships for many months -- if ever. Still, we can't be positive. Reckon's only leash is her implanted set of compulsions and desires -- which Sims tells me Reckon calls the 'Black Voice.'"

"Jesus! 'The Black Voice.' Like in a low-budget horror flick."

"Exactly," Carson replied, looking quite satisfied with himself, "and that's exactly what those who oppose our goals will experience -- absolute and utter horror."

"And then they'll be dead." Edmiston shook his head in both amazement and admiration. "I've got to hand it to you, Alex. This is a helluva solution to our mutual problems." He raised his chipped pink beer glass. "Here's to Reckon," he said.

"Thank you, Richard," Carson said, his full features flushed with triumph, his voice practically

purring.   He lifted his own glass.   "Here's to
Reckon, indeed."

EIGHTEEN

Just how Rikka Thorsen managed that look of shy boldness intrigued Virgil Merrill. He'd seen the tall, dark girl over in the fiction section when he first entered the library. She seemed to be browsing. He settled in at a reading table with the new copy of *Newsweek*, and was halfway through, working from the back of the magazine, when Rikka sat down opposite him.

"Evening, Sheriff," she said, her brown gaze both compelling and cautious, but her smile wide.

"Good evening," he replied, smiling back at her, closing the magazine. "Finding anything?" he asked. Somewhere behind those warm eyes, he wondered -- briefly in law enforcement mode -- was Ricky Jo Mullin watching him? Somehow, without knowing why, he didn't think so.

She slid a thick trade paperback across the table. "Have you read anything by this author?"

Merrill turned the book so he could read the title, felt his smile broaden in surprise and delight. *Howard Waldrop*, for god's sake! *Night of the Cooters*. "Yes, I have," he replied, "and he's good. *Insanely* good." He opened the book to the first story, saw it was the one he remembered, the Texas landing of H. G. Wells' Martians. He handed the book back to Rikka. "I'm betting you'll like this, and they should have a couple more Waldrop collections, if they haven't gotten swiped. He's one of the more popular little-known short-story writers in the country."

"Can you suggest anything else? I read pretty fast."

Merrill thought for a moment. "Maybe Robert Crais. He's over in Mystery. Elmore Leonard -- same place. And Neal Stephenson's *The Diamond*

Age. A nice upbeat view of the future, about a little girl named Nell who changed the world."

Rikka's eyes grew thoughtful. Her smile became more intimate. She seemed momentarily older. "A girl who changes the world. That sounds nice. I'd like that." She stood up, the Waldrop in her hand, her smile reflective, her mood definitely indrawn.

"Well, good luck," Merrill said, rather lamely, intrigued by this new aspect of Rikka Thorsen.

She snapped her fingers. "Oh, I almost forgot. I met Walt Whitaker out in the woods on Monday. He was working on some water bars, and let me help. His opinion of you's pretty high." Her eyes danced, full of mischief.

The sheriff shrugged, unaccustomed to compliments, and feeling like a fool for letting this young girl disconcert him. "Walt and I've known each other a while," he said finally. "He's one of the good guys."

"*I* thought so." Rikka glanced down at her watch. "Well, your good guy promised to buy me a beer at the Green Chain at nine o'clock, so I'd better get my books together 3
and checked out. I should at least run a brush through my hair before I meet him. See you -- and thanks, again." She turned to go, then swung back around, and regarded Merrill seriously. "You know, Sheriff, you're right about Walt -- not that everyone in town hasn't been pleasant to me since I got here. But he's certainly not the only good guy around. You're pretty special yourself." She looked down at the table top, her eyes hidden by long lashes for a few seconds before she brought her gaze back up to his, color in her cheeks. "I hope that didn't sound too presumptuous or corny."

"No, not at all," Merrill replied, the words coming out quicker than he wanted. "I'm just not used to kind words from people in your age group."

"I'll have to remember that," Rikka said, all the boldness and mischief back in her eyes and voice, "and behave myself in the future."

Merrill grinned at her, unable to do otherwise. "You do that. And enjoy your beer with Walt. Just be careful of the clientele at the Green Chain."

"I'll do my best," she said, and crossed her heart, "and I'll see you later."

He watched her walk briskly back into the stacks, her back straight as a string, her movements as fluid as warm oil. Her shoulders, Merrill thought, were almost as wide as his, her arms were corded with long muscle, and her chest would never make the cut on 'Baywatch,' except maybe on the older lifeguard, David Whatshisname.

So why was his heart tripping along at half again its normal pace?

The sheriff knew that question didn't bear close scrutiny, at least not at the moment. He went back to his magazine, trying to rekindle interest in the current crisis in the Middle East, and forced himself not to look up when Rikka Thorsen left the library five minutes later.

Once she was gone, Merrill relaxed to a degree, enough to manage an appreciative chuckle when Ms. Endicott, the all-too-sharp librarian, remarked, as he checked out a few books, "Sheriff's got a girlfriend."

"Thanks, Helen, but I don't think so. I have grandchildren almost as old as Ms. Thorsen."

"She may know that, Virgil," Helen Endicott replied, without looking up, pushing her glasses onto the bridge of her nose. "She spent most of the afternoon yesterday going through back issues of the *North Cedar Sentinel*."

"Maybe she just got interested in local history."

"Ummm. Maybe. But most of the articles she copied had pictures of you or your family."

73

"Really?"

"Really, Virgil." Ms. Endicott looked up at him now, her expression an odd mix of speculation and curiousity. "I must say, though, that I prefer a wholesome interest in a single older man to some of the 'how-to' books she was reading a couple of weeks ago, *Defense Techniques of the Navy SEALS* and such."

"You're kidding!"

"Not really. She usually reads fiction and psychology texts, in fact I think she's read every one of the latter we have. But I suspect now she's concerned that she might run into whatever helped to clean up the area by finishing off the Dilts boys."

"She said she was going to meet Walt Whitaker for a beer at the Green Chain this evening. Maybe she thought she needed some tips on self-protection."

Ms. Endicott laughed -- librarian-quietly. "Sounds like she's playing the field, checking out all the town's elders."

His mind at a full gallop, the sheriff gathered his books. "Could be, Helen." He smiled down at her. "She might not be heterosexual, you know."

"Be still, my heart," the librarian replied, clasping her bosom in feigned rapture. "But seriously, she's not a lesbian, Virgil. We can tell these things."

"*I* certainly can't."

"Even though you don't live in a fantasy world -- like most men -- you still have an old-fashioned way toward women. It's very appealing, but it's a bit of a blind spot, I think."

"Thank you, I think."

"I'm not sure it was a compliment, Virgil. And you should probably get home so you can be near the phone."

Merrill felt his brow furrow. "Why's that?"

74

"So you'll be available when they phone in the riot at the Green Chain. It might be too much for the local police."

"Very funny." He started for the library entrance. "Good evenin' to you, Helen."

"You, too, Virgil. And don't forget to buy condoms." Her muted laughter followed him out the door.

NINETEEN

One of the nicer things about North Cedar was that its small size made everything close. Rikka's house was only a short distance west of the library, and the Green Chain only about three blocks south. She dropped off her books, brushed her hair, and was out the door not more than ten minutes after leaving the library.

As she walked, she thought about her conversation with Virgil Merrill. She'd given him something to think about, for certain, but it hadn't been easy. When she'd been safely back in the library stacks, she'd hugged herself in sheer relief. Every ounce of her new self-control had been needed. And he'd reacted the way she'd hoped, with interest. He'd *liked* her, had regarded her as a friend. Even as a *woman*. Her sensitive nose had told her that much, had sensed his hormonal response.

Rikka smiled to herself, as she walked down the slanting sidewalk, hands in her pockets. It had been *perfect*.

On a Thursday night, the Chain was about the closest thing North Cedar had to a social center. Friday nights and weekends saw the campgrounds and larger restaurants along the river turn into party spots, but with one work day to go in the week, most of the folks in the popular bar were probably locals, and it wouldn't be crowded or noisy.

Still, as Rikka approached the Chain's open front door, there were rows of vehicles lining each side of the street, mostly crew-carrying crummys and pickups sporting the names of timber-related businesses. There was even an old Dodge Power Wagon A-frame. The sound of jukebox Country music punctuated by bursts of loud laughter spilled out into the warm night, along with the smells of hot bar food and cold beer.

Apparently the socializing wasn't as quiet as Rikka had supposed, and her mouth began to water from the smell of the food. Sometimes it seemed she was always hungry. She smiled to herself, seeing a sign in the bar's window, 'Home of the 24-Oz. Logger Burger.' A couple of those ought to fill her up, and she could get some nachos to share with Walt.

And Walt Whitaker would be easy to find, Rikka thought, as she walked into the Chain. There shouldn't be that many people in the place sporting a snow-white hair and beard.

There weren't. Walt waved at her from a table against the far wall, just beyond the end of the long bar that faced the door. Around the corner behind him, Rikka could see another room with much better lighting, several pool tables, and at least one darts board.

To the best of her fragmented memory, she'd never been in a bar before. Of course, even though her ID said that she would turn twenty-two in July, Rikka knew she'd been born in 1980, and thus would only be nineteen this year.

Not that any of that made one bit of difference. She waved back at Walt and threaded her way around and between people and tables. As she approached, he stood and held a chair for her, slipping it beneath her as she sat down.

"That was certainly chivalrous," Rikka said, smiling up at him, and grabbing a menu as Walt reclaimed his own seat.

"Well," Walt replied, filling a second glass from the pitcher of dark beer in front of him, "this is a mostly polite community, with mostly civil inhabitants." He slid the glass over to Rikka, then looked around the crowded bar. "And a fairly quiet bunch tonight. Myron, the larger gentleman behind the bar, takes a dim view of altercations which might affect the value of his real estate and its furnishings. Any sort of significant beef winds up outside in the street."

Rikka looked over at Myron, who was tall and not laterally-challenged. He wore a black T-shirt with the words, 'You're not in Cicely, this ain't the Brick, and I'm not Holling,' in block white letters. When he saw Rikka looking, he nodded to her, teeth bright against his neatly-trimmed dark brown beard.

"Clever shirt," Rikka commented, lifting her glass to her lips, and taking a long draft.

"Wanta see another one?" asked a perky voice to her right.

Rikka turned. A petite brunette in jeans and another black T-shirt stood between her and Walt, an expectant smile on her face. She held an order pad in her left hand, a pencil in her right. Her shirt's message read 'I'm not Shelley.'

"Definitely clever," Rikka agreed, and held out her hand. "I'm Rikka Thorsen. And I love the *Northern Exposure* re-runs."

"Us, too." She shook Rikka's hand. "I'm Patty Black. And I thought up these shirts. Fortunately, my dear husband had room for all that information on his, and mine has the one he bought for me down in Texas a couple years back just beat all to hell."

"What did it say?" Rikka asked, glancing at Walt, seeing his smile, and knowing he knew.

"'Hooters' Reject,'" Patty said, laughing. "I wouldn't wear it, of course, at least not in here." She cocked her head at Rikka. "Did you say *Thorsen*?"

"She's Ida Murtchison's grand-niece," Walt put in.

"No relation to...?"

Walt shook his head, still grinning. "Don't think so. She's strong enough, though."

"Do tell," Patty said, looking Rikka up and down. "You *do* look like you could manage a day's work."

"In about three hours," Walt said.

"Whatever you say, Walter," Patty replied, laughing. "Now what can I get you folks?"

"I'm *starved*," Rikka said, "I'll have two Logger Burgers and an order of nachos to split with Walt. And more beer in a bit."

Patty Black's eyebrows practically disappeared beneath her short bangs as she wrote on her pad. "You're not just *starved*, girl. You're hungry enough to eat the ass end out of a dead skunk." She looked at Walt. "You want anything more than your half of the nachos, Walter?"

"No, that'll do. I had a bite earlier. And Ms. Thorsen might not eat as many nachos as she thinks she can, 'specially not after those burgers."

"Hey, I did over thirty miles on foot today!" Rikka protested, knowing that she'd gone closer to fifty. "I deserve some significant grub."

"I'll see that the cook gets it going," Patty said, sticking her pencil behind her right ear. "Be just a few minutes. Nice to meet you, Rikka." She tapped the order pad. "And I do hope you come in often, with this kind of appetite."

"I like this place," Rikka said, topping off their glasses as Patty returned to the bar. "What's this beer?"

"Cedar Stout," Walt answered. "Patty and Myron do a little microbrewing on the side. It's popular with the locals." His gaze suddenly lifted over Rikka's head. "And here comes one of the larger locals now."

"Excuse me," said a deep voice from behind and above Rikka, "but did I hear your name is 'Thorsen?'" She'd never heard a voice like it.

Heavy and thick, it's rumble seemed to fill the room. Their table fell into shadow. Rikka looked up.

And up.

And then up some more.

The largest right hand she'd ever seen descended from somewhere near the ceiling.

"I am Ole," the voice said. "Ole Thorsen." He barely pronounced the 'h' in Thorsen. Above the hand was a leg-sized arm attached to shoulders a yard wide, on which rested a proportionate neck and head. Just now, the broad face wore a friendly smile, for which Rikka was profoundly grateful. She gingerly took his offered hand. Her fingers didn't reach across his palm. "Rikka Thorsen," she replied, deciding that if this man had said "Fee, fie, fo, fum," it would have been more appropriate.

"A great pleasure," Ole said, taking a chair -- which creaked alarmingly. He didn't release Rikka's hand until he was seated and peering into her face, squinting in concentration.

"You are not related to us, I think," he announced, massive forearms resting on the table. His bright blue eyes were small, even smaller when he smiled, and set deep below beetling brows. Freckles splashed over a burned and peeling pug nose. "Myron says you are living in the old Murtchison place. Ida was a good person. I will ask my grandmother if, if fact, we are related, though your skin is dark, not so Scandinavian. Where do your people come from?"

"Longview," Rikka replied, thinking that even a presumed connection with Ole Thorsen wouldn't be a bad thing.

"Ah," Ole said, nodding ponderously, "there are trees and mills there, so perhaps..." He rose from the chair, a nearly geologic movement. "We set up tomorrow on a BLM timber parcel on Boundary

Ridge. An early start for us. We begin cut next Tuesday, after Memorial Day weekend." Ole gestured toward the bar, at a man near his size. "Sigge and me have a busy day tomorrow. He is my little brother. Not so big as me. Spent too much time chasing girls, missed too many meals. Even got married." He shook his head in mock dismay, then brightened again. "Erika is a good woman, though, and my little niece and nephew show promise."

"Nice to meet you -- cousin," Rikka said, standing and shaking Ole's hand again. This time, she applied some significant pressure, and was pleased when his expression showed approval.

"Hoo, you are a powerful lady," he said, grinning. "Next time we arm-wrestle for who buys beer. I wish you a good evening." He turned to go, and Rikka saw the picture of a leaping dolphin on the back of his white T-shirt, with the message, 'Buy Only Dolphin-safc Tuna.' She hadn't thought loggers would be interested in such things, though clearly anyone the size of Ole Thorsen would be have to be non-selectively omnivorous.

Sigge had left the bar while they were talking, and met Ole near the front door. They spoke briefly. Both men raised fists the size of Easter hams to Rikka before leaving, ducking out the door.

"You'd think a town this size would have fewer surprises," she said to Walt. "It seemed quiet the first couple of months I was here."

Walt looked apologetic. "I should have thought to ask you about the Thorsens. They've lived around here for a coon's age. Nice family, all good workers. Sigge's kids, by the way, are both under ten and almost my size. Probably what Ole meant by 'promise.'"

In the woods, Rikka thought, smiling at Walt, size probably really *did* matter. She reached over and touched his hand. "Just let me know if there's any more surprises you can think of that you might want prepare me for."

"Probably none the size of Ole," Patty Black said, coming around the table and setting down a tray loaded with their food. "Right, Walter?" She rested a hand on Rikka's shoulder. "Sorry to eavesdrop, hon, but that's what we do here in North Cedar, mind everybody's business."

"We've all gotten used to it," Walt said, reaching for the nachos.

"At this point, it's almost a family thing," Patty added, lifting Rikka's twin Logger Burgers off the tray and placing them in front of her.

"A *nice* family," Rikka replied, grinning at the pair of them as she started in on the first burger.

And she found she meant exactly that.

TWENTY

Even with a highly-sophisticated scrambler on both ends of a phone conversation, Dick Edmiston much preferred to pass on orders in person, during daylight hours, and in a public place. In this case, that was impossible, and the Memorial Day weekend began tomorrow after work hours. Time had gotten critical, so he'd gritted his teeth and made the call, violating his own rules.

"The thing we spoke of," he said to the people he knew were listening inside a Ford Expedition parked next to a particularly wild stretch of the North Cedar River. He paused, waiting for a response.

"Yes," came the reply, somewhat brittle with electronic manipulation. Edmiston thought he could hear the sound of rushing water in the background, though it might just be the scrambler.

"Go ahead with Plan One. They will begin falling at that site on Tuesday if they're not stopped. The person I mentioned in our last conversation should be held
accountable."

The voice on the river gave a short, barking laugh. "Good. Consider it done."

"Saturday night?"

"Yes. We'll contact you on Tuesday." The line went dead.

Edmiston replaced the phone in its cradle, switching off the scrambler. His hands steepled on his desk top, he sat in silence, contemplating. For better or worse, he thought, the die had been cast. Planet Prime! would fight destruction with destruction, serving notice to the faceless corporate entities who raped and despoiled the land.

Battle was joined, the old war began anew.

And, although he didn't want to implicate his fellow environmental activist, if a trail developed, it would all lead back to Alexander Carson's doorstep.

Perfect.

TWENTY-ONE

Tourists and campers began trickling into the North Cedar recreational area during the month of April, with a surge at the start of fishing season on the last weekend of the month. May remained steady, while the weekends grew heavier, filled with boat trailers and tackle-laden fishermen. Memorial Day weekend was the true beginning of summer, with traffic jams at the docks and stifling crowds that would continue unchecked through Labor Day.

Virgil Merrill hated those three summer months to the very depths of his being. His work load quadrupled, even with the town cops, game wardens, and campground rangers doing regular overtime.

There didn't seem to be anything too stupid for the tourists to try. Having enough money to afford a four-wheel-drive SUV or Volvo was no guarantee of even a lick of common sense, and folks from the Midwest added to that a complete lack of appreciation for the function of gravity.

They didn't seem to realize that if you were climbing up a fairly loose and steep slope, and lost purchase, you would likely roll or topple all the way to the bottom. In this country, the bottom could be a long way down and generally had water -- sometimes fast and deep. So, if you were alive when you entered the water, there was considerable likelihood that you might not stay that way.

Merrill had plucked people -- both alive and dead -- off of sandbars, the boom logs stretching behind the dams, and jams of logs jill-poked in canyons. He'd felt helpless and angry over the dead, and just plain angry over the sheer nitwittedness of the fortunate survivors.

He looked out at the deceptive beauty of the river as he drove the Caprice down past the Dew Drop on his way to the office. The rising sun shone off the riffles and wet rocks on either side of the main current, and ground fog lay silver in the trees on the opposite side. That timeless allure would claim at least one careless camper or fisherman before the weekend was out, maybe two or three. People convinced that anything so lovely couldn't kill you in less time than it took to draw a deep breath.

Wrong. And more wrong if you were a petty timber rustler or big-time Ukrainian pot farmer, because something new and incomprehensibly lethal lurked in the deep forests, something with its own moral vision and the ability to enforce it.

There would be lots of people traipsing around those woods over the next few days, and some of them might not come out under their own power. Yet legitimate timber operations had been unmolested, folks like Walt Whitaker and Rikka Thorsen were out there most days, and none of them had been picked off. Two incidents simply didn't make a pattern, even though fourteen people had died in them.

As he swung onto the highway, Rikka still on his mind, the sheriff made a mental note to have Helen Endicott show him on the library computer exactly what material on covert operations and personal defense Rikka had been perusing. Merrill wasn't sure *why* that might be important, but something told him it was.

Rikka Thorsen had preoccupied him entirely too much lately, and last night's little encounter at the library hadn't helped alleviate that preoccupation. Pulling up in front of his office, the sheriff resolved to put her out of his mind until the holiday weekend was past.

Easier said than done, he thought, as he climbed out of the patrol car, thick Samsonite briefcase in hand. Try as he might to avoid it, his professional curiosity kept dragging his personal interest in her direction.

Darned kid, anyhow.

"Mornin', Darla," Merrill said heartily, striding into the office in his best law-enforcement manner.

Deputy Darla Kuhn -- the person who really ran the place, he always said -- looked up at him, then sat straighter, her hazel eyes narrowing. "My, we're full of piss and vinegar this morning, aren't we?" She looked at him closer. "It's all a facade, though, isn't it? You're well aware that we're about to enter the Season of Hell, and you're just being brave. How flipping noble."

Merrill nodded and removed his campaign hat, still moving in the general direction of his private office. "Yup, that's it. School's out in two weeks. Your husband will be off down to Corvallis to work on his Masters', and you'll be practically alone, 'cept on weekends. You'll be workin' your tail to the bone in here." He put his hat flat against his chest, tried to arrange his features in an expression of pity. "I don't need to tell you, Darla, I *feel* your pain."

"If we weren't so completely in the same boat," Darla replied, "I might accuse you of insincerity, but the worst I can say is that your ironic nature is uncannily accurate. Tom *will* be gone to OSU during the week, I *will* be overworked and underpaid, and I *won't* be able to work out as much as I want, but that's the way it goes."

"You're not using real big words," Merrill observed, "so you must not be *too* upset." He looked her over carefully. "And you appear pretty fit, as skinny as ever."

"From most men in your age group in this town, I'd take that as an insult, but I've seen pictures of your wife. She wasn't any heavier than I am. And your kids used to be the same, even though I haven't seen any of them except Kathy for a couple of years." Darla was thirty-five, two years older than Merrill's eldest daughter, an attorney working for Multnomah County, in Portland.

"They're still about the same," the sheriff replied, "and except for being brunette, having a bunch fewer freckles, and bein' so snippy, you'd almost pass for one of mine."

Darla laughed, her voice fond as she looked at her boss. "I could do worse for a dad. Kathy says you always had time for your family. My dad's a workaholic of the first order, too busy turning a buck buying and selling property to do much more than recognize us kids."

"Says the woman who's bustin' her butt all Summer, while her husband goes to school," Merrill said. He sat his hat on Darla's desk, his briefcase on the floor, and walked over to the coffee machine, picking up his cup. "I wish I had an answer to that problem for you, Darla. When I was a kid, dads worked and moms didn't. Most dads worked hard trying to provide. Didn't mean they didn't love their kids. Just because your father has made it big doesn't turn off that need to work his ass off."

He rotated the spigot, filling his cup. "And that's the trap. Easy to get into, hard to get out of. Reason I moved up here after I started workin' for the Sheriff's Department. I wanted to have time for Deb and the kids, instead of being on the fast track to bein' High Sheriff down in the County seat. Not as much money, but a lot more satisfaction. Worked out real fine while it lasted." He held up his cup. "You want some?"

"No, already had some," Darla answered, and he saw pity in her gaze, something he'd never wanted to see.

"Oh, shit, I'm sorry," he said, suddenly uncomfortable. "Didn't mean to sound bitter, or make you think I feel sorry for myself."

Darla sighed. "It has to leak out once in a while, Virgil. Otherwise you wouldn't be human. You're one of those people who plan their lives, and just about the time you figured you had it pretty much worked out and together, and relaxed a bit, fate dealt you a nasty blow. Undeserved and unexpected, I know, but life has a way of doing that."

"You sound like me."

"I've had a good teacher for the past three years. Now, why don't you tell me about your new girlfriend?"

He barely avoided spilling his coffee. "*What!*"

"Don't act innocent. I stopped by the library to return some books last night, right at closing time, just after you left. Helen gave me all the juicy details. I think I've seen this Rikka Thorsen around. Isn't she the big girl who walks like her engineers used a different set of blueprints than they used for the rest of us?"

Merrill regarded her balefully. "I think I liked this conversation better when I was feelin' sorry for myself. Why don't you grab the duty clipboard and come into my office?" He took his hat and briefcase and stomped out of the room.

"Oooh, a show of passion!" Darla replied, retrieving the clipboard and following him. "Also an avoidance of the question. A sure sign of guilt in anyone's book, methinks. Was there then a *rendezvous* last evening, after the library?"

Tossing his hat onto the hat rack in the corner, the sheriff sat down behind his desk. He couldn't quite decide whether to smile and simply explain the situation, or start yelling. The former won out.

"This is how I see it, Deputy," he said, leaning back in his chair and crossing his arms over his chest. "Rikka Thorsen is new to our community. We have come into contact, mostly at the library. She is bright, inquisitive, and seemingly alone. A nice and nice-looking person -- so she won't be alone long -- but it would take an imagination with considerable leaping ability to put the two of us in a situation even remotely unclothed or immodest. She is, for God's sake, well under half my age, and cannot -- repeat, *cannot* -- be sexually interested in me. Plus, she met Walt Whitaker for a beer at the Chain last night."

"Helen mentioned that, too. Maybe this Thorsen has OGS."

"Let me guess -- Old Guy Syndrome?"

Darla grinned. "Very quick. Or maybe she's looking for a new daddy. Any psychologist will tell you those people are out there."

She *has* a daddy, Merrill wanted to say, but he's probably putting in his days in a meth lab or some low-risk prison, and may not even remember that he has a daughter, or -- more likely -- thinks she's dead.

"You're thinking," Darla said, sitting down with the schedule clipboard in her lap. "That's promising."

"She's reserved," the sheriff slowly answered, looking over Darla's head, "and she treats me pretty much as an equal, without our knowing each other well. She likes the town and the people, thought Walt Whitaker is a 'good guy', quote-unquote. There's a sort of reluctant boldness about her that I don't know if I've seen before."

"Helen said she went through the old *Sentinels* looking for stuff about you. That says something.

And, remember, you *always* believe the best about women. It's your nature."

"Well, Rikka Thorsen's sure not *stalking* me."

"If she starts, you should probably notify the local police. It's out of your jurisdiction."

"Oh, that's *real* funny. Why don't we put Rikka away for the moment, and you tell me what's on that clipboard?"

"Before I do, by the end of the day, I want you to decide whether you want to tell me whatever it is you're holding back about Rikka Thorsen. I know you, Virgil, and I know there's more. I recognize that expression. I would never accuse you of improprieties of any sort, but you're keeping something to yourself."

"You women are too observant," Merrill replied, "but you're right. I got curious about Rikka Thorsen, and made some unofficial inquiries. Not just real sure what we've got, though. Probably should have run it by you earlier, but no law was being broken, so I let what I knew marinate."

Darla lifted the clipboard, ran her right forefinger down the short list of names and notations on its single sheet. "Well, before I get started on this, are we going to have our little chat about your sweetie around mid-afternoon, say right after you talk to the two Japanese journalists?"

"That sounds fine." Then what she'd said sunk in. "*What* Japanese journalists?"

"Kenechi Sonada and Noriyasu Kogawa, with the *Tokyo Star*. They wish to ask about the 'forest killer,' as Sonada put it. His English is very good, by the way. Their company owns a home at Sunriver for employee use, so I don't think this is more than a break from a golfing vacation."

"Oh, Christ." Merrill cast his gaze upward. "Maybe someone will drive their motorhome into the river, and I can cancel."

91

"Probably not, and it gets better. Your first visitor at nine this morning is one Malcolm Brown. From his efficient Brit accent and reason for speaking to you, I would say he's *the* Malcolm Brown."

"The Sasquatch fellow, right? I read his book. Damn good perspective, very fair treatment of the subject."

"Thank you, Mister Book Person. He did say he only wanted to share some thoughts with you. Apparently he gave a talk in Eugene last night at the Hult Center, wants to stop by on his way back up to Portland."

"A hundred miles out of his way." The sheriff stroked his chin thoughtfully. "He must have something important to 'share,' then. I might actually *enjoy* that. What else?"

"Nothing at the moment."

"What I needed to hear," Merrill replied.

TWENTY-TWO

After introducing himself, while the sheriff did paper work, Malcolm Brown spent a long, slow fifteen minutes going through Darla's notes on the fourteen deaths. Then he read the coroner's report, finally replacing everything in the correct folders and laying them back on Merrill's desk.

"Well, Sheriff," Brown said -- in a Northeast Irish accent overlaid with years of service in the English Special Air Service -- "what you have here appears to be a large, very powerful, tool-using primate with some arboreal tendencies, acting alone." His blue eyes twinkled, vivid against the darker background of a medium tan and a greying crewcut.

Merrill thought for a moment. "In the trees, huh? I wondered about that."

"Perhaps I should have inquired as to the height of the lower branches. The trees, I gather, are huge, old examples of their kind, grand and tall?"

"Yeah. The lower branches start twenty feet up, some thirty, some even more."

"Oh, dear," Brown replied, his tongue flicking his thin mustache, "then my clever scenario just leapt into the loo."

"How's that?" the sheriff asked, having a pretty good idea what Brown's answer would be.

"Too many of the laws of biophysics are being violated in these two incidents. Let's leave the tree issue for a few minutes and go back to the two locals who lost their heads. I've been witness to the aftermath of several small aircraft crashes, as perhaps have you. Quite frequently, when the aircraft stops abruptly, the only unsupported portion of the passenger's body -- the head -- will be thrown down and forward. The chin contacts the upper chest and becomes a fulcrum. The spine is severed, the skull erupts through the facial covering and shatters the windscreen. The facial integument, musculature, scalp, and so forth are ripped vertically to permit this."

"Pretty gruesome," Merrill responded, glad that Darla was on the other side of a closed door.

"The key point is that the neck musculature remains behind. And, similarly, the spine also can be broken by twisting, as in popular action films." Brown tapped the folders he'd just examined. "I've not seen anyone sufficiently powerful to accomplish what happened to these unfortunate gentlemen, everything above the clavicles essentially removed in one swift and sudden motion."

"Our county coroner said the same thing," the sheriff said, and went on to explain Doctor Cameron's computer program and its findings.

"Bright fellow," the Irishman said. "Well, then, since what happened was clearly impossible, let us return to the Ukrainians. Someone had to plunge down from overhead into the final group of four men, who, had they any training -- and they had -- were positioned back-to-back and firing into the darkness. A three hundred and sixty degree field of fire. A perfect grouping against an attacker without any sort of projectile weaponry, wouldn't you agree?"

"Seemed to be," Merrill replied.

"So, a primate, and here by 'primate' I mean a human being, does the impossible. He rips off two men's heads, complete with the associated neck and shoulder musculature. Then, a week or so later, this same immensely powerful individual drops a minimum of twenty vertical feet from a tree limb, and lands perfectly amongst four men with automatic weapons. He stuns -- let us postulate --

three of them, cuts the standing man's throat, then finishes off the others, all in a matter of seconds."

"Your Ukrainian scenario sounds at least possible," Merrill said.

Brown grinned widely. "Oh, yes, if our killer were a trained acrobat in superb physical shape, who also happened to be incredibly lucky." He stroked his chin. "Though I'm a bit put off by that twenty-foot drop. Aren't you?"

Merrill lifted his hands out, palms-up. "What, then?"

"Nothing," Brown answered. "What I described in both instances was precisely what must have occurred. A primate strong enough to remove someone's head simply by pulling would be too heavy to climb trees -- as is the male Gorilla, for example. And someone who -- by dint of natural agility, training and unusual good fortune -- killed those last four Ukrainians would almost certainly weigh considerably less than two hundred pounds."

"I think you just used Occam's Razor on both the up *and* the down stroke."

"Oh, splendid, Sheriff," Brown laughed. "But, yes, the simplest answer, as William of Occam -- and many others -- have said, is the only answer. We are trying to explain this in human parameters. And that is not possible. I believe what you are looking for *is* human, you understand, but not as are we. Someone who has lifted humanity's bar to the next level in speed, strength, and precision."

"You forgot 'see in the dark,'" Merrill added.

Brown leaned back slightly, without seeming to alter his ram-rod posture. "True," he admitted, "but that follows perfectly, doesn't it? *All* the senses: sight, hearing, smell, touch. You have an awesome and fearful opponent, Sheriff." Brown laughed again. "I shall feel much safer when I board my flight to Vancouver late this evening after my talk in Portland, and can place considerable distance between myself and this superhuman killer."

Merrill gave Brown a quick smile. "Now you've got *me* scared."

"Hardly," Brown replied dryly, still smiling. He reached into the pocket of his blue cotton short-sleeved shirt, brought out a business card, and handed it across to the sheriff. "This is my home number. Let me know when you have any new information. I'll help if I can."

After examining the card briefly, Merrill stuck it into his card Rolodex. "You've already helped me a bunch."

"Nonsense," the former SAS-man said. "I've merely somewhat refined information you already had. You'd thought of the trees, only were reluctant to accept it. I would add, however, that I believe these killings are in response to perceived transgressions of some magnitude. None of the smaller marijuana operations -- the so-called 'mom and pop' plots -- have suffered, you said? And no legitimate timber workers have been attacked?"

"Not so far."

"It should be very interesting, then, to discover who shall be the next victims. Just who will merit death." As he finished speaking, Brown stood, apparently ready to leave.

"Yeah, right." Merrill said, getting to his own feet.

The two men went into the outer office, Brown very gracious and polite when Darla asked him about his books. "I just completed revisions on the Sasquatch book," he said, and the new edition should be in stores by Christmas, a few things removed and quite a number of pages added. I even tackled the very valid concern of just how such large creatures manage to travel over long distances undetected. They definitely seem to migrate."

"And your theories are..?" Darla asked, dimpling at Brown.

"One is that they may simply be very cautious. Near-human intelligence should permit good route choices, as well as offer low visibility. They seem to keep to higher elevations during the warmer months, but prefer heavy timber and ready access to water. Without the option of hibernation, they have to be where there is adequate forage. In fact, that is the largest single problem with the existence of an animal of such size. What do they eat on a year-round basis? There are plenty of green and growing things during summer, but *winter* is a different matter."

"What other theories are there on their seasonal movements?" Merrill asked. A lot of loggers reported sightings and evidence of Sasquatch activity, but, in most cases, what they saw -- or *thought* they saw -- could just as easily have been a lighter colored black bear.

"Well," Brown said, with a sheepish grin that made him look years younger, "a bit distant one is that they utilize the old natural 'ley-lines' and geodetic force-fields so dear to the hearts of occultists. The geodesic nodes of convergence are supposed to allow instantaneous travel between them, and might even connect parallel worlds. As I said, *most* far-fetched."

"But that's the one you favor, isn't it?" said Darla.

"I'll never tell, Ms. Kuhn," Brown answered, "and I'm not just being coy and clever. I am known for being an adventurous fellow, a good researcher, and a stone-reliable presenter of ideas and theories. A sort of 'Indiana Brown,' if you will. Going out on some cracked-pot limb does not serve me well in terms of image, financial backing, or book sales." He put his right hand over his heart, smiling mischievously. "So, please, do not impugn my honor. And, should you tell anyone, I will, as always, deny all."

"I'll read the new edition," Darla said. "I promise."

"Wonderful! Then my journey was not in vain." He turned to Merrill. "I almost hate to leave, Sheriff, but I must get to Portland and check through my slides before tonight's lecture. Thank you for your time, and yours, too, Ms. Kuhn."

Merrill followed Brown out to his rental car, an unremarkable dark blue Nissan Altima. He sensed a hesitation about the Irishman, as though something had been left unsaid. When they shook hands, Merrill asked, "Anything more, Mister Brown?"

The smaller man looked up at the sheriff. "Yes, there is. Yours is not the first story of a physically unique, unkillable human which I've encountered. There are four others. One in Colorado, two in the Himalayas, and one from Black Dragon Mountain in upper China. The others are less recent, more of the stuff of rumor and legend, but very similar to yours."

As he spoke, Brown got into the Nissan. He rolled down his window, and started the engine. "One more thing, Sheriff. Don't limit your search to the male sex only. The Chinese example was female."

TWENTY-THREE

Memorial Day weekend got off to a slow start, an unexpected blessing. A little after four in the afternoon, a comparatively unstressed Darla Kuhn came into Merrill's private office. She left the door open about six inches so they could hear the phone, then sat opposite her boss.

"Did you *see* their car?" she asked.

"No," Merrill replied, looking at her with puzzlement. "Something special?"

"'64 289 V-8 candy-apple red Ford Mustang, glass-pack mufflers. Didn't you *hear* it when they left? That *incredible* rumble?"

"Yeah. Paperweight fell on the floor. I thought it was a log truck. Those two Japanese guys had a *Mustang*? Shit, I would've *killed* for one of those when they first came out."

"What'd they want?"

"Apparently, this is designated monster day. They read about the 'continuing mystery' in the *Bend Bulletin*, didn't have a tee-time this afternoon, and thought they'd have a chat with me. I didn't realize how many homes at Sunriver are owned by Japanese corporations, how much golf they play. They were nice enough people, though. I think they were disappointed when I told them their <u>Arigami</u> - - their word for monster -- is probably human." Merrill held up two business cards, in both English and Japanese. "I told 'em I'd be in touch."

"An outright lie. Tsk-tsk," Darla said, laughing. "And now, I believe you said you were going to discuss your girlfriend with me?"

Without a word, Merrill removed the thin file with the Ricky Jo Mullin/Rikka Thorsen information. He handed it across the desk, then watched Darla as she went through it. Her breath caught several times, her eyebrows did a few jumps and twists, and she looked at him sharply twice.

As she read, Merrill opened the large drawer on the left side of his desk and brought out a small basketball about six inches in diameter. After shutting the drawer, he spun the ball on his right index finger for half a minute, then, watching his deputy, tossed it idly from one hand to the other while Darla finished.

When she was done, Darla fixed him with what he admitted constituted a fair imitation of his own sternest look.

"This isn't one of your jokes?"

The ball now spinning on the palm of his left hand, Merrill said only, "Nope."

"Then what does it mean? This, what?..*resurrection*?.... cost someone time and money." Darla pointed at the booking photograph of Ricky Jo. "This person is nearly gone, Virgil. We saw cases like this when I was in school in Monmouth. We'd tour the treatment facilities. Right at the end, they look like this." She drew a finger across her throat. "Croak City."

"Nice term for our nation's troubled youth, you cynic, you," the sheriff replied, chuckling. He set the ball down on his desk, in a loop of phone cord. "Whatever happened to her must have taken about five-six months, judging from her last arrest. Somebody -- apparently altruistic -- yanked her off the street, and paid for her treatment. Then they purchased and refurbished Ida Murtchison's little bungalow on 4th Street, provided 'Ms. Thorsen' with a monthly stipend, and here she is. One of us, blending in. Slick as a whistle and just as clean."

"What does she *do*?" Darla asked.

"Works in her yard, hikes a lot since the weather turned nice. Supposedly, she's taking a break after

100

college -- only we know there wasn't any college. Used to see her Jeep up in the woods, but these past two weeks, I think she's been walking from her house. Earlier this week, she ran across Walt Whitaker, helped him build water bars on some motorcycle trails. She says she liked Walt. I expect Walt liked her. I plan on calling him this evening, stand him to a few beers, ask him about our Ms. Thorsen."

Darla kept studying Rikka Thorsen's file, re-reading bits of it, and then returning to the booking photograph, shaking her head. "I'm going to have get a good look at her. I just can't imagine that such a physical wreck could be restored." She lifted her gaze from the picture to Merrill. "You know, as much time as she spends up in the woods, she could be the killer's next victim."

"Don't think so," the sheriff replied, "since she's just hiking around. The deaths have all been people who were exploiting federal lands for their own profit. The Dilts boys were timber thieves. The Ukraininans cleared brush, put out rodent bait, and fertilized their young plants. A *big* operation."

"There are *lots* of pot-growers out there," Darla protested.

"Just little mom-and-pop things," Merrill scoffed. "They stick a dozen or so plants in the ground, leave 'em to mature, maybe check on 'em every couple weeks. Deer eat half the crop, bugs get some of the rest. It's all low-effort, low-impact. Maybe they sell some of it, but most is for home or medicinal use. Doesn't really harm the environment."

Darla looked at him quizzically. "So you've decided this is like the monetary limit to qualify a sin as mortal -- in the eyes of the Church -- a hundred bucks, or whatever it is now? Get to a certain point and the Angel of Death rips you a new one?"

101

The sheriff thought about that. "My best guess," he said. "These aren't opportunistic homicides, I'm almost sure of it. Someone waited for the Diltses. Someone actively scouted the Ukrainians."

"So your sweetheart will be safe?" Darla's smile was pure evil.

"God, I hope so," Merrill intoned piously, looking wistfully over Darla's head. "I'd hate to lose her so early in our budding relationship."

"You don't realize it, Virgil, but you're about half serious."

"Only with respect to what she represents. Who put her here, and why? Hell, this is the best mystery that's turned up around here in years. My money's on some federal agency. The question is, which one? Has to be Interior or DEA."

"You're not putting me off that easily. We can come back to this subject at a later date, you know."

"I'd be awful surprised if we didn't," Merrill said, picking up the little basketball again. "Who's on duty this weekend?" The County always put two deputies on patrol in the area on summer weekends.

"Gina Vasquez and Ray Hoppman," Darla answered.

"Good choice." Merrill approved of female-male officer pairings. Rowdy campers were generally more inclined to behave themselves if a woman deputy was part of the duty team. Even people who wanted to be out-of-control seemed to get themselves together in front of a female officer.

"And," Darla continued, "Carvel Hunnecker is back on duty the first of the month. Got the wires off his jaws yesterday."

"Oh, crap." Carvel Hunnecker was the other Game Warden, Greg Dickson's slightly junior partner. In March, Hunnecker had made the mistake of going to visit Ellen Jean Hollis -- his somewhat-estranged girlfriend -- to try and

102

reconcile. He'd fondled her ass while she bent over her freezer, and Ellen Jean'd backhanded him with a frozen steelhead, breaking his lower jaw in three places.

"I knew you'd be thrilled. What is *with* him, anyway?"

"Oh, his dad was a B-movie actor in the late fifties and early sixties. Made six 'Hunnecker the Jungle Man' films, and a slew of other bit parts, mostly beach movies. Shows up in a lot of old late-night stuff. Came back to Oregon with Carvel's mother, settled on a farm down in the valley." Merrill chuckled. "The kid was raised with his dad's stories, plus albums filled with Hollywood memorabilia, and my theory is that he felt cheated out of a movie-brat childhood. Good-lookin' young girls in skimpy swimsuits seem to trigger his sense of loss at not being totally screwed-up, make him grumpy. Since the lake and campgrounds are full of bikinis and what not during the summer, Carvel spends most of that time irritated. Takes it out on people."

"You're kidding!"

"Nope. And he *hates* the Beach Boys."

Darla looked at him with sudden understanding. "So *that's* why you play their CDs whenever he's here. I always wondered about that. You sneaky old devil!"

Grinning modestly, the sheriff put his basketball back in its drawer and brought out a small stack of CDs. "Yup," he said, thumbing through them. "'Bout time to get the machine loaded up for the season, too. Hate to take up too much of Carvel's time."

"You should be ashamed," Darla said, shaking her head.

"Not me," Merrill grinned. "Just bein' practical."

103

The sun hadn't quite dropped over the horizon when Virgil Merrill strolled onto his front porch and settled into one of several carved wooden lawn chairs he'd brought out of storage the previous weekend. He lifted a non-alcoholic beer from the small Coleman cooler beside the chair, snapped it open, and took a couple of sips. Then he re-read the library print-out Helen Endicott had given him.

Rikka Thorsen's reading list, composed mostly of novels, anthologies, psychology books, and memoirs. He was pleased to see that she'd read everything he recommended, then remembered what Darla Kuhn had said that afternoon, and winced. Hearing those words had made him realize for certain that his interest in Rikka wasn't entirely professional, though he'd pooh-poohed it at the time.

Merrill smiled to himself. Well, interest or no, he wouldn't be getting into any nineteen-year-old shorts any time soon. An absurd thought, anyway.

The key titles on the list had been checked out right before the Dilts boys met their maker. The sheriff let his gaze drift down the page. Four books altogether: *Deadly Fighting Skills of the World, Stalk and Kill, The Way of the Warrior, and U.S. Marines Close-Quarters Combat Manual.*

He read them through again, and felt the same dull unease dribble down his spine, heightened a bit more, perhaps, with each re-reading. Malcolm Brown's remark that the killer could be a woman kept repeating in his mind. Plus, she was well under Brown's weight limit of two hundred pounds.

All quite ridiculous, of course, his common sense told him, but he couldn't quite push that nagging doubt away.

He glanced up from the sheet of paper, at the lowering sun shining through the branches of the Red cedar next to his front sidewalk. Just after eight-thirty. Walt Whitaker should be here in a few minutes. Merrill had phoned the older man before leaving his office, caught Walt on his way to the Safeway. Walt had agreed to show up for a beer and a chat right around sundown.

The sheriff figured the easiest way to deal with the situation would be to ask Walt straight out if there was anything unusual about Rikka Thorsen. An afternoon spent building water bars should provide plenty of insight to someone as observant as Walt.

When the sun had slipped below the western foothills, Walt came up the sidewalk at his usual brisk pace, his posture the envy of any Marine drill sergeant. A career habit of shifting his mailbag from one shoulder to the other while doing his route apparently had kept Walt from having the usual mailcarrier hip, shoulder, or back problems.

"Evening, Walter," the sheriff said, as Whitaker opened the gate. "Got a cold one waitin'."

"Sounds plenty good," Walt replied, plopping down in the chair on the other side of the cooler. When he'd selected a bottle of Henry Weinhard's and opened it on the end of the cooler, he took a drink and smacked his lips. "Hits the spot. Long day up in the woods today, clearing winter fall off a couple of trails. And just in time, too. Folks were already pulling into the trailheads by noon, gettin' in a few hours of riding before they head for the campgrounds."

The fleeting thought came to Merrill that perhaps a campground full of people would be outright

105

slaughtered over the weekend, but that didn't begin to fit his homicide motivation scenario. He was fairly certain on that one, although he'd told the on-duty deputies to cruise though several of the more remote camping areas, just in case.

"How heavily are those trails used?" he asked Walt.

Walt considered for a moment. "On the nicer weekends, 'bout fifty percent of capacity, mostly family groups or purely recreational riders. These trails are a little too smooth and slow for the go-fast speed worshippers. They head east to the desert. The folks who come here are inclined to stop and smell the roses, look at the scenery. Not that there aren't places where you throw caution to the winds, crank that throttle open, and go like hell. There are. It just isn't all the time. Some people *like* all the time."

"Oh," the sheriff replied, nodding. He leaned toward Walt. "Say, I heard you had Ida Murtchison's grandniece, Rikka Thorsen, helpin' you up in the woods the other day. She looks to me like she could put in a good day's work."

"Funny you should ask," Walt said, taking another pull on his bottle. "I've never seen anything like her. First she dug a water bar trench in twenty minutes that would take a really fit grown man half again as long. Then she ran alongside my motorcycle to the next water bar. I went fairly slow, and she sweat pretty good, but she never got even close to out-of-breath. By the time we finished two more water bars, we were a good twenty miles from town, so she agreed to ride behind me coming back. The whole way, it was like she wasn't there, she was so perfectly balanced on the machine." He grinned at Merrill, then laughed. "An amazing young lady, the sort I'd want

106

for a daughter or granddaughter. Except I think her parents probably came from the planet Krypton."

The sheriff laughed along with his guest, ignoring the twisting sensation in his stomach. "Anything else?" he asked, trying not to appear too interested.

"She ate two logger burgers at the Chain last night, half a plate of nachos, and drank a pitcher of beer. Swear to god, I think she could've put away even more. Oh, and Ole Thorsen came over and introduced himself."

"Supergirl and the World's Biggest Galoot, huh?"

"They really hit it off," Walt said. "Ole treated her like they *were* related, and Rikka said afterward what a nice guy Ole was."

"Don't you think she sort of expects everyone to be nice, Walt?" Merrill asked quietly, still sipping his beer.

Before answering, Walt looked around for a second or two, as though searching for something, his right hand fluttering. He frowned, sighing in frustration. "You know, Virgil, I smoked a pipe for close to thirty years, quit when I was fifty-five. Even after fifteen years, whenever I try to do any deep thinkin', I start to reach for that damned pipe."

"Sorry, Walter," the sheriff said, amused, setting his empty can down and reaching for a full one.

"You don't have to smirk."

"Sorry." Merrill popped the can top.

"S'all right. Anyway, to answer your question -- you're right, but that's not it, exactly. Rikka's kind of like someone raised outside our society. We expect *them* to be foreign, look foreign, talk with an accent. She doesn't have any of that, but there are missing spots in her knowledge that even a city kid who suddenly found herself in a little hick town like this one wouldn't have."

"Yet she has quite a lot of confidence."

"True," Walt said, letting more Henry's roll down his throat. "And she's not afraid to ask questions about things. Hell, she looked around the Chain last night like she was at Disneyland, takin' it all in, askin' about this or that. She went to school in Corvallis?"

Merrill nodded. "Yup, graduated early -- in February. Came up here to recuperate from bein' educated." Left unsaid was the fact that Rikka Thorsen hadn't much of a life until she got here. That, the sheriff suspected, was why everything interested Rikka so much -- it was all new. "Anything else?" he asked.

"She picks up things real quick. I didn't have to explain somethin' more'n once. She remembers every word you tell her. And her hearing's real good. There were some elk up on a ridge top near one of the water bars. I saw her head come up about five minutes before I heard even the slightest noise." Walt swallowed the last of his beer. "And I think her ears wiggle."

"*What?*"

Walt reached for the cooler, flipped the top open, still talking. "When she first hears a sound, they twitch toward it. She tries not to, but I saw 'em move every once in a while, when she thought I wasn't looking. Some people can actually do that, you know. The ear muscles are still there on all of us." He stuck his fresh bottle against the cap remover and levered the cap off.

"I'm guessing that in animals it's an automatic response," the sheriff said. "We had enough cats and dogs over the years, and that's how it seemed to work for them. So you think she sort of stifles it after that first little flick?"

Walt considered that for a moment. "Yeah. She didn't do it at all last night in the Chain, though."

"Noise comin' from all directions, maybe, and in an unthreatening circumstance. But I bet if someone made a sudden loud sound, it'd happen." Merrill leaned back and crossed his legs, looking at the red blooms on the clematis cloaking his white picket fence. He tapped his beer can on the arm of his chair. "Interesting that so many odd physical characteristics would crop up in one person. None of 'em by themselves too unusual. Taken together...well, let's say it's real strange."

"You didn't offer me a beer just to pick my brain about Rikka Thorsen, did you, Virgil?"

"Not exactly," Merrill replied. Without mentioning any names, he gave Walt a short version of his conversation with Malcolm Brown, and their consensus that the lone killer had to be holed up somewhere along a twenty-mile stretch of the North Cedar River.

"It couldn't be Rikka!" Walt protested. "She's just a young girl."

"Now don't get all het up, just because I asked about her. I agree. It can't be her. Not just because she's such a nice kid, either. There are plenty of pleasant sociopaths runnin' around out there. No, Walt, whoever did the Dilts boys and those Ukrainians had received considerable training along the way. Training takes time. Nobody in her age group has had the time. Simple as that." He uncrossed his legs and stretched his arms into the air, yawning. "Chances are, though, it's somebody new in the area, and that's what we're lookin' for. Somebody in the twenty-five to thirty age group with a military background. You run across anybody who fits that description recently?"

"No," Walt answered, tugging thoughtfully on his beard, "not that I recall. What's Marv Bullock have to say about this?"

Merrill snorted. "In an election year, even if the killings have taken place on federal lands technically not in his jurisdiction? Let's just say that good old Marvin would just love to have one of his own make the collar. And preferably me and not some up-and-comer who might get swept into office on the high tide of an adoring public."

"I hadn't thought of that," Walt said, tugging on his beard again. "Sure makes sense, though."

"Believe it," the sheriff replied. "Marvin Bullock does a hell of a job, but he does understand the fickle nature of the political winds."

"So you want me to keep my eyes and ears open for some ex-Green Beret with homicidal tendencies?"

"And an environmental agenda -- maybe. I'm gonna have a word with Charlie Wamic, Earl Pogue and a few of the other old-timers. See if they can do the same thing. Might scare up something."

A sly grin crept over Walt's face. "Will there be a reward?"

Merrill reached down and picked up another Henry's, holding it out to the retired postman. "I think you're drinkin' it, Walter."

TWENTY-FIVE

The circa-1960 Virgil Merrill didn't look all that different from the 1999 version, Rikka Thorsen thought, as she examined copies of yearbook pages and newspaper articles. He was a bit more relaxed around the eyes then, and sterner about the mouth. She grinned to herself. Jocks having their picture taken probably all tried to look grim as death. Every team picture taken since the invention of the camera seemed to confirm that.

Rikka sat back in her chair, a pencil between her teeth, studying the computer-rendered history of the Merrill family through forty years of photographs and memories. At first it was only Virgil and Debra at the U of O, and never together, except for one dance photo in 1960 at the Junior Prom. For him it was basketball, lettermen, and ROTC; for her, ski club, tennis, and biology.

Debra Diane Morgan had been a relaxed, short-haired blonde, tall and slender, generally with a wide smile on her freckled features. Someone I would have liked, Rikka mused, looking at Debra Morgan's tomboy grin, had I been alive then and known her. How was it that the Fates took a person like that, and left people like Rikka's parents, whose concept of fun always involved drugs and booze, and who felt that personal responsibility was for other people?

Rikka shuddered at the thought of her parents. The rewired brain that Doctor Sims had given her persisted in dredging up memories long-vanished, gradually filling in a million-part puzzle. Except when she was very small, few of Rikka's recollections of her mother and father were remotely positive. They had either been high on something and useless, or straight, depressed, and uninterested. She couldn't even remember their names.

Nor did she want to.

Ever.

It *would* happen, though. Her healing mind would restore that information, along with everything else, thanks to Sims.

She shouldn't complain. Rikka owed all of her new existence to Maureen Sims, and once she completely mastered the Black Voice, her life would be in order. She clenched her right fist in triumph.

A sharp pain stabbed through her hand. Rikka looked down in surprise at the splintered pencil sticking into her palm. She'd removed it from her mouth without realizing, then snapped it in thirds when she made the fist.

After tossing the bits of pencil into her wastebasket, Rikka held her hand palm up under the halogen desklamp, watching the wound heal. Her body even absorbed the tiny slivers under her skin. Within ten seconds, no trace of her injury remained.

Thank you, Doctor Sims.

Rikka moved rapidly through the Merrill file, making sure she'd scanned everything in the proper historical order. The *Sentinel* had treated the Merrill family's arrival in North Cedar thirty years ago as a big event, with pictures of the sheriff, his wife, and their three small children. The paper'd also included a shot of his high school basketball team, in Drain, south of Eugene in the Willamette Valley. Drain was even smaller than North Cedar, another little lumber town that hadn't had the recreational potential afforded by the North Cedar River or the lake, and had thus been hit harder by the loss of timber revenues.

Virgil Merrill had muscled up in college, Rikka saw. She smiled at the boy in the high school picture. He'd been pretty bony then. Still broad-shouldered and thick-wristed, with a no-nonsense expression on his young features, but decidedly skinnier.

The Merrill offspring, shown in numerous newspaper articles over the years, favored their parents. David, the eldest, and Maryanne, the youngest, both looked like their mother, with platinum hair and freckles. Kathy, the lawyer and middle child, square-featured and almost certainly red-haired, was a virtual female copy of her father. God, Rikka thought, studying the tall, somber girl's picture, she must be hell in a courtroom, with those pale eyes that could probably bore right through you.

Satisfied that she'd gotten the file entered into the computer properly, Rikka returned to the shot of the high school basketball team. Maybe she should've gone to Drain, snooped around there a bit. Plenty of people ought to remember the high-scoring center from the class of '58 -- the 'Drain Adding Machine.' She wondered briefly what pea-brained sports reporter had thought *that* one up.

Anyway, the sheriff's folks might even still be alive. Not that she could talk to them. Virgil Merrill seemed like someone who kept in touch with his family. A curious female stranger on his parents' doorstep would be a large mistake on her part. Still, Drain was something to consider at some point in the future.

She went back to the team picture, clicking her mouse to isolate and enlarge Merrill's face.

Forty-two years ago he'd been maybe a year younger than Rikka was now. Almost a lifetime, yet she found herself drawn to him -- the one person she'd met locally who she was positive could be dangerous to her.

God, this was stupid! And foolish. Rikka cradled her face in her hands, her gaze still on the screen, wishing she could will her growing moth-to-the-flame fascination away.

Knowing she couldn't.

There was irony in the attraction. Rikka knew it was mutual. She'd been close enough to the sheriff at the library to smell his interest and recognize it as sexual.

Rikka might be more aware of his response than he was, though she doubted it. Merrill knew himself well.

"I'm sorry for you, Virgil," Rikka spoke aloud to the young features on the screen before her, touching the glass with the tip of her right index finger. "Everything in your life must've seemed close to perfect. Then, five years ago, your wife died of ovarian cancer." She felt her eyes mist. "You must be terribly lonely sometimes." Rikka leaned back and folded her arms across her chest, her brown eyes still locked on the screen. She blinked a couple of times to clear her vision.

"You're not the only one," she said, very softly.

TWENTY-SIX

By noon Saturday of the Memorial weekend, the
Thorsen brothers had positioned the tall Skagit
yarder-tower in the center of the old Sharkey's
landing. Cabled down, the
four-foot-thick steel and aluminum column
telescoped sixty feet into the sky from its six-
wheeled undercarriage. While Sigge checked the
tension on the cables, Ole tested the winches and
the cable-wound drums which snaked felled logs up
to the landing.

Most of the early logging operations in Oregon
had involved narrow-gauge railroads punched into
roadless stands of old-growth timber. The logging
crews rode in on the trains to camps where they
stayed for weeks at a time, living in tents and
wolfing down five thousand calories a day. Steam-
driven portable donkey engines yarded the huge
logs up out of canyons and along ridgetops onto
waiting rail cars, and the trains carried the timber to
the mills down in the valley.

A time of romantic legend gone forever, Ole
Thorsen knew. Big trees cut by big men working
from first light to sundown. You still saw the
stumps of those forest giants in some stands of
mature second- and third-growth trees, and rusting
cable winding down the ridges.

'Getting out the cut' had meant something in those
days, when a growing America demanded wood for
homes, furniture, stoves, and fireplaces. Ole
frequently wished he had been alive then, listening
to tall tales around the campfire, and riding the little
train out of the woods on a Saturday night, intent
on beer, gambling, and women in the roistering
timber towns at the railhead.

Arvid Sharkey had been alive during the glory years of logging, and was still around when Ole and Sigge's father was a boy. Thankfully, Sharkey hadn't lived to see the current state of the timber industry, where operating decisions were made in boardrooms instead of on-site, and family-owned operations had become novelties.

Change had been inevitable. Ole knew that. Planting hybrid trees which grew at twice the rate of the older Douglas fir, maintaining watercourses and riparian zones, and preserving shaded spawning beds for trout, salmon, and steelhead. All good and necessary things. Forest Management had evolved into a science, which explained why both he and Sigge had degrees in Forestry from Oregon State.

And there were still Thorsens on the land. That was very important in the eternal scheme of things.

Satisfied that the equipment would be ready to go on Tuesday, Ole walked away from the tower's base, smiling and giving Sigge the high sign. Sigge's wife Erika and their two children should arrive shortly. Ole rubbed his hard stomach, which was threatening to gnaw a hole in his backbone. Erika would bring lunch with her. He was fond of his sister-in-law for any number of valid reasons, one of the strongest being her ability to prepare hearty food in quantities that even Ole found gratifying.

He stood on the edge of the landing and looked east, down into Perkins Creek, a couple of hundred feet below, through the remnants of morning mist glowing in the sunlight near the water's surface. Sigge's kids might enjoy some fishing this afternoon, or maybe just a hike along the stream, looking for frogs. His brother and Erika would welcome the time to themselves, and Ole could bask in his role as favorite uncle.

116

Only uncle, he reminded himself. Erika had no brothers to provide competition for him. When Arno and Jan were just little crawlers, Ole would lie down on the floor, and they would climb over him like puppies. Now that they were grade-schoolers, they tried to wrestle their big uncle down to the ground, shoving and tugging at him until he finally collapsed, wailing in feigned distress.

Life was very good, Ole reflected, although his parents frequently questioned him concerning changing his marital status. A wife might be a good thing, Ole realized. Someone to share more than tales of hunting, fishing, sports, or the woods. A person could only drink so much beer, slap so many people on the back, before the sameness of life began to get boring.

Perhaps he would get to know that Rikka Thorsen better next time he saw her at the Chain. The girl had a grip like no woman he'd ever met. And damned few men, either. Worse yet for his ego, Ole suspected that she hadn't been bearing down during their handshake.

A very interesting woman.

He bet she couldn't cook worth a darn, though. Of course, he thought, stroking his stubbled chin, looking down at his feet, there were other things men and women could do together besides eat.

The occasional movie or concert, for example. He chuckled deeply to himself, then bent down to the ground. In front of his boots, a dull line of rust, half-covered with dirt, had caught his attention.

He poked at it with a forefinger, dislodging a long iron rail spike. He picked the spike up, turning it in his hand, flaking off the encrusted clay with one large thumb. The spike's head still showed flats from the gandy-dancer's hammer, eighty years or more ago.

Ole looked around the edge of the freshly-gravelled landing. How many more spikes lay under its surface? Dozens, maybe hundreds, along with heaven knew how much broken crockery, silverware, and other non-burnable trash. He tossed the spike in the air and caught it, one of the few things left of the original logging operation. The cook sheds, the bunkhouses, the equipment, even the rails, had all been removed or gone to rust like this spike. In another eighty years, maybe even the landing itself would be over-grown. Probably not, though, Ole thought. There were several ridge trails that converged at this point, and elk, deer, hunters, and fishermen would certainly keep those open.

And it would still be called Sharkey's Landing, in all probability. There would be no evidence of the Thorsen brothers, however, and no one would recall a two-hundred-acre logging show run before the turn of the century.

Lost in thought, Ole didn't hear his brother come up behind him. "What do you have there?" Sigge asked, putting one big arm around his older brother's shoulders, and peering down at Ole's hands.

"Just an old spike," Ole replied. "I'll take it home to Papa."

Sigge roared with laughter, the sound echoing off over the treetops. "Papa has at least a hundred pounds of old spikes that you carried home with you when we were little! Give me that! I'll throw it over the side." He reached around Ole for the spike.

"No, it's mine!" Ole laughed, lifting the spike over his head, dancing sideways away from Sigge, holding his brother off with his free hand.

When Erika and the children arrived five minutes later, in their emerald-green Chevy Suburban, the Thorsen brothers were still chasing each other

118

around the landing, scuffling like a pair of slightly-undersized Grizzly bear. Only when they became aware of three sets of amused eyes staring at them through the Suburban's windows, did they stop, wheezing with laughter, sheepish expressions on their faces.

TWENTY-SEVEN

Surrounded by nitwits and fanatics was not the way Charles D. "Chuckie" Morberg wanted to live his life. Damned fine thing the money was good, he thought, as he hiked resolutely through the darkness, one of a group of five, carrying a backpack filled with plastic explosive.

Bunch of kids, too, all of them less than Chuckie's twenty-eight, though he looked ten years or more younger. Green as grass these four were. They had the courage of their convictions, a strong sense of their moral high ground, and their parents' checkbooks.

Chuckie was happy to deal with the latter, and willing to put up with the rest. He'd gone into the Army at eighteen, right after high school, volunteered for Special Forces, taken demolition training, and then in mid-1990, had been sent off to the Middle East and Operation Desert Storm.

When he landed back at the Demolition Training Center in 1993 -- this time as an instructor -- most of his illusions about life were long departed. After a few months deciding which direction he would go, he'd left the military and offered his services to the highest bidder.

As it turned out, there had been quite a few highest bidders. Chuckie now owned two condos and an impressive portfolio of stocks and bonds. All of which made him feel

much better about being stuck cohabiting with a bunch of granola-crunching, lentil-lapping, party-line-spouting enviro-Nazis. Planet Prime! rhetoric was not his cup of tea.

On the other hand, he'd only have to put up with it through the Fourth of July. Then Chuckie would be off to Spain, doing a little work for the Catalan

Separatists. A job both more dangerous and more lucrative. The Spanish were all too familiar with explosives, and Barcelona existed on a twenty-four hour bomb alert.

Even so, Chuckie figured a blond and blue-eyed American, to outward appearances only in his late teens, would be able to move around Spain easily.

It could be fun.

A different deal entirely from rural Oregon. The local nimrods here had no clue the kid flipping burgers at the Flint Lake Marina was not what he seemed.

But, hey, life was full of nasty surprises.

The two dark figures moving ahead of Chuckie suddenly stopped, and the one in the lead raised a hand. Until he spoke, Chuckie didn't recognize Brian Hibbs. These people all dressed alike, in polarfleece and dark-dyed cotton, so he had a hard time otelling them apart. Except for Mimsy Borogave. She wore some kind of natural herbal bug-repellent that smelled vaguely like maple syrup, so he knew she stood right behind him, her left hand on his left shoulder, kneading his trapezius, breathing in his ear.

"We're about a half-mile from the landing," Brian said. He shone his hooded flashlight on a double strip of bright pink ribbon dangling down from a vine maple limb. Even in the dim light Brian's narrow eyes held a zealot's glow.

A raving loon, in Chuckie's book.

"Good," Chuckie replied, looking to the east. A quarter-moon was barely visible through a line of mature fir. It had just risen over the north face of Mount Jefferson. He flipped his watch cover open. Nearly twenty-three hundred hours -- eleven o'clock. "How much closer do we have to get to have a good view of the landing?" he asked.

121

Matt Wagner, Brian's second-in-command, answered, his slower and deeper speech containing none of his leader's excitement. "There's an open spot about a quarter-mile away from where they'll be set up, at a slightly higher altitude. If you use our night-vision binoculars, you'll be able to see everything."

Chuckie nodded, and snapped his watch closed. Wagner was the easiest of the group for him to stomach, although Mimsy certainly knew how to fuck. Problem was, about the only time she shut up about the environment were the three minutes just before and just after she came. At least she was predictable. He liked that in a woman.

For a while.

"Okay," he said, "get me there, and I'll take care of things while you people wait."

Jeremy Hampson, no taller and even skinnier than Chuckie, spoke up from beside Mimsy. "Hey, we're supposed to help."

Whiny little shit, Chuckie thought, the kind that went home from Boot Camp about fifteen minutes into the first day. Chuckie went on professional mode. "You have. You got me out here. Now let me do my job." He grinned at them in the moonlight, spreading his arms wide. "Big bucks for the big risks, ya know."

No one had an answer to that. They all knew Chuckie wasn't on board for altruistic reasons. Hampson looked from one of them to the other, seeking support. Finding none, he began to pout, his soft features drawing in on themselves. Chuckie just looked back at him. Jesus, the cops get ahold of this wimp, he'll spill everything in a second. Might not be a bad idea to do something about that possibility, before he left for Spain.

For that matter, these people all knew more about him than he wanted, but he'd known that would

122

happen going in. Chuckie had been hired for his expertise, nothing more. Though they didn't like to admit it, Planet Prime!'s demolition people had, in recent years, succeeded mostly in having things either go off prematurely or blowing themselves up.

From a strictly professional view, Chuckie found that both completely hilarious and a good measure of the skills possessed by most environmental terrorists, who apparently thought that *wanting* something to work correctly was somehow enough. Nail bombs, as an example.

Of course, sometimes ignorance cut both ways. He would not have guessed that moon- and starlight could provide sufficient illumination so that five people could walk three miles through the forest without flashlights.

They'd left the Ford Expedition parked about a quarter-mile from the entrance to this trail, pointed away from the trail and on the opposite side of the road. Chuckic had insisted on that, as well as walking well off the road to get to the trail. He'd have preferred to hike the ten miles from their cabins at Lautenbach Hot Springs, but that really wasn't feasible. On a holiday weekend, people might remember a group of well-outfitted hikers at night. They probably wouldn't notice another Expedition.

The trail rose gradually to a small knoll, and, in the distance, near a saddle further down the ridge, Chuckie could see the landing. A yarder-tower stood just west of the landing's center, with two enclosed trailers -- one obviously living quarters -- on opposite sides of the tower. A pick-up and a Suburban were parked near the travel trailer.

"Shit," Brian Hibbs said, looking through his binoculars, "just the tower and an equipment trailer, and someone's there. I'd hoped there'd be a harvester or two, and maybe a forwarder."

Sounding disappointed, he handed the binoculars to Chuckie.

Chuckie snorted. "Like I'd know what *those* are," he said, studying the site, trying to pick the spots to place his charges, to bring the tower down. His companions waited behind him, Hampson audibly fidgeting, Goretex or Klimate or some other waterproof fabric rustling.

Wagner cleared his throat, keeping his voice low. "Harvesters do what the name implies. They grasp the trunk, cut the tree, lift it horizontal, then cut it into sixteen-foot lengths. From there it can go onto a truck or the forwarder -- which looks something like a tractor with a wagon on the front. In most of the Cascades and a lot of the Coast Range, though, the terrain is too steep to use harvesters and forwarders. This site is like that, so they're using a tower. The conventional loaders and skidders'll probably be brought up on Monday evening."

"You know your enemy," Chuckie said, impressed.

Wagner's answer sounded almost sad. "Forestry degree from Oregon State. I wasn't happy with modern forest practices, so I elected to help speed up their evolution."

"I think *I'll* do that," Chuckie replied, smiling at Wagner. "So, if I take down their tower, they won't be able to log?"

Hibbs shook his head and shrugged. "They'll borrow or rent one, get it back up here within a few days." He raised a fist in the moonlight. "But our *message* will be clear."

"Right on," Hampson said, squeaky and irritating.

"Fucking A," said Mimsy, right behind Chuckie, and he heard a rising note of excitement in her throaty voice. It sounded more personal than environmental.

Wagner said nothing, and Chuckie wondered how committed to the cause he still was. Was it flagging devotion, or was he just more in tune with reality?

"You want anything done besides the tower?" Chuckie asked. "I can deliver more bang for your buck -- if you want."

They thought about that for a minute. Finally, Hibbs asked, "Can you put the equipment trailer over the side?" He looked at Wagner as he spoke, and the latter nodded.

"No problemo," Chuckie answered. He handed the binoculars back to Hibbs, reached into his belt-pack and brought out his ex-military night-vision goggles. After switching on the batteries, he donned the goggles, adjusted them, then turned to the four Planet Prime! members and smiled. "Back in a bit," he said, and walked away down the trail to the landing, feeling his adrenaline kick in.

He always liked this part best.

TWENTY-EIGHT

A slow, careful ten minutes brought Chuckie along the ridge to the edge of the landing. He stood in the moonlight, his hand resting on the butt of the CZ 75, its safety off, nestled in its holster under his left armpit. His position was too exposed. All it would take was one person getting up to piss, and he'd be spotted.

Not one hell of a lot he could do about that, though.

As quietly as he could, keeping his gaze on the occupied trailer, Chuckie squatted, removed his backpack and unzipped it. He glanced around the area, mentally noting how many detonators and cubes of Semtex he'd need. If he did the equipment trailer -- and he saw no reason not to -- it would take a double load of explosive on both that and the base of the tower. One each on two of the cable anchors made four detonators and six cubes.

Unwrapping the charges and detonators one by one, he made his way around the landing, pressing each detonator into its respective glob of explosive before switching on the tiny receiver. The equipment trailer gave Chuckie pause for a minute or so, but at last he found a position on the frame that would pivot it against the wheel chocks and flip it off the landing and down into the canyon below.

When he was completely satisfied that everything had been done correctly, Chuckie backed away from the landing the way he'd come, his backpack in his left hand and the CZ in his right. A hundred yards into the trail, mostly screened by tree limbs tipped with the fuzzy tufts of new needles, he turned and walked swiftly back to the waiting quartet of environmental saboteurs. Jeez, he thought, they looked like an ad from a Patagonia catalog, all clumped together for a picture during the ascent of some useless mountain.

"Well," he said, stepping over an oblong boulder, "I think we're all ready." Though he doubted she could see him all that well, he winked at Mimsy.

"Took you long enough," Hampson in that irritating voice of his.

Chuckie regarded him levelly for a moment, then raised the CZ and stuck it against the little twerp's nose. "And your point *is*?" Chuckie asked quietly.

Hampson went absolutely still, his eyes widening in fear. His face looked like he was going to cry, and he began to quiver silently. His lips moved for a few seconds, trying to form words. "N-nothing," he choked out at last.

"I thought so," Chuckie replied, grinning at Hampson as he holstered the CZ. He heard Wagner release his held breath, and Mimsy touched Chuckie's right hand with warm fingers. Chuckie looked at her, saw her parted lips, and knew things were going to be moist at the cabin tonight. *You ain't seen nothing yet, babe,* he thought.

"Okay," Chuckie continued, "if there are no more questions, let's finish up." He turned toward the moonlit landing, and brought the transmitter from the inside pocket of his light nylon jacket. Pointing the device at the scene in the distance, he depressed the activating button.

Explosions ripped the base of the tower, the two cables, and the equipment trailer. The trailer popped up on its rear end, balanced for an instant, then bounced over the edge of the landing and into the canyon. Gravel and dust obscured the lower third of the tower. It began to topple, slowly at first, then faster.

Crashing directly onto the occupied trailer.

"Oops," said Chuckie, without any conviction whatsoever.

TWENTY-NINE

Ole Thorsen woke up in an upside-down tangle of chainsaws, hardhats, peaveys, and logging chain, wedged against the back wall of the trailer. He had just enough time to realize he'd heard an explosion, and then the trailer was tumbling downslope, gaining speed, throwing Ole and everything else alternately into walls, floor, and ceiling.

They were falling into the canyon. The explosion had blown the trailer off the landing.

Curling into a ball, Ole held his ankles, and tucked his head into his chest. The trailer began to come apart around him. Chain and peaveys spun away into the darkness, striking sparks on the boulder-strewn canyon wall.

Something slammed into his head, and the world went grey, then black.

THIRTY

After his Saturday evening workout, Virgil Merrill had showered, slipped into clean sweatpants, a U of O T-shirt, and an old pair of Chuck Taylor All-Stars, and gone for a walk. A block away from his house, going on midnight, he heard the distant sharp double-blast of the explosions from the direction of Sharkey's Landing.

He stopped and looked north into the dark ascending rows of timbered ridges, waiting for another blast. When nothing more came, the image of the Thorsen brothers heading out to the mountains with their logging equipment earlier in the day flashed into his mind.

What he'd heard hadn't sounded like dynamite, exactly, but far too loud for a weapon. He turned and ran back to the house, grabbed his cell-phone, and left a message on the office recorder. Vasquez and Hoppman would check in every half-hour, know he was up in the hills, checking on what he'd heard. Probably wasn't anything significant, anyway.

Then he threw on a light cotton jacket, picked up his patrol car's keys and his Glock, and headed out the door, mentally running an inventory on the rescue equipment he kept in the trunk.

Five minutes later, he was off the pavement and drifting the corners of the wide gravel road out of town, ten miles and a half-dozen intersections from Sharkey's Landing.

THIRTY-ONE

When he came to, the first thing Ole realized was he was lying on his back, half-covered by running water. The second was that at least one wall of the trailer lay on top of him. Also, he thought, groaning, his head felt like the railroad spike he'd found earlier had been driven through his skull.

Most of the rest of him hurt, too. As much as he could, he flexed his arms and legs, gasping in pain, almost losing consciousness again. Nothing seemed broken, but everything *hurt*.

He was in Perkins' Creek, he knew that much. And Sigge, Erika, and their kids must still be on the landing.

The landing. He had to get back up there.

Reaching around with his right arm, searching, Ole found a long handle, and slowly drew it close enough to feel the other end. A jointed arm, a pointed metal tip. A peavey.

Good. Ole brought his knees up to his chest, sliding them along the inner surface of the wall pressing down on him. He ignored the red streaks in his vision. The wall shifted, raised. He stuck the point of the peavey into the wood paneling above him, and pushed.

Only one wall. It wasn't that heavy, no more than four hundred pounds. Grunting with effort, clenching his teeth to keep from screaming from pain, Ole shoved upward, then wedged the peavey between the wall and the stony creek bed.

He fell back, shaking, lying in the cold water until his vision cleared and his panting slowed to normal breathing. The water felt so good flowing around him, cool and soothing against his abraded skin, bruised muscles, and aching joints.

But he had to get back to the landing, find Sigge, Erika, and the kids. Gritting his teeth again, Ole rolled out from under the wreckage of the equipment trailer and into the open air. On his knees, he looked up at the landing. Nothing but blackness showed against the star-strewn night. The moonlight hadn't reached down to the creek yet, but the illuminated canyon rim was stark and silent.

No flashlights. No voices. Gathering his breath Ole shouted into the darkness.

No answering shout came from above.

He shouted again.

Still nothing.

Why didn't they answer? He began to crawl downstream on his hands and knees, away from the steep canyon wall, toward the more gradual timbered slope a hundred feet away. He could use the trees to pull himself up.

Every movement, no matter how small, hurt. Ole had to stop twice on his way to the trees.

Ten minutes later, he grasped the smallest trunk he could find and stood up, swaying, in the stream. Jagged flares of light blossomed behind his eyes at the effort.

He heaved his body out of the water, planted his feet at the base of the first tree, reached for the second.

One tree at a time, Ole Thorsen began his tortuous climb out of the canyon.

THIRTY-TWO

Blood dripped slowly from between the layers of the crushed and flattened trailer, reduced to a stack of splintered plywood and aluminum sheet on a bent frame. Virgil Merrill wasn't sure how many people had been inside, but he was sure no one had survived. The big six-wheeled telescopic tower that had landed on top of the trailer had weighed probably fifteen tons. No signs of life. After circling the wreckage once, he shut off his flashlight, and slowly turned three hundred and sixty degrees, his gaze probing the darkness surrounding the landing.

Marzipan. He'd recognized that smell the instant he opened the car door. Frigging Semtex. Whoever did this had professional connections, had probably known *exactly* what they were doing. They weren't simply vandals who saw an opportunity to have some fun with dynamite, and took it. Perhaps they hadn't intended to kill anyone, just take down the tower, but Merrill wasn't at all sure of that.

Close to forty-five minutes after the explosion, they likely weren't still out there. They had been, though. Hiked in, quietly placed the charges, then watched the explosion from a distance.

Merrill wondered what went through their minds when the tower hit the trailer. He pushed the thought away. Better to examine it later, when this was all sorted out.

Satisfied that nobody sat on the northern slope cradling a sniping rifle -- knowing that a real loon would already have taken him out -- the sheriff returned to his car and started making the calls.

The first went to Vasquez and Hoppman, then the auxiliary clinic at the lake, who would relay in an ambulance from down in the valley. He made certain they understood that this was a pick-up only, with no need for a helicopter or any sophisticated life-support equipment. Knowing they'd need some way to raise the tower off the trailer, he then called Jurgen Alcorn, who skinned cat for the Thorsens. An unbelieving Alcorn already had a loader on his lowboy, and once the sheriff got him calmed down, agreed to bring it up to the site immediately.

Then a final call. "Is this Old Fool Central?" Merrill asked, when Fred Cameron answered, on the sixth ring.

"Christ, Virgil!" Cameron said, more alert than the sheriff had expected, but still muzzy. "This better be something important."

"Fred, I hate to bother you, but we've got at least two homicides up to Sharkey's Landing. One or both of the Thorsen boys. Somebody dropped a yarder-tower on their trailer. Since there's two rigs here, my guess is both Ole and Sigge."

Any residual trace of sleep vanished from the doctor's voice. "Is one vehicle Erika's Suburban?"

Unwillingly, the sheriff found his gaze going to the big green Chevy. "Yeah," he said reluctantly, his heart dropping into his gut, "seems to be."

"Holiday weekend, probably Sigge, her *and* their two kids."

Merrill sagged against the side of the Caprice, his eyes closed, squeezing his forehead with his right hand.

When he didn't reply right away, Cameron sounded concerned. "Virgil, you okay?"

"I'll be all right. Just hadn't thought about Erika and the kids. Christ on a bicycle!" He paused and sighed, his hand still kneading his forehead. "You want to come up here, do the post on-site? I got

133

Jurgen Alcorn on his way with a loader. We'll have 'em out soon enough."

"Of course. Just let me put a fresh roll of film in my camera, check my traveling bag, and I'll be there."

"You know the way?"

"Virgil, I've fished Perkins Creek as much as you have. It'll take me less than an hour."

"Take your time. Jurgen won't be here by then. And, Fred, drive carefully. We don't need to lose anybody else."

"Thanks, Sheriff. Wise of you to remember that physicians in their sixties all drive like maniacs."

Merrill laughed, hollow and unconvincing to his ears. "Just didn't want your shift lever to end up in an embarrassing location, Fred."

"Damn, you're vile sometimes," Cameron laughed, then, "see you in an hour or so."

"Yeah, 'bye," Merrill replied, and hung up. He looked around the landing after dropping the phone onto the Caprice's seat and closing the door. Time to check out the whole area, maybe look at that trail to the north. Nobody'd arrive for close to half an hour. Hefting the flashlight, he snapped it on and walked to the upended base of the fallen tower.

Hell of a hole, the sheriff thought, shining the light into the crater, and real smart charge placement. The guy knew he couldn't blow the thing down directly, so he undermined it. Cute.

Next he inspected the frayed cable ends, tied off on choker collars encircling old stumps on the east side of the landing. Neatly wrapped and neatly blown. A real talent, the bomber had, and probably a shitload of training. Who in hell would do something like *this*? And *why*?

Beyond the southernmost cable, right at the edge of the landing, a stray beam from Merrill's big light caught the rim of a second crater and the sharp outline of a snapped and twisted trailer tongue.

Ah! the sheriff thought, the Thorsen's equipment trailer. The rest of their heavy rigs would have come up on Monday, along with the water wagon, so the bomber only had a limited number of targets. Fred had been right. Sigge and his family had come up for a weekend of recreation, and paid with their lives.

He walked to the edge of the landing after studying the warped trailer tongue for a moment, stepping around seedling fir scattered along the perimeter. Pointing his flashlight down into the canyon, Merrill picked up a fist-sized rock and tossed it into the depths below him, watching it fall through the column of light. A dull thump followed by a splash sounded from the creek.

There, at the very bottom, he could make out the wreckage of the trailer, sections of roof, floor, and walls folded like giant playing cards around boulders and logs left from the winter and spring runoff. The contents of the trailer littered the margin of the stream at the base of the canyon wall, a jagged line of hand tools, snarled chain, and shattered boxes of ribbon and marking paint.

And something else, against a particularly large boulder. Merrill couldn't quite see it clearly. He leaned over the edge, lifting the flashlight over his head.

A *bed*. And next to it, tangled sheets, red-spotted. Blood.

The other rig -- the *pickup*. *Ole*.

Muttering an oath, the sheriff sprinted the thirty yards to his car, unlocked the trunk and took out the two hundred-foot coils of nylon rope he kept for this sort of situation. Running back to the tree line downstream from the ruined trailer, he tied off around a foot-thick fir, looped the second coil around his left shoulder and began backing downslope through the timber.

Thirty feet down, he heard something on the hillside below. Bracing himself against a tree, he shone his flashlight between the dark trunks of the lower timber, and onto a large blood-encrusted figure wedged against the bole of a fir fifty feet below him.

"Ole!" Merrill shouted, "Is that you? It's Virgil Merrill."

The answering grunt was incomprehensible, so the sheriff dropped lower, shouldering his way through the big trees, playing out his rope until he stood beside the injured logger.

One eye swollen half-shut, his face a mass of bruises and contusions, Ole's breathing was ragged. He was drenched in sweat. Shock, Merrill realized. He put his right arm as far as it would go around the bigger man. "C'mon, Ole, let's get you out of here."

"Not so easy, I think," Ole replied, his voice weak. He attempted a grin made lop-sided by swelling.

Merrill smiled back. "Yeah, well, if I get pooped, I know you'll get me out. Let's get this rope around your waist. I'll go back up, bring the patrol car over part-way, hook the winch to the rope, and haul you up."

Swaying despite his grip on the tree, Ole mulled that over for a few moments, then gave up. "Yeah, sure," he said, finally, blinking his good eye. Suddenly he grabbed the sheriff's arm. "Sigge, Erika, the kids. What about them?"

Merrill shook his head. No use trying to hide the truth. "The tower fell on their trailer, Ole." He continued shaking his head. "I'm sorry."

Burying his face against the sheriff's chest, gripping Merrill so hard the sheriff thought he'd crack a rib, Ole sobbed only once. Then he straightened up, his expression determined. "First we get me out of here, Virgil. Then we get the bastards who done this."

"Fair enough," Merrill replied, and double-looped the rope around Ole's waist and tied a slip-knot. He folded Ole's hands around the knot. "Stay on your feet and we'll be okay. I'll winch slow. Remember, if you lose your footing, and it starts to drag you, pull the knot loose. We don't want to wedge you against a tree and damage you any more than you are already."

"Yeah, yeah," Ole agreed, "but I think I'm plenty damaged now. Don't know how much more I have room for."

"None, I hope." The sheriff began climbing back up to the landing, hand-over-hand. "Have you out in a jiff."

It took ten minutes, with Merrill keeping one hand on the winch controls, and the other on the winch cable, his patrol car's headlights illuminating the scene. If there was still someone out on the northern hillside, watching, they'd know when Ole appeared over the rim of the landing that there was a survivor. An itch of apprehension burned between Merrill's shoulder blades, half-expecting the high-powered rifle slug that never came.

At last Ole rolled over onto the landing, lying on his left side as his hands feebly worked at the knotted rope. The sheriff knelt down beside the huge logger and jerked the knot loose, then covered Ole with the heavy wool blanket from his trunk.

He positioned himself so that Ole couldn't see the crushed trailer, and spent the ten minutes until Vasquez and Hoppman arrived talking softly about everything and anything except the deaths of four innocent people, two of them children.

There would be more than enough time for that later.

THIRTY-THREE

Even wearing civilian clothes and carrying a bouquet of roses, Virgil Merrill felt horribly conspicuous and uneasy walking through the main entrance of Valley Memorial Hospital, early Sunday evening. He didn't care for hospitals, and liked this particular one least of all.

Deb had died here.

The final two weeks of her existence were contained within these walls, he had been at her side for most of it, and each and every sight and smell brought it all back to life.

Or death, actually.

He walked directly to the elevators, each step stirring memories long and mercifully buried, rising like dust from the carpet. He knew what he'd gone through in the years since Deb's death had been a sort of denial, but he also knew that denial of terrible experiences helped a person recover.

And he'd thought he'd *been* over them. Now he wasn't so sure. At least he'd had the foresight to bring some chewing gum, so his jaws didn't lock up on him.

The elevator doors opened and the sheriff stepped inside, punching the third floor button. His finger had lingered near and almost pushed five, the floor Deb had been on. Three, however, housed no terminal cases. Ole Thorsen, beat to hell though he was, would live.

In fact, Ole might be as sore as a human could be, but there had been no broken bones, only two nearly-dislocated shoulders and more bruises and scrapes than even Ole's body had square inches of skin.

As Fred Cameron had explained to Merrill, their biggest concern was that the deep bruises in Ole's arms and legs might pass a clot into one of his lungs or his brain.

So Ole, wired up to more monitors than were decent, and pumped full of blood thinners and pain meds, was technically only under observation for the next few days, unless the batteries of tests and X-rays had missed something.

The senior Thorsens, Hakon and Katie, had gotten to keep *one* of their sons, at least.

The doors slid open and the sheriff turned left, knowing the room numbering system by heart. Room three-seventeen would be on the right, with an outside window facing the parking lot.

Merrill paused for a second and took a deep breath before entering the room. Ole's folks would be in there, and he would be on the receiving end of their questions.

Sure enough, Hakon and Katie were seated beside their son's bed, Katie with her right hand under Ole's pillow, and Hakon with a burly arm around his wife's shoulders.

The head which came up when he walked in, though, didn't belong to either of Ole's parents. The sheriff found himself looking directly into the fierce brown gaze of Rikka Thorsen.

"Good evenin'," he said, nodding and smiling to her, trying to keep from showing his surprise, thinking that Rikka looked as though she expected someone to come through the door with a gun, intent on finishing Ole off.

She smiled back at him, rose from her chair, and walked around the end of Ole's bed to him. The momentary hostility left her face completely.

"Let me get those in some water, Sheriff," she said, grinning sweetly at him as she took the bouquet. She wore a cobalt-blue long-sleeved silk blouse, tan cotton slacks, and loafers whose color matched her blouse perfectly. Her short black hair looked as though it had received well over the traditional hundred brush strokes, and a Celtic cross pendant hung from a golden chain encircling her neck. Even under these circumstances, she was breathtaking.

"It's the Sheriff," Rikka announced to the senior Thorsens, who still hadn't noticed either his entrance or Rikka's greeting. She lowered her voice as she turned away to get the empty vase on Ole's nightstand. "I knew you'd come," she said, and winked at him.

His heart missed a beat.

Hakon Thorsen stood, Merrill's height but twice as wide, and shook himself like a bear getting the kinks out. He smiled at the sheriff, the act in no way diminishing the misery that cloaked his face and body. "Good of you to come by, Virgil," Hakon said. "I expect you've had a pretty busy day, haven't you? And I don't have to tell you how we feel about you getting Ole out of that canyon." Unspoken was the question of who had done this terrible thing, who had destroyed a large part of the Thorsen family.

"Wish neither of us had this day, Hakon," the sheriff replied, wishing, too, that he had his hat so he'd have something to occupy his hands.

Katie Thorsen -- tall, angular, and going grey -- stepped around her husband and hugged Merrill. "Oh, Virgil!" she sobbed, her head on his left shoulder. Tears wet through the thin cotton of his shirt.

Nothing made him feel more helpless than grief, his own or someone else's. He patted Katie on her broad back, not knowing what else to do, glad that she didn't feel as sharp and raw-boned as she looked. "I'm so sorry, Katie," he said, his own eyes getting moist.

"I know," she replied, gulping as she released him and stepped back, "and I know you're doing everything you can." She brushed her hair away from her face, the tears off her cheeks, then indicated Rikka, who was in the tiny bathroom, filling the vase with water. "You already know the *other* Thorsen, I see."

"Uh, yeah, we met at the library," Merrill said, then quickly shifted the conversation to the reason they were all in this hospital room. "We know that there was only one person on the landing. He or she walked in from the north along the ridgetop. There were at least two other people up at the edge of the old cutover." He stopped to gather his thoughts. Lack of sleep was making them drift more than he liked. "They all wore boots with Vibram soles. I don't have to tell you how many of those there are out in the hills this weekend. We ran Marty Gilbride's dogs in at daybreak, along the ridge trail north. They tracked three miles out, to Boundry Road, and that's where the trace stopped. A rig parked there, we figure. By the time the dogs got to Boundry, there'd been so many fishermen, mountain bikers, and other folks gone through, any worthwhile tire tracks were long obliterated."

Merrill stopped, acutely aware that he was telling these poor people that he didn't have shit on whoever had killed their son and his family.

"I *can* tell you," he continued, "that whoever set the charges had professional training. He or she -- and I'm saying 'she' because the person had smaller-than-average feet, and conceivably could have been female -- used Semtex, a plastic explosive, with electronically-activated detonators. After placing the charges, the individual *backed* away from the landing into the timber, so we have two sets of identical footprints pointing in the same direction. Like I said, a pro."

141

"A *woman* could do such a thing?" Katie asked.

"I'd like to think not," Merrill replied, "but there are women receiving training in non-traditional areas these days."

"And money talks," Hakon Thorsen put in, shaking his massive head in bafflement. He slammed a big right fist into the palm of his left hand. "God-damned environmental nuts!"

Rikka had finished with the roses, and now stood to the sheriff's left, her arms folded across her chest. Even before he looked at her, he felt her presence tugging at him. "Sharkey's Landing," she said in her low voice, her head tilted to one side. "That's up between Perkins and Ramage Creeks, right?"

"Yeah," Merrill answered, raising his hands palms-down in the universal gesture for calm. "Look, Hakon, don't be too quick to point the finger of blame. Sure, it might be someone with an environmental activism tie, or it might be that somebody simply doesn't like Thorsens very much."

"My boys didn't have any enemies!" Hakon rumbled loudly, and Katie grabbed his left arm as if to restrain him. He started to shake her off, then remembered where he was, and subsided, giving his wife a quick smile and patting her hand.

"How about *you*?" asked the sheriff. "Anybody have any reason to get at you through your sons?"

Hakon shrugged. "Not like this, I think. But a man doesn't spend his whole life in one place without making some 'not-friends,' as my old man would say."

"Think it over," Merrill said. "If you come up with any names, I'll do some checking."

A low moan from the bed interrupted his words, and all four of them instantly turned in that direction.

Though his right eye was still badly swollen, Ole Thorsen had both eyes open, and was regarding his surroundings uncertainly. He looked first at the monitors taped to his arms and chest, then at the sheriff, standing at the foot of the long bed. His battered lips formed a parody of a smile. "I feel better than on the hillside, Virgil."

Katie Thorsen almost threw herself onto the bed before she remembered why Ole was there, and restrained herself, but the term 'relief' didn't begin to express the depth of the expression on her face.

"Glad to hear it," the sheriff replied.

"I'm sorry I couldn't help Sigge," Ole said to his parents. A single tear ran from his damaged eye and rolled down his cheek.

"We're just glad you're going to be all right," his father said, his tired voice thick with emotion, and Katie Thorsen choked back a sob.

A barely audible growl came from Merrill's left. He glanced at Rikka. Her hands were clenched at her sides, and the tendons in her neck stood out like logging cable. Slowly she turned her face to his, and what he saw blazing in her eyes bore no resemblance to anything human. He'd seen lesser degrees of that look in Viet Nam, in the eyes and on the faces of men who'd lost friends in combat.

"You okay?" he asked.

She nodded, and whatever had transformed her features gradually receded, as though Rikka was physically forcing it away, back down into some internal cage. "Sorry," she said, with a self-conscious grin, when her face had returned to normal.

Hakon and Katie, occupied with their son, apparently hadn't noticed Rikka's reaction.

They spent the next half-hour taking Ole through what had happened prior to his trip down into Perkins' Creek. The Thorsens' ability to discuss the

143

matter dispassionately amazed the sheriff. Occasionally, pain would flicker over either Hakon's or Katie's faces, but otherwise they were surprisingly calm. The pain medication Ole was on, some sort of hydrocodone or oxycodone cocktail, seemed to make him slow without actually affecting his memory or his judgement.

Worst for Merrill were the protracted periods of silence where Ole tried to recall events. The sheriff would start to fall asleep in his chair, and Rikka -- who said nothing during the entire conversation, only listened -- would reach over and tap the back of his left hand sharply, smiling to herself.

It was both unprofessional and embarrassing. He felt like an idiot.

Just after five o'clock, Ole ran down, overcome as much by his own memories as by his injuries and the drugs. The sheriff had taken a few notes in the small spiral notebook he'd tucked in his shirt pocket before he left home, and he would incorporate those into the computer report he'd already composed at his office.

"Sharkey's Landing, huh?" Rikka said, standing and stretching. "Mind if I go up there and have a look?" she asked Merrill.

"Things are pretty well cleaned up," Merrill replied. "The demolition people went over everything with metal detectors and sifted the areas immediately adjacent to the explosions. I doubt you'll find anything. But go ahead, if you want."

"Good," she said, and bent over Ole, whispering in his ear and patting him on his less swollen cheek. She straighted. "I'll be by tomorrow. Get some rest." She turned to the sheriff, poking him in his ribs. "And you get some rest, too, after maybe some coffee. I won't be around to keep you awake on your way back to North Cedar." She hugged Katie, and shook Hakon's hand, saying that she hoped they really *were* related, then walked out the door, after one more wink at Merrill.

The hospital room, small though it was, seemed empty without her. "Such a nice girl," Katie said. "She met Ole at the Green Chain this last week, came by here when she heard about..." Katie's voice faltered, and Hakon put his arm around her again. Exhausted by his efforts to recall the night's events, Ole had begun to drift back to sleep.

"I better get back to the office for an hour or so," the sheriff said. "I'll see that you're updated as things progress."

"I hope you nail the bastards to the wall, Virgil," Hakon Thorsen said, and Katie nodded emphatically.

"I'll try," he assured them. He repeated Rikka's actions, hugging Katie and shaking hands with Hakon, then asked Ole, "What did Ms. Thorsen say to you before she left, if you don't mind my asking?"

"Something which I approved of. She said she would find them all and kill them slowly."

Taken aback, Merrill asked, "Do you believe she meant that?"

With an effort, Ole shook his head. "No, not really." He smiled. "I think it would not be slow."

THIRTY-FOUR

Clouds were rolling in over the Cascades when Rikka arrived at Sharkey's Landing. She eyed the towering thunderheads carefully, calculating how long until the storm hit -- and if it would. Just after six-thirty, the sun still streamed in from the cloud-free west. She had an hour, anyway, she figured.

Quickly she changed clothing, hanging her slacks and blouse in the Cherokee, and tucking her Italian loafers under the driver's seat, socks inside them. Standing in her sports bra and panties, she pulled on her hiking shorts and a T-shirt, laced her boots on, and set out to find out all she could about the killers before the rain washed their trace away.

First she walked the perimeter of the landing, then she crisscrossed it. By the time she set foot on the trail north, she had identified the scents of Marty Gilbride and his dogs. From there, heading north on the trail, she could easily separate those smells from those of Merrill and the female deputy, both of whom had accompanied Gilbride.

When she reached the point overlooking the landing from which the charges had been detonated, she had the distinct odors of eight people and five dogs. She trotted rapidly along the trail.

It was all quite simple. Except to take the occasional pee, no one had left the route taken by the killers on their way in, and the dogs didn't hunt about in their search. Just as the sheriff had said, though, the trail ended at the gravelled edge of Boundry Road.

Rikka walked parallel to the road only a short distance before picking up the killers' attempt to throw off any searchers. She smiled as she moved quickly to the west, pushing aside fir and alder branches and going around clumps of Vine maple.

When their track popped back out on Boundry, she stopped in the shadows and studied the road both ways.

Then she walked directly across the road, to the spot where the killers had parked. Here their scents were the strongest they'd been since the point overlooking the landing, and without the overlayer of the law enforcement people or dogs.

Rikka spent fifteen minutes examining every square foot of the small area. When she'd satisfied herself that she'd gotten accurate olfactory impressions of each of the five individuals, she retraced her route to the landing, running the information over in her mind as she ran back along the trail.

She knew she could identify each and every one of them again. The big question, of course, was their destination after leaving their parking spot. The way they'd probably gone took them back to the main highway. From there, they could go anywhere.

Still, Rikka was satisfied with her efforts. She knew how many and which sex, and she knew which of them had placed the charges that had killed Sigge, Erika, and their children, and injured Ole. Now she needed only their names.

No one else had that information, however, except the killers themselves.

The rain, when it began, heavy but warm, did nothing to dampen her spirits. She was wet by the time she saw the landing and her Jeep, and completely drenched when she stuck her key in the lock.

Heading back down into the still-clear valley, with the river sparkling in the lowering sun, Rikka ignored the puddles of water dripping onto the floorboards. She toweled off her hair with one hand, steering with the other.

The sheriff, she thought, would be quite pleased.

And the next three or four hours would be most interesting.

THIRTY-FIVE

Though he kept an eye on the clouds looming to the north and east, Virgil Merrill's primary interest was getting the hell to bed and bagging some sleep. North Cedar stayed dry, but the mountains were really catching it, rain sheeting down in buckets like a coyote pissing on a flat rock.

Typical early summer storm in the Cascades, an inch an hour for two to three hours, then over -- until the next one.

Fatigued he might be, but he chuckled when he looked toward Rikka Thorsen's place as he headed to his own home. Sharkey's Landing was probably practically under water. Rikka, if she'd been up there in the past couple hours, must've gotten soaked.

There was her Cherokee, though, parked in front of her house. It did appear, he noticed, to be quite clean, so she hadn't entirely escaped the deluge. Still chuckling, he turned right and drove the three blocks home, hoping he'd be able to keep his eyes open long enough to get out of his clothes and into the sack.

His briefcase, when he'd hoisted it out of the back seat, seemed to have gained twenty pounds or more. Sure as hell, the sheriff thought, even though he was in good condition, thirty-eight hours without a wink of sleep was a younger man's game.

Arguing with himself about whether to grab a bite and shower, shower only, or just crash, Merrill didn't see Rikka Thorsen until he was halfway between his front gate and the porch.

She sat on his porch, in shorts and a black Oregon State sweatshirt, her long tanned legs stretched down the steps, leaning back against a support post, arms folded in her lap, eyes closed.

The sheriff stopped and blinked a couple of times to make sure he wasn't seeing things. No, she really *was* there.

"About time," she said, without opening her eyes. "I've been waiting a half-hour. A fine way to treat an unpaid volunteer."

He sat down on the opposite side of the steps, his briefcase between his knees, and smiled in spite of his fatigue. "You okay?" he asked.

"Of *course*," she snorted, her eyes still closed. A smile tugged at the corners of her mouth.

"Any revelations that'll keep me awake for the next few minutes?" Bone-tired as he was, he couldn't help looking her up and down, admiring the way she was put together.

"There were five of them," Rikka answered, "four men and a woman. One of the men placed the charges. He had more in his knapsack, I'm fairly certain. They were parked west of the trailhead about a half-mile."

"How come you know all this, and I don't?"

"Because dogs can't talk, so they couldn't tell you what they knew." Her smile widened. "*I* can."

The sheriff sighed, running his left hand over his crewcut. "Maybe I'm so tired my brain's stuck in neutral, but are you tellin' me you *smelled* all these things. Is that correct?"

Rikka's eyes opened, so dark a brown they were almost black. Guileless and innocent. She nodded. "Got it in one, Sheriff, as they say on those BBC mysteries. And I should point out that, during my volunteer efforts, I nearly drowned." Her smile was close to full-on now, her gaze teasing.

"Let's go in and get some tea," Merrill suggested, grasping the railing and, with some effort, pulling himself to his feet. "You can tell me all about this gift of yours."

150

"Give me a hand up," Rikka said, reaching out her right hand, cocking her head mischievously.

"You're daring me, aren't you?" the sheriff asked.

"Whatever you say," she replied, still grinning, wiggling her fingers.

He'd never touched her before. Her hand was muscularly hard, like grabbing onto mahogany covered with a thin layer of dense polymer. And warm. Incredibly warm.

A sharp tug on his hand, and Rikka stood beside him. Her face was inches from his, her lips slightly parted, exposing the white edges of her front teeth. "Tea, you said?" she asked, innocence returned.

"Sure." Merrill released her hand, and unlocked his front door, holding it open for her. There seemed to be what the people-skilled called 'an interpersonal dynamic' going on here. He could almost see Helen Endicott and Darla Kuhn's faces grinning knowingly at him, and could almost hear their laughter.

Rikka stopped in the entryway, standing on the slate. She looked left into the living room, at its gleaming maple floors and Middle Eastern area rugs, and the beige-and-blue upholstered furniture which he and Deb had purchased just the year before Deb had been diagnosed.

"This is beautiful," Rikka said softly, taking it all in, then looking at him with genuine compassion. At that moment, Merrill realized that this girl *had* done exactly what Helen Endicott had told him. She had actively researched him and his family, and in some strange way he couldn't manage to sort through in his weariness, her interest seemed well-intentioned.

"Thank you," he said, walking around her, leading the way to the kitchen. She followed close on his heels, near enough so he could feel her body heat. In the kitchen, he motioned her to a chair in the breakfast nook, poured some distilled water in the teakettle, and sat the kettle on the gas Jennair before bringing out his assortment of tea bags.

"You know," Rikka said, selecting a good green tea after a short search, "if you invite a vampire over your threshold, they can enter your home at any time -- forever." Her smile held a speculative element, trying to gauge his response.

"Is that right?" Merrill said, bringing down two ceramic mugs, setting one in front of her. "But that's not how you got your sense of smell, is it? Being a vampire?" He sat down opposite her, grinning. "Though, to be honest, my personal experience with vampires is rather limited."

"No, I'm not a vampire, if such things exist," Rikka replied, her smile strengthening, "but all my senses are extremely acute, for whatever reason."

"Must come in handy," the sheriff said, "and not just for tracking people. Can you pick out individual conversations in a crowded room?"

She regarded him with what he hoped was respect. "Yes."

"I'd pay good money to be able to do that," he said. The kettle began its pre-boil chatter, and he got up to get it before it started to whistle. Pouring the hot water into her cup, he asked, "See in the dark?"

Rikka nodded, twirling her tea bag in the cup, with a cautious smile. He wondered for an instant how those lips would feel on his, then decided there wasn't much question about that. At least not one that wasn't foolish.

Merrill doodled his own tea bag for a few moments, looking through the steam at her, thinking about his conversation with Malcolm Brown, and the Irishman's views about the killer. "How about emotions? Man in my line of work learns to read people a bit. Body language, facial

152

expressions, tone of voice, those sorts of things. Alcohol or lack thereof on the breath; size of pupils, sometimes. You can probably beat me all hollow on that score."

Her long lashes veiled her eyes for a heartbeat. If she weren't so dark, the sheriff would almost have thought she blushed. She might be thinking she'd told him more than she should have.

"I don't much like being around people without self-control," she replied, "or if they've been drinking or doping, and riding an emotional rollercoaster. I can smell the basic emotions, fear, anger, hunger -- which is a lot like desire -- elation, all that stuff. So children, whose scents are so pure and clean, are the most fun to be around in groups. Adults in groups aren't, unless they have a communal feeling, like the people at the Chain. And uncomplicated, good-natured people like Ole are great, or Walt, who's so steady and so positive."

"I see," he said, nodding. "Can you smell a lie?'

"Oh, yes," she said, grinning for the first time like the kid she really was. "Every time."

Merrill took a careful sip of his tea. "I forgot to ask if you wanted sugar," he said.

"No, you didn't. You knew I wouldn't want it. Our wavelengths aren't so far apart." She watched him steadily.

"You sure of that?"

"Uh-huh." She held her cup against her lower lip, gripping it with both hands, tilting it to drink. Her gaze never left his. Steam condensed on her lashes.

Christ, she was good-looking.

Time to change the subject. "At the hospital," he said, "when Ole came to and talked about his brother, you got upset. Don't know if I've ever seen anybody look quite that way."

153

"Yes, you have," Rikka said, her expression smug. "You aren't exactly lying, Sheriff, but you *are* holding back. Viet Nam, I'd guess."

She was like an intelligent polygraph. He realized he was trapped -- likely in more ways than one. And not all of them unpleasant.

"Would you really like to kill them?" he asked.

"Ole told you what I whispered in his ear," she said, still looking over the rim of her cup. "*That's* cute. And, no, I wouldn't *like* to kill them. That wasn't what I said. I *will* kill them, if I can find them. And if they stick around the area, you can bet I will."

He laughed. "You're sitting in the sheriff's kitchen, telling the *sheriff* you're going to kill someone?"

"I tend to be very direct, or haven't you noticed?"

Here came that trap again. He'd thought he'd side-stepped it. Apparently not. In his current state, she was too fast for him -- and entirely too focused.

"I'm not sure I've ever seen anybody look more tired than you do right now, either," she continued, without giving him time to speak. "When'd you sleep last?"

Merrill shrugged, covering a yawn. "Friday night. I think."

"Poor baby. You need to get cleaned up, get some food in you, and sleep until noon tomorrow. Why don't you shower, while I put something together in here?" She rose from her chair, took both their cups. "And don't look so incredulous, Sheriff. Me cooking food for you should *not* get a bigger response than my saying that I'll kill whoever murdered Sigge and his family."

"Cooking is more of a surprise," Merrill admitted.

154

"No doubt." She put the cups in the sink, opened the door beneath it, and dropped the tea bags into the garbage. "What's in your fridge?"

"Eggs, tofu, yogurt, non-fat milk, low-fat mayonnaise, sliced smoked turkey, probably some bacon to get me through the occasional need for something unhealthy. Some spare batteries. A ten mm. Beretta in a Zip-loc freezer bag."

"Good," Rikka said, opening the refrigerator door and peering inside, "I can use the Beretta if the bacon comes after me." She looked over the top of the door, and made a shooing motion with one hand. "Go. Get cleaned up. I can find the pots and pans on my own. I'll try not to burn the place down."

"You do that," the sheriff responded, yawning again as he stood and walked across the kitchen toward the master bedroom. He stopped in the doorway and studied Rikka for a second or two. Why was he letting this kid push him around? Watching her as she rooted around in his refrigerator, the way she moved, and the little faces she made, he knew. He was neither too old nor too tired to miss that one.

Oh, well, Merrill thought, shucking his clothing in the bedroom, he *was* for sure too damned tired to analyze anything more than superficially.

The shower, as hot as he could stand it, restored him somewhat. He threw on a nearly-new pair of summer-weight sweatpants and the same UofO T-shirt he'd worn Friday evening, then brushed his crewcut and headed back to the kitchen.

As he went down the hall, the smell of whatever Rikka'd prepared -- he could definitely smell tofu and bacon -- made his mouth water. Hungrier than he'd thought.

Rikka had just poured the second glass of milk when he entered the kitchen. Folded paper napkins lay beside two gleaming plates, the Melmac he'd resurrected after Deb had died and he couldn't stand using their wedding china.

"I couldn't find candles," she said, bowing from the other side of the table, "and I used most of the bacon and the rest of the eggs."

"Smells great, looks edible," he said approvingly, holding her chair for her. When she was seated, he handed her the napkin, then took his own place.

"We should have wine," Rikka said, gazing at the plates and food with a little frown.

Merrill shook his head. "Half a glass of wine, and you'd be lugging me to bed."

The frown disappeared, replaced by a sneaky grin. "We should have wine," she repeated, an octave lower.

Unable not to smile, the sheriff grabbed a serving spoon, and ladled what looked like something from a Dr. Suess childrens' book onto their plates. The dark bits, he guessed, were bacon. "You're too quick for me," he said, when Rikka indicated she had a big enough helping.

"Not really," she scoffed, taking a forkful. "You're just super-tired and preoccupied."

"That's the truth," Merrill answered, chewing cautiously on his first bite. "This's pretty good." Then he had a thought. "Taste is part and parcel of smell. How do things taste to you?"

Rikka tapped the tines of her fork on her front teeth. "Hmmm. More subtle, certainly. Better recognition of components. Otherwise about the same." She dug back into her food. "Good enough explanation?" she asked, between bites.

"Sure. Just thought I'd ask."

They ate in silence for a few minutes.

When the sheriff felt comfortably full, and his milk was half empty, he said quietly, "You know, my wife's been gone five years, and this is the first meal I've had in this house with someone who isn't a family member." He yawned. Fatigue had begun to re-assert itself.

"I'm not surprised, knowing you," Rikka replied, her plate bare of food, and her milk empty. She wiped her lips with the napkin, then steepled her arms over her plate, lacing her hands together and resting her chin on her fingers. "We both have history, Virgil, yours longer and far, far better than mine. Tonight, we don't need history."

Rikka stood, came around the table, and bent her head to his, cradling his chin in her left hand.

"We need *this*," she said, very softly, and kissed him.

As it turned out, she was right.

And he wasn't nearly as tired as he thought.

THIRTY-SIX

The morning sun outlining the bedroom windows on the inside of the mini-blinds generated enough radiant heat to warm the side of the sheriff's face. He lay on his back, eyes closed, covered only by a sheet, drifting, feeling better and more rested than he had in ages.

The real world might be out there somewhere, but it touched no part of him.

Jesus, had he really had sex with someone a third his age? Probably. He could feel crusts of dried body fluids on his upper thighs, crotch and abdomen, and his dick felt like it had been wrung dry, maybe several times.

"Brought you some coffee," said a voice, from above and to his right.

Merrill smiled, but kept his eyes shut. "If you're Rikka Thorsen, I'll take coffee. If you're not, you can leave."

A throaty giggle. "This Rikka Thorsen, she must really be something, huh? Hauled your ashes big-time?"

He opened his eyes. Rikka stood beside him, nude, holding a cup of coffee. Merrill let his gaze range up and down her body, marvelling that anyone so perfectly constructed could find an old fart like him desirable.

"If you say 'perky,'" Rikka said, with a warning glare, "I'm gonna dump this on you."

"Just wishing I was a poet," Merrill said, reaching out and touching her thigh.

"*Definitely* better than 'perky,'" Rikka replied, smiling warmly at him. She sat down, lifting the sheet up so her bare butt pressed against his side. "It's nine o'clock. You should drink this, shave, and get cleaned up, lover. Darla said the TV crews will be here by noon."

"*Darla*?" he asked, a cold knot suddenly forming in his stomach. "TV crews?"

"She seems very nice. We chatted for a while. And it's just the Portland stations. Darla said no helicopters. They'll be coming here, to the house. Darla thought that much congestion down at your office would clog the highway."

"Oh, *Christ*," he said, and closed his eyes again. Rikka shifted beside him. He heard a 'clink' as she set his coffee on the nightstand, then felt her heat descend to him. Her mouth found his. "M-mmm," she murmured, the tip of her tongue probing between his lips. "I can taste *me* in there," she said, giggling.

"Oh, Christ," Merrill said again, less emphatically, stroking her lower back. "You're not kiddin', are you? You really talked to Darla, and there really arc TV crews?"

"Sorry, but yeah," Rikka replied, "and you're supposed to call Marvin Bullock."

"You told Darla who you were?"

Rikka nodded. "The moment I answered the phone, she started to laugh, and, even though she said she wasn't sure I wasn't your daughter Kathy, I think she knew." She kissed him again, then lay on his chest, her face too close for him to focus on. "You guys talked about me, huh?"

"Yes," he answered, hoping he didn't sound as exasperated as he felt.

"Darla said she'd be over about eleven. I'll fix breakfast while you clean up. Drink the rest of your coffee." She pushed up off him and the bed, walked to the door and leaned against the jamb, arms akimbo, her legs crossed at the ankles, looking at him. She smiled, an introspective and private smile that included only the two of them. "That was good last night, wasn't it, Virgil? No one ever made love to me before."

"Hard to believe that."

"Oh, *yes*. I've been *fucked* innumerable times, and one of my father's drinking buddies forced himself on me and in me -- *raped* me -- when I was twelve, but nobody ever *loved* me." Unshed tears glistened in her brown eyes.

Not knowing what to say, he managed only, "I'm sorry."

Rikka did her husky laugh again. "Don't be. You might not have needed me as much as I needed you..."

He interrupted her, raising his right hand. "I did. In a different way, maybe, but just as much, Rikka.

"Okay." She lifted her chin. "Say my name again. Please."

"Rikka."

"Nice, very nice. In the heat of passion, drawn out more, that was nice, too."

Merrill felt like a kid with his hand caught somewhere besides the cookie jar. His face warmed.

"You're blushing!"

"Sorry. Can't help it."

"No, it's sweet." Her expression turned serious. "Look, the life you had and wanted slipped away five years ago. The rug wasn't pulled out from under you so much as part of it was cut away. You didn't fall through the hole, but my guess is it was a near thing."

"Yeah, it was," he answered. The words didn't come out easily.

"Well, I'm not a patch on that rug, or even a whole new one. I'm just me. You're you, and we don't have any history together except last night. I just want to tell you that I won't be drifting away anytime soon. Unless you chase me off."

160

"I won't." He looked at her steadily. Deb had that same expression on her face when she'd come home with the results from her preliminary tests. Fear, uncertainty, hope, all somehow occupying her features simultaneously. "I won't, Rikka," he repeated. "I swear I won't." Then he grinned at her, her standing nude in a doorway where he'd never thought to see a woman standing nude again in his lifetime. "If you don't mind my asking, though, just what is it we're doing here?"

She returned his grin. "Some of those psychologists I've been reading would say 'sleeping with the enemy,' pointing out the adversarial natures of our two age groups, but I wouldn't say that. We seemed profoundly *non*-adversarial. What I *will* say is that if you don't get your butt in the shower, you will not get breakfast before your daughter Kathy gets here. So get going."

Merrill stared at her in horror. "*Kathy* is coming here?"

"She called at eight, just before Darla. Said she was going to walk the dog, and then she'd be down, that she needed to get out of Portland."

Maybe, he thought, he could just pull the sheet up over his head and hide for the rest of the day. Instead, he took a deep breath, swung his legs out of bed and sat up. He lifted the cooling coffee from the nightstand. "That rug you mentioned," he said, draining half the cup. "I think somebody's got a hold on the edge of it."

He got to his feet slowly, feeling his joints pop. Too long in bed. His shoulders and butt hurt, and he had a good idea why. The reason stood in the doorway, regarding him with fond amusement, trying not to laugh.

"Don't you dare!" he said, gripping the back of his neck with both hands, and popping the vertebrae.

"What, laugh?" Rikka asked innocently. "And *why* would I do that?"

"My point exactly," Merrill replied, heading for the bathroom, pleasantly surprised at how good he *did* feel.

"Sorry I can't come with you and scrub your back," she said, "but I have to fix breakfast."

Puzzled, he looked back over his shoulder at her. "There's food left in the fridge?"

"Not really. I went to the Quik-E Mart, got some things. It's eggs again, and marinated tofu pups cooked with the rest of the bacon. I'm not much of a cook. Mostly I do quantity."

"After last night," the sheriff said, "I think I know why you need the fuel."

Rikka bit her lower lip and looked at him hungrily. "There'll be a reminder later, Virgil."

"You *are* direct, aren't you?"

"You love it."

"And you should get some clothes on before Kathy gets here."

"Sure. Now go get clean."

In the bathroom, slipping a new blade in his Gillette Sensor before lathering up, Merrill studied his face in the mirror. Eyes clear, no new lines anywhere, brain
functioning, all systems seemingly on line. Most of all, there seemed to be no trace of guilt.

God, he thought, I feel good.

And had been.

THIRTY-SEVEN

Though Rikka no longer ovulated, and guessed that Maureen Sims had thereby eliminated any hopes Rikka had for motherhood, she found Virgil Merrill's concern over his daughter's impending arrival delightful and amusing.

"So, Virgil," she asked the sheriff, who stood in the dining room, looking uneasily out the window, "Kathy is going to come in yelling at you and hitting me with a stick?"

Even from ten feet away, Merrill's glance at Rikka held a clear element of anxiety. "You talked to her. How'd she seem?"

"Nice enough. Surprised, of course, to hear a woman's voice instead of her father's. Unspoken questions, naturally. Spoken questions, for sure, but reasonable. My name, and why she hadn't heard it before. She puts her sentences together like you do, very careful phrasing, with maybe a lawyer's edge. Her golden retriever/Wolfhound mix's name is Sam. She does not drive like a bat out of hell, like her dad, but should be here by ten."

"Sounds like you talked to the right Kathleen Merrill," the sheriff replied, with a short laugh.

"Is she your favorite?" Rikka asked, as she pushed tofu pups around amongst the frying bacon.

Merrill looked at her sharply. "She say that?"

"In so many words, later in our conversation."

"She might be right. David was very close to his mother. He and I got along well enough -- still do -- but he didn't just *look* like his mom. Maryanne -- the baby -- figured out early that both sides of her bread could have butter on it, so she dealt with both her folks equally." He paused and stroked his chin. "Kathy always came to me first, and she looks like me, so, yeah, I'm more comfortable around her.

She's tougher on me than the other two, though, and she doesn't mince words."

"Well, I just hope she's hungry," Rikka replied, scooping the meat and faux meat onto a plate covered with paper towels, and sticking the laden plate into the warm oven. Next she drained the frying pan leavings into an old cup and set the cup on the counter.

"How did you learn to move so efficiently?" Merrill asked, momentarily turning away from his scrutiny of the street outside.

Rikka grinned at him, pouring beaten eggs into the pan. "You didn't ask that last night."

"Hell, I was half-a-step behind, and tryin' to catch up." He laughed. "Damn kid, anyway."

"That was why it worked, you know. You cared about me. Unlike most guys, you weren't the only one there."

Reaching up with his right hand, the sheriff felt around in the empty air above his head. "Can't seem to find my halo, though."

"Too bad," Rikka said dryly. "We could play ring toss."

"Even after a good night's sleep," he said, looking sourly at her, "my wit's no match for yours."

Rikka shrugged. "I'll bring you up to speed. We'll have a training session later." Motion on the street in front of the house caught her eye. "Does Kathy drive a white Subaru Forester?"

Merrill turned slowly around. "That's her."

"I'll just continue looking domestic here," Rikka said, "while you greet her." She slid a spatula under the eggs and flipped them over. "Or did you want to do it the other way 'round?"

"Real funny," he said, walking across the slate entryway to the door and opening it.

Humming to herself, Rikka brought out three plates and set them beside the stovetop. She heard

Virgil yell, "On the lawn, Sam! On the lawn! Here, boy!" then the sound of claws on the slate, followed by panting. She looked at Merrill, saw him whirling around on the entryway, holding the front paws of a large golden-brown dog who seemed to be attempting to lick his face off.

The moment the sheriff released the furry monster, it bounded toward the kitchen and Rikka, tongue lolling. Rikka had a glimpse of a tall, red-haired woman coming through the doorway, a look of frustration on her features, then the dog leapt at her.

"Sam!" Rikka shouted, and held out her arms as Sam slammed into her. She ended up pinned against the counter, Sam resting his front paws on the counter top, while she hugged him to her. "You're just happy to be out of the car, aren't you, boy?" she said into one fuzzy ear, scratching his back as the big dog grunted with pleasure, his hairy tail wagging so hard he nearly over-balanced them both.

Over the top of Sam's head, Rikka saw Kathy Merrill hug her father, and peck him on one cheek before coming into the kitchen. Like Rikka, she wore shorts and a sweatshirt, and was the same height.

"Hello," Kathy said coolly, gripping Rikka's right hand around Sam's bulk. She indicated Sam, with a thin smile. "You're not what *I* expected, but the dog's convinced."

"Hi," Rikka replied, shaking hands. "They say dogs are hard to fool."

Kathy laughed, the same short choppy sound as her father's. "I've often wondered just who 'they' are." Kathy's face was thinner than her father's, her cheekbones more prominent, but otherwise a carbon copy. More freckles than her father, too, though far fewer than her mother or siblings.

Kathy's eyes, though, were the first feature anyone would notice. A band of green haloed the pupils of Virgil's blue eyes, allowing him to express a certain visual warmth when he wished. Rikka had seen that frequently, and loved it. His daughter's eyes lacked any trace of green. Rikka found herself looking into a gaze the exact shade of pale blue found inside thick Arctic pack ice, and just as devoid of life.

Smelling curiosity without disapproval, Rikka released Kathy's hand, eased Sam down to the floor, then locked her own brown gaze with Kathy's chilly blue. "Would you like some breakfast? We're just about to sit down."

"Sam will expect you to set a fourth place," Kathy said, jerking a thumb at the dog, who, greetings over, stared at the panful of eggs with the look large dogs reserve only for that most sacred of all things, food.

After turning off the low flame, Rikka divided the heap of eggs equally onto four plates, set three of the plates on the table, then, after first filling a water bowl, placed the fourth on the floor with the bowl. She knelt down and rubbed Sam's neck, sliding the plate under his eager nose. "Here you go, Sam. Eat up."

"That'll last about five seconds," Merrill observed, fetching silverware from a drawer, watching the dog attack the food.

"Probably," Kathy agreed, "but with Sam, it's the thought that counts."

Rikka pulled the plate of bacon and tofu pups from the oven and set it in the middle of the table. "Here it is. Whatever's left, Sam gets." She smiled at Kathy. "With your permission, of course."

"Granted," Kathy said, grinning and dipping one freckled hand in Rikka's direction, "and he'll love

166

you for it." Her eyes had thawed a bit, Rikka noticed, thinking that was a good thing.

The meal progressed quietly. Sam finished his own food and sat patiently on his haunches on the floor, attentively watching the humans, his expression hopeful.

"Just how did you two meet?" Kathy asked, as she forked a few pieces of meat onto her plate.

"At the library," her father replied.

"Oh. Do you live here in town, Rikka?"

"About four blocks away."

"How convenient," Kathy said, then stopped and put down her fork, looking at her plate. "I'm sorry. I didn't mean that quite as snide as it sounded."

"But a *little* snide?" Virgil asked, grinning at his daughter.

Returning his grin, Kathy said, "I work with *lawyers*, for God's sake, Dad. Lawyers *do* snide."

"Yeah, no shit. Except my darling daughter, of course."

"Thanks loads." Kathy waved a fork-impaled tofu pup at her father. "I hate to disabuse you, dearest father, but I do snide and worse in the courtroom."

"But you don't cry, do you?"

"No, I kick their butts. When conditions permit and the law allows."

"Why do I think that this conversation is a replay of prior conversations?" Rikka asked, slipping Sam a small piece of bacon.

"Dad frequently reminds me we're on opposite sides of the law," Kathy said, giving her father a quick false smile.

Merrill smiled at Rikka, winked, and stood. "I'd better go phone Marv Bullock and get his thoughts on my press conference." He picked up his plate and glass, setting them in the sink.

"Won't he want to be here?" Kathy asked

"Don't think so," the sheriff replied, resting his butt on the counter edge, sipping the remnants of his Barcelona blend. "Marvin doesn't like to waste his time, 'specially during an election year. If we had someone in custody, or even some good information, he'd be up here in a second. Until I got here to the house last night, and discovered Rikka'd been up nosing around at the homicide scene, I knew only that they'd used Semtex, and we had four bodies."

Kathy turned to Rikka. "What did you do?"

Rikka shrugged. "What your father said. Nosed around. Literally. Found out there had been one person setting the charges, four others waiting up on the ridge, one of them a woman."

"Whoever set the charges was very well-trained," Merrill added. "A thoroughly professional job, I'm sorry to say." He went on to explain the homicides in sketchy detail.

"You have that precise a sense of smell?" Kathy asked Rikka.

"I went to Oregon State," Rikka replied, indicating her sweatshirt. "What with all the farm animals on campus, it just sort of happens."

"Uh-huh," Kathy said, in doubting tones. "I think you've been spending too much time around my father, and those farm animals aren't the only things full of shit."

"Got a better explanation?" Merrill asked, grinning at them both.

"No," Kathy answered, glaring at her father, "but I know there is one."

"Maybe," he said.

"Go call Marvin," Rikka told him, "and Kathy and I'll get acquainted."

"Sounds mighty folksy," the sheriff said, heading for the telephone in the living room, taking his coffee with him.

168

When her father seemed out of earshot, Kathy looked at Rikka for a few moments, apparently gathering her thoughts. "I want you to know, Rikka," she finally said, "that I bear you no ill will, but this is, quite frankly, the hardest half-hour I've ever had in this kitchen. Even after Mom died, every time I came here, it was still the house I grew up in, and both my folks were essentially still here. I just didn't *see* my mother here any more. Now, today, for the first time, that's not true."

"I didn't have anything like your family as I grew up," Rikka replied, "but I think I understand, and I'm sorry. I don't know what else to say. Don't think it's any easier on your dad."

"Probably not," Kathy admitted. "He and Mom were so devoted to one another. Has he talked about her at all?"

Rikka shook her head. "Not much. Some."

"He won't say much, if I know him. Those emotions he considers positive he shares, particularly with family and friends. The negative, the private things, those he bears alone. He held us all together, including Mom -- her as long as he could -- during her illness. And beyond that, of course. Anyone who knew him at all could see he was suffering, but he controlled it so incredibly well." Kathy shuddered. "I felt so helpless. He supported us unselfishly and uncomplainingly, and every time I came here after Mom died, I kept half-expecting to find him dead. For months after the funeral, I'd think every phone call would be Fred Cameron with bad news."

"Not his style," Rikka said, shaking her head again. "He's fatalistic, ironic, reserved, and dry, but suicide would be a weakness he couldn't permit himself. He'd feel he was disappointing people."

"You know," Kathy replied, as she sat her emptied plate on the floor for Sam to clean, "that's *exactly* right. Are you *sure* you went to Oregon State?"

Rikka laughed. "Picked up my diploma at Administration in February, General Science major." She wondered if Doctor Sims had managed to insert her name in the University's records by now. A phony diploma hung on the wall above Rikka's computer, a scanned and composited document that looked genuine, but Sims had encountered initial difficulty in getting inside the Oregon State computer system.

"What does a General Science major do?" Kathy asked. Sam had slicked up her plate, and was now regarding Rikka with intense devotion.

"Hang around North Cedar, for now," Rikka answered. "When the weather turns in the fall, I'll think about what I want to do with the rest of my life. Until then, I'm coasting."

"What about Dad?"

Rikka sat up straighter, ran her fingers through her short hair. "Yeah," she said, letting a faint smile form on her features. "Well, this was unexpected, in a way. If he wants, I'll stick around."

"You make it sound so *casual*," Kathy said, frowning.

"I'm trying not to upset you, Kathy." Rikka thought for a moment. "Let me put it differently, then, more like I feel. He's going to have to chase me away. Is that better?"

"Much," Kathy laughed. "You know, I suppose I knew this day would come. Analyzing my thoughts, I guess I had hoped for some denim-clad country woman, middle-aged and maybe given to line-dancing and sad songs of loss, remorse, and broken-down pickups."

"Someone you could feel superior to, who'd be no threat to your mother's memory?"

"Ouch!" Kathy replied, wincing and looking mildly alarmed, but still tickled. "Too close for comfort."

She reacts exactly like her father, Rikka thought. "How about a waitress or hairdresser, who calls everyone 'Hon,' and pops her gum?"

"Even better," Kathy agreed. "Or maybe a child of the Sixties..."

"Sure. Ample breasts, ample hips, in tune with all the world, and totally organic. Long dresses, sandals, a headband with a feather in it, and hair down to her ankles. Buddha and the Kama Sutra." Rikka found this actually enjoyable.

"...and instead," Kathy continued, giggling, "I get a woman pentathlete who's younger than I am, and who my dog likes."

"Fate moves in mysterious ways," Rikka said.

"A small part of me *hates* you," Kathy said quietly, her gaze hardening.

"A larger part of me envies you," Rikka replied, regarding Kathy levelly. "I will never know your mother. I will never know your father's hopes and dreams when he was younger. I will never be a part of your family."

"I hadn't thought of those things," Kathy said.

"I hadn't, either, until just now, but they're true, all the same, and you need to know that. But, all that aside, I think your father is the finest man I've ever known. And I think we can agree on that much." Rikka extended her hand across the table to Kathy, raising both eyebrows.

After looking at Rikka's hand for a long moment, Kathy took it in hers. They shook cautiously, and Rikka knew she had won an important concession.

"You will *not* be my stepmother," Kathy said, still holding Rikka's hand.

"And I won't try to be, counselor," Rikka answered, releasing her grip. "Are we done with the first round?"

"Yes," Kathy said, her laugh again echoing her father's, "and I couldn't have said it better myself."

"Thanks," Rikka replied, and gave Sam her plate.

THIRTY-EIGHT

Seated in his study in his favorite leather chair, nursing a glass of Bernkastler Doktor Spaetlese, Alexander Carson watched -- for the third time -- his tape of Virgil Merrill's meeting with the Portland press.

The sheriff was no demagogic orator, but neither was he a tongue-tied bumpkin. A tall, broad-shouldered, knuckly man, Merrill's answers and explanations were delivered in calm factual tones, cut and dried, with no extra verbiage. His manner of speaking suggested that he had spent the movie theatre experiences of his youth watching films featuring John Wayne and James Stewart.

Standing in front of a two-storey home -- possibly his own -- on a sunny holiday weekend, a female deputy beside him, Merrill forced the press to respect him, and then did not betray their trust. Carson thought that to be an art few modern politicians understood, and fewer carried off with any style. He conceded a certain grudging admiration for this rural lawman.

There was, however, a nagging familiarity about the man that bothered Carson. On this third viewing, hanging on Merrill's every word, he tended to ignore the camera's occasional pan of the front of the house, and almost missed the brief glimpse of the two young women in shorts seated on the shaded porch behind the sheriff. Hastily he stopped the tape and reversed it frame-by-frame, until he had a mostly clear view of the pair. He heard his breath catch, then catch again.

He lifted his cell-phone from the end table next to his chair, and dialed.

When Dick Edmiston answered, Carson said, "This is Alexander Carson, Richard. I have some good news and some bad news concerning your recent efforts in the North Cedar area."

Edmiston laughed. "I just spoke with my people down there, Alex. There is no bad news. They got away clean."

"Quite possibly. I agree. However, do you remember last year when two of your lesser lights -- Crawford and Sutton -- were arrested for placing a thirty-foot banner on the Steel Bridge in Portland, protesting the plight of the Marbled murrulet?"

"How can I forget those two nitwits?" Edmiston groaned.

"Just so," Carson replied, "and the poor bridge tender over whom the banner fluttered when it detached. Now she can't even hang her laundry out during the summer months, because the wind whipping the sheets disturbs her so much."

"You didn't do so well in the courtroom, either, Alex. The County's lawyer chewed us up bad."

"Nonsense, Richard. The loss in the courtroom was virtually pre-ordained. My task became to simply limit the monetary strike on the senior Crawfords and Suttons -- old and dear friends -- who begged me to save their offspring from the pain of incarceration. And I succeeded in that."

"Yeah, yeah," Edmiston said, "but that cold-eyed redhead had you dead to rights in the courtroom."

"*That's* the bad news, Richard. Have you seen the six o'clock news on Channel Two?"

"No. I thought I'd catch the eleven o'clock, later tonight. What's the problem?"

"I just watched the media interviewing the local sheriff in North Cedar, one Virgil Merrill, a tall, red-haired gentleman who handled the media monster far better than one would expect."

"*Merrill*? That was the lawyer's name, wasn't it?"

"Precisely, Richard. *Kathleen* Merrill. The sheriff is her father, apparently. She sat on the porch behind him during his question-and-answer session with the press. Occasionally, the camera would pan over her, so I am quite certain of her identity. This may be bad, Richard."

"How so? Nobody's come looking for my people. The expert we hired out of California seems to be a real pro. So what's the deal?"

Carson spoke slowly, with emphasis on each word. "The 'deal,' my friend, is that four people -- a young family -- are *dead*. Though it might be unintentional, and a case could indeed be made that this is true, it is *not good*. Watch this sheriff on the news; tape it. This man is no fool. Your people are trespassing on his territory. He knows the terrain, he is familiar with the locals, he knows there were five individuals involved in the incident, and he knows one of them was a woman. *How* he knows those things baffles me, but if he is like his daughter, he is *relentless*. It will be *personal* with him. Having a family trust fund and the supposed moral high ground will *not* protect the perpetrators of this deed. If you leave your people in place, have them take great care."

"And what's the *good* news, counselor?" Edmiston asked sarcastically.

"Oh, ye of little faith," Carson intoned, chuckling. "It *is* good news, Richard. Unless I am badly mistaken, Maureen Sims' creature is seated next to Kathleen Merrill on the porch. In fact, I'm sure of it."

"This is important?"

"Think, Richard. *Think*! Somehow she has insinuated herself into the community and their sad little lives. What does this tell you?"

"You can deal with the sheriff, if you have to?"

"*Exactly*, Richard."

"Sims would loose her pet monster?"

"*Exactly*, Richard. The Black Voice will speak."

THIRTY-NINE

Locking her condo's front door behind her after a five-mile run, Maureen Sims lifted a bath towel from her coat rack and wiped her sweaty face as she walked into her kitchen. She rummaged in the refrigerator long enough to select a bottle of orange juice, then walked into the living room and snapped on the television.

Taking a seat on a small, brown leather ottoman, the towel draped around her neck, the doctor drank from the opened juice bottle, and watched the six o'clock news.

Some environmental yahoos did this, she thought, as she watched Virgil Merrill's news conference. Alex Carson will know all about it. She would call him after the news was over.

Listening to the sheriff's slow, deep voice as he described what little the authorities knew about the homicides, Sims was profoundly puzzled. She could think of no way anyone could have discovered how many people were involved, and that one was a woman -- unless one of the killers had broken ranks and ratted the others out.

And that hadn't happened. This canny, dry-witted upholder of law and order would have at least alluded to an outside source of information.

Then she saw Reckon sitting on the sheriff's front porch, her dark head down close to that of another young woman, this one red-haired like the sheriff. The two talked quietly, hands in front of their mouths, occasionally glancing up at the speaker's back.

Doctor Sims began to giggle.

She knew how the sheriff had come by his information about the killers.

Carson -- the pompous idiot -- would not realize what had happened, and the environmentalists might well have a very rude awakening in the near future.

In fact, she was *certain* of it.

The question was, how soon?

She decided not to call Carson.

Instead, laughing so hard she nearly blew orange juice out her nose, Maureen Sims went to take a shower.

FORTY

Eleven hours after the conclusion of his meeting with the media, the soft but insistent chiming of his cell-phone awakened the sheriff.

He fumbled the phone off his nightstand with one hand, while turning the clock face with the other. *Midnight*, he thought in irritation. Christ. This better not be somebody wanting a frigging quote. He rolled onto his back, brought the phone up to his mouth. "Hello," he said.

"Virgil!" came the voice of Fred Cameron, decidedly amused. "Talked to Darla earlier, and just wanted to check on you, make sure you were holding up okay."

"Sorry to disappoint you, Fred," Merrill replied, quickly getting the drift of the conversation. "Everything's all right. I'm fine." He paused, looking over at Rikka, who lay propped up on one arm, watching him. "Is this one of those crank calls?" the sheriff asked.

Cameron laughed. "Oh, *no*. I didn't interrupt anything, did I?"

First covering the speaker, Merrill handed the phone to Rikka. "Here," he said, grinning at her. "It's for you."

FORTY-ONE

"Just riding," Walt Whitaker called it, on those rare days when he went out without his little chain saw and all his other assorted tools. Freed from that extra weight, the XR-250 felt light as a feather under him, and almost as responsive, whizzing rapidly down the sun-dappled trails.

On this Friday after Memorial Day, his ostensible purpose was to check those signed routes which had been heavily-used over the holiday weekend, see how they'd held up. So far, things looked good. Except for the trails drenched in Sunday evening's thunderstorm -- which were still slippery in the shaded areas -- everything looked fine.

They should, in Walt's estimation. An incredible number of volunteer hours -- not just his -- had been spent grooming and maintaining the extensive trail system. State and federal funding never seemed to be quite adequate, and politicians were always trying to divert designated trail monies for other purposes. Trail users, be they hikers, horseback riders, mountain bikers, or ORV folks, frequently had to fight to retain funds which, in many cases, came from their own purchased use permits.

This made little sense to Walt, whose pragmatic approach to the situation didn't allow for political agendas and radical notions. His parameters tended to be limited to making trails eight feet wide, eight feet high, and free of significant obstacles. Anything beyond that was unnecessary malarkey. He just couldn't see it.

He also didn't see the three-eighths-inch plastic-clad cable stretched across the trail fifty yards ahead of him, five feet off the ground.

FORTY-TWO

"Three were here," Rikka said, straightening up from where she'd been kneeling beside the trail, "two men and a woman." She wiped moist duff off her hands, her brown gaze sifting through the patterns of sunlight and shadow slanting down through the canopied forest. "One of the men was part of that group of five who killed Sigge's family, Virgil."

"Looks like Hakon's knee-jerk remark at the hospital was right, then," Merrill replied, sighing. "We've got ourselves a nest of eco-terrorists somewhere in the countryside, or at least someone pretending to be." He tweaked the still-strung cable, watching it bounce, sun flashing off the clear plastic coating and woven steel beneath. "Good thing Walt was standing up. If he'd been sitting, this would have broken his neck."

"Or taken off his head," Rikka added, "and, thanks to his chest protector and his helmet, he's only got a few broken ribs, a cracked collar bone, and a mild concussion from rebounding into the ground."

"Steep price to pay for having a good time."

"Not as steep as Sigge," Rikka growled.

"You're starting to get that look again," the sheriff said, studying her face.

She looked up at him, her eyes nearly glowing. "You *bet* I am. What if, instead of Walt, who wore all the right gear, this had been some kid with just a helmet, boots, denim pants, and a jersey? He'd be hurt worse, maybe killed. All so some stupid fools could 'make a statement.'"

"I don't pretend to understand their motivation, and I seem to remember that the Unabomber started out doin' this sort of thing," Merrill said, walking over to one end of the cable, "but I *do* have to stop them. Now, let's take the evidence down before someone else comes along and clothslines themselves."

Five minutes later, they walked side-by-side up an Elk trail which led to Headquarters Grade, one of the old railroad lines into the forest. The cable-stringers had used the same route, and Walt had ridden his almost-unscathed motorcycle out on it. The knobby imprints of Walt's tires wound ahead of them, in among the big second-growth trees. Rikka marveled that the elderly postman had been able to even stay on the machine, let alone navigate out to the road, then ride along it until he found someone to get help. She and Virgil had followed the EMT rig to Walt, then back-tracked to the cable.

"He said starting it was the hardest part," Rikka remarked, trying to distract the Black Voice, which bubbled threateningly inside her.

"Sure," Merrill said, his long strides eating up the distance back to the Caprice. "Every time his foot hit the bottom of the kickstarter's travel, it must have seemed like somebody stuck an icepick in his ribs."

"He said he almost blacked out."

"Not surprisin.' I sure as hell wish I could get a handle on these people." They'd come to a large clear space in the canopy overhead, and were walking through waist-high salal, green with fresh spring growth.

"Whatever they're driving uses BP Super-92 gasoline," Rikka said casually, "so it's probably a good-sized vehicle."

"What!"

"Well, probably. That's what I smelled where we parked your patrol car. Until I sensed them, I didn't know it was their rig. Walt uses Texaco in his bike, so it wasn't him, and you use Shell."

181

Merrill stopped in the trail, regarding her with astonishment. "How in hell do you know *that*?"

Rikka grinned at him. "The additives. I went around to all the local stations on Tuesday. Gasoline kind of over-powers my nose, but I can still differentiate the additives."

"Well, I'll be good God-damned! Is there no end to what you can do?"

"After the past few nights," Rikka replied, looking smug and grabbing his butt, "I'm going to assume that's a rhetorical question."

FORTY-THREE

"El Supremo on the Opex line," Darla said, leaning around the sheriff's half-opened office door.

Merrill grimaced, and picked up the phone. He'd gotten a statement from Walt at the hospital yesterday afternoon, but hadn't been able to reach Marvin Bullock before he went home for the day. "Mornin,' Marvin," he said. "How are things down in the State Capital?"

"Oh, just dandy!" Bullock answered, in his usual semi-angry tones. "Projected figures have Ross County leading the state in per capita homicides so far this year, and our senators and representatives in the State House are asking embarrassing questions."

"That's interesting. I don't suppose the Tourist Board can turn that to our advantage, can they?"

"Jesus, Virgil!" the high sheriff exploded. "This is an *Election Year*." The words were underscored. There was a significant pause. Merrill kept quiet. "What I called about, is," Bullock continued, "do you have anything new?"

Darla still stood in the doorway, looking concerned. Merrill grinned at her. "Well, yeah. One of the people involved in the Thorsen murders helped place the cable that damn near killed Walt Whitaker. And they drive a good-sized rig which uses BP Super-92 gasoline."

"Environmentals, you think?"

"Looks that way. Or some sneaky bastards that want us to think so."

"How soon?" A typical Bullock remark, designed to force the conversation farther down the line.

"Marvin, I wish you wouldn't pull this shit with me. It'll be over when it's over. We're not close. I figure we'll have another incident or two, unless we get lucky. You need to be prepared to keep back-filling and stone-walling."

Bullock made a sound like a calf frustrated at reaching its mother's teats. "All right. I can do that. I know you won't fail us, Virgil. I'm just catchin' some heat here." Another pregnant pause. "You think there's any connection between this and that first bunch of deaths?"

Now it was Merrill's turn to pause. "Yeah, I do, but I don't think it's the same people involved."

"How so?"

"I'm not sure, but my mind won't equate up close and personal with stringing a cable across a trail or detonating plastic explosive from a distance. Besides, the average group of self-important environmental activists would have been badly chopped up by those Ukrainians. So, for me, at least, things just don't line up quite right -- yet."

"Well, Virgil, let me know when they do -- and the sooner, the better."

"Don't worry," Merrill answered. "I've already signed up for a double podium, so we can share the limelight at the press conference. You have any preference on the color of the banners, or should we just stick to the traditional red, white, and blue?"

Bullock laughed. "Thanks for puttin' things in perspective. And let me know the minute something breaks. Talk to you then."

"You bet," Merrill said, but the line had already gone dead.

"He pissed?" Darla inquired from the doorway.

"Not really," the sheriff replied, massaging the back of his neck with his left hand. "He's just bein' the man in the hot seat, and tryin' to transfer some of the heat in my direction. Eighteen homicides in three weeks are definitely more than Marvin

184

Bullock -- or any of the rest of us -- need. Most years, this part of the county gets one or two."

"The only BP in the area is down at the lake, isn't it?," Darla asked. "We're not going to keep somebody down there checking vehicles, are we?"

"You volunteering?" Merrill asked, cocking an eyebrow at her.

Darla shook her head.

"No, then," he said. "We don't have enough additional info to narrow it down, and most of the rigs going to the lake are fairly good-sized. It'd be a needle in several haystacks, a waste of time."

"Thank you. So, what exactly do we do next?"

Merrill shrugged. "Wait for another shoe to drop. We know there's at least seven of them. They're probably living in a cabin or two belonging to some family member, or maybe rented for the season. There are close to a hundred cabins available locally, up and down the river. They could be part of the seasonal job market, and living separately, just get together to do their thing. Or they could be driving in from the valley."

"Virgil, how do we know how many of them there were, each time, and what kind of gas they use, and we still don't know who they are?"

"Shut the door and sit down," the sheriff said, after a long look at her. He gestured to the chair. "C'mon, sit."

"O-kay," Darla replied, regarding him narrowly as she sat down.

"It's Rikka," Merrill said, leaning forward, his hands folded on the desk. "She has some unusual talents."

"So I gather." Darla paused in false innocence, then continued more sincerely. "She seemed nice on the phone, and even nicer at your place last Monday. Kathy clearly liked her, and I would have

185

thought anybody who'd gotten that close to you would have been a hard sell to your daughter."

"That's not what I meant by talents, but their gettin' along puzzled me a little, too. They were alone in the kitchen for about twenty minutes while I was in the living room, on the phone to Marv, and my guess is that they hammered out some sort of working agreement then. Kathy's tough and hard-headed, and Rikka's no shrinking violet, but I didn't see any marks on either one of them."

"Kathy's always enjoyed telling you what to do," Darla observed.

Merrill snorted. "Shit, Kathy's always enjoyed telling *everybody* what to do, from the time she could talk. A natural-born lawyer if I ever saw one."

"But Rikka's talents you were referring to had something to do with the *case*?" Darla inquired sweetly, grinning.

"Yeah," he said, managing a weak grin in return, cussing himself for not doing better. "She has a very keen sense of smell. She went to Sharkey's landing, checked it out, walked all the way to Boundry, identified five distinct individuals, one a woman. One of those five strung the cable that got Walt. And Rikka can identify brands of gasoline by the odor of their additives. We parked on Headquarters Grade, at the top of the same elk trail the cable-stringers went in on. Whatever rig they drove burned BP."

"These talents," Darla said. "They must have been part of the Ricky Jo Mullin Improvement Package, paid for by some unknown benefactor?"

"Not your average re-hab center," the sheriff agreed, "that's for damned sure. Her other senses are affected, too, not just smell."

"You mean like taste, sight and hearing?"

"Yup."

186

"Is she as fit as she looks?" Darla asked, reaching out and patting her boss's left hand, resting on the desk top, smiling at him in reassurance. "I'm not angling here, Virgil. I'm just wondering."

Merrill sat back in his chair and crossed his right leg over the left, resting his right ankle on his left knee. He reflected on Darla's words for a few moments, then spoke. "More so's my guess. You've seen how muscular she is, and Walt says she's a workin' fool."

He didn't want to say how Rikka's skin felt, how those dense, powerful muscles slid so smoothly underneath it, flowing and ebbing under his touch. How her warm, moist mouth drove all rational thought from his mind. Instead, he said, "She's heavier than she looks, too."

Darla began to snicker. "I'd pay money to know what went through your mind between those last two sentences.

"I'll never tell."

"You just did, Virgil. You just did. And now you look like someone who has a very sour dill pickle caught in his throat."

"It's not nice to make fun of older people," Merrill replied. "Remember, if it weren't for Rikka Thorsen, we wouldn't have enough information on these cases to fill a thimble, so I'm gonna put off wondering just what happened to make her the way she is until this is all over. And even then, when it's all over, I might not. There are some things in this world that don't need a whole bunch of scrutiny."

"I think I read that line on the second page of the Book of Merrill."

"Probably you did," the sheriff said, laughing, "but that doesn't make it any less true."

"I suppose not," Darla agreed. "You know, watching you and Rikka on Monday showed me just how much the two of you are alike. Not as much as you and Kathy, perhaps, but close. Rikka's had a horrendous life, according to your file, and I think that's part of it. The degree of pain she's experienced."

"How so?"

"Her *eyes* are the same age as yours."

FORTY-FOUR

Up before first light, Rikka had been in the forest depths for nearly an hour when the sun lifted over the Cascades. After Walt's collision with the cable, she'd sat down with Virgil and mapped a series of seven search grids bracketed by the major roadways into the hills. Each morning she ran the trails of one grid, hoping to discover either evidence of new activities by the five -- now seven -- terrorists, or, with luck, the terrorists themselves.

Tonight she would go out at eleven o'clock. Virgil had been adamant that the perpetrators would not do their work in daylight, and Rikka agreed.

Eventually, she would find them.

The Black Voice would speak.

They would die.

Leaving her Cherokee at the house after showering, Rikka meandered off to the Dew Drop Inn for breakfast. It wasn't a slow meander. Nearly twenty miles of up-and-down trail had raised what Virgil would refer to as 'a powerful hunger.'

Thinking of the sheriff made her smile as she walked down the sidewalk to the restaurant. Not just because they spent most nights together; that unfettered joy had been almost expected. Mostly it was the sheer *delight* Rikka found in his company, the intimacies other than physical, the mingling and intertwining of their lives.

Maureen Sims had done her the greatest favor of her life.

Then she recalled her words to Virgil the morning after their first night together.

"Sleeping with the enemy."

Was *that* an understatement.

FORTY-FIVE

Two nights later, an hour after midnight on Monday morning, at the edge of a recent Timber Sale, Rikka found three of them, all part of the seven she'd detected, preparing to spike trees.

FORTY-SIX

Thrilled and excited to actually be in charge of a
night tree-spiking group, Jeremy Hampson didn't
immediately notice the tall young woman standing
in front of the Ford.

Jeremy hunched over his work, with the rear
hatch raised, transferring dozens of eight-inch steel
gutter spikes from a large bag into smaller rubber-
banded packets.

He looked up. She seemed to suddenly just *be*
there.

Clad simply in a dark T-shirt and black jeans,
with hiking boots on her feet, she stood alone in the
center of the skid road where Jeremy had parked the
Expedition. He saw no sign of his companions,
Kiki Bridges and Alden Peterson.

"Hello," Jeremy said, the quaver in his voice
betraying his surprise. "Can I help you?"

She remained quiet for a moment or two, back-lit
by a three-quarter moon just past zenith. "My name
is Rikka, and, as it happens, you *can* help me. I
have a problem with anger-management. Your two
friends helped to de-fuse it to an extent. First, tell
me who you are."

"Jeremy Hampson," Jeremy replied, managing to
hold the quaver in check.

"And your friends?" She took a step or two
closer.

"Alden Peterson and Kiki Bridges."

"Kiki was the girl?" Something lumpy dangled
from her right hand. Jeremy wanted to look at it,
but he couldn't take his eyes off her face. As though
he could hold her self-admitted anger in check if he
didn't look away.

"And you're staying around here?" She came
another step nearer.

"Uh, yeah. My folks have a couple of cabins by Lautenbach Hot Springs." Cold sweat dribbled down his ribs.

"How many of you are staying there?"

"T-ten, now, but that varies." Jeremy tried to remember if there was anything in the Expedition that could be used as a weapon.

"Are the four who were with you the night you murdered the Thorsens all there now?"

"Wh-hat?" Jeremy stammered. "I don't k-know what you're talking about." He grabbed onto the edge of the hatch to steady himself.

"Let me refresh your memory, then, Jeremy. Murder. There were five of you that night. One -- a guy -- set the charges while the rest of you watched from up the ridge. You were one of the watchers. Another was a woman."

"I didn't do *anything*," Jeremy nearly wailed.

The woman -- Rikka -- raised what she held in her right hand, hanging by its hair. "He's lying, isn't he, Kiki?"

Jeremy looked into Kiki Bridges' dead eyes, drooping half-opened in her severed head.

"That's right," Kiki said, startling Jeremy so bad he nearly fell to the ground. The killer manipulated Kiki's lower jaw with her left hand. "He was there. He watched. He deserves to die."

"N-n-no." Jeremy shook his head.

Rikka began to smile. A remorseless deadly smile. "Think about it, Jeremy," she said, her voice cold as liquid oxygen. "You told me where to find the others. I don't *need* you any more." She came closer.

Jeremy looked around wildly. "Where's Alden?"

"I cut his throat back in the trees, while he was taking a piss. He's probably done now. Should we go see?"

192

"N-n-no," Jeremy replied. "Don't kill me!" he pleaded, and began to cry.

"You. Useless. Little. Pus-ball!" Rikka said slowly. "You stood by while four innocent people were killed, two of them children, and you think you deserve to *fucking live*?" She held Kiki's severed head up in front of his face. "Say good-bye, Kiki."

"Good-bye, Jeremy," said the head.

"Never thought of myself as a ventriloquist," Rikka said, throwing the head over her left shoulder. It spiraled away into the darkness, landing with a faint sodden thump among the trees.

Before Jeremy could turn and run, or cry out, her right hand shot out and grabbed him by the throat. She pulled his face up to hers, squeezing his neck so tightly that he could barely breathe. The cartilage of his voice box began to grind together. Choking, he stared into her rage-twisted features, flailing his arms ineffectually.

"You've known a few minutes of terror, dickhead," she said, her eyes practically glowing. She squeezed harder and lifted Jeremy's feet off the ground, "but your pain and suffering is *nothing* compared to what's gonna happen to the guy who planted the explosives. Your folks' cabins are about to be re-decorated."

Her grip tightened.

Jeremy tried to scream, and couldn't.

He tried to breathe, and couldn't.

He tried to live.

And couldn't.

FORTY-SEVEN

The Black Voice had not overwhelmed Rikka. She had feared it might, when she came face-to-face with one of those who had killed the Thorsens.

Instead, she had harnessed that dark tide and ridden it, forced it to do her bidding, binding her anger and channeling it into her hands and blades.

Tree-spikers, she thought in disgust. Aware of what could happen when a chain saw -- or more likely a trimmer saw at the mill -- bit into the tree's trunk and impacted the heavy steel spike. Breaking up, sending a stream of shattered metal into the saw operator and those nearby.

And they did it anyway. Then, safe and anonymous, read about the consequences of their actions in the newspapers.

Wink-wink, nudge-nudge.

But she'd finished three of them, and now she knew where the rest were. Forty-five minutes to get to the Hot Springs, then perhaps another half-hour to ferret out which cabins the killers occupied on the ninety-nine-year-leased government lands adjacent to the privately-owned springs.

Rikka turned the key in the Cherokee's ignition with a great deal of satisfaction.

One of the Thorsens' killers down, four to go.

FORTY-EIGHT

Matt Wagner had not done well in the two weeks since the Thorsen family had died on Sharkey's Landing. Ordinarily somewhat solitary, he had retreated further into himself, drunk more wine than normal in the evenings, and slept fitfully, getting up frequently during the night.

No longer a problem, Chuckie Morberg thought, as he let Wagner's body slip down the short muddy bank and into the Lautenbach River. Spread-eagled, clad only in warmup pants and a T-shirt, the corpse spun slowly away into the main current and rapidly moved downstream.

He watched Wagner disappear in the undulating water. Poor schmuck. Just shows what can happen when you develop a conscience.

Humming softly to himself, Chuckie headed back in the direction of the cabins, being careful to place his boots on either logs or the larger rocks. They'd find Wagner within a week or less, no question. The little river emptied into the lake well above the dam, and bodies had an unfortunate tendency to float to the surface eventually.

Chuckie had used an eight-inch stiletto only three-eighths of an inch wide, driven it directly into Wagner's heart from behind while the forester-turned- environmental activist stood on the river bank. An excellent instrument and technique that had served Chuckie well a time or two previously. Now to get back to the cabin before anybody -- Mimsy, for example -- woke up and wondered where he'd gone.

Of course, he'd made a point of fucking Mimsy until her ears bled earlier tonight, so she should be sleeping soundly.

That got him to thinking that he had only a couple of weeks left here. He reached into his pants pocket and felt the duplicate key he'd had made for Mimsy's Toyota Corolla. If Wagner floated up in the next two weeks, Chuckie might have to make a run for it, and he made a point of never using a vehicle that could be traced to him.

He also made a point of always being ready to run. At the moment, he wore a cotton shirt under a light cotton jacket, jeans, and his old zipper-sided jump boots from Airborne school. His CZ 75 nestled comfortably under his left armpit in a nylon holster, with cash and passport in his hip pocket.

Just a kid out stretching his legs from having one too many beers after he got off work down at the marina.

Every time he left the cabin, even if it was only to take a leak in the middle of the night, Chuckie dressed and pulled on his boots. And he never went *anywhere* without having his pistol within easy reach.

He approached the cabins cautiously, keeping an eye out for anyone else going or coming from the outhouse. The cabins had been built by that little prick Hampson's family right after World War Two, and the cheapasses had never forked over for a drainfield and septic tank. Even the interior wiring was a little marginal, but it, at least, had been modernized a few years back. Each cabin had a sixty-watt porch light to help outhouse returnees find their way, and Chuckie could see the area between the two cabins fairly well as he moved through the forest.

When he was fifty yards away, his vision partially obscured by a line of young vine maple, Chuckie thought he saw a shadow pass from the larger cabin to the smaller one he shared with Mimsy, Brian Hibbs, and Hampson. He tensed, stopped, and

196

watched for a few moments, then began walking at an increased pace. Maybe Hibbs had been over shagging one of the women in the big cabin, the sneaky little shit.

Then, thirty feet from the cabins, Chuckie saw something long and white laying in the doorway of the big cabin, right at the edge of the porch light's circle of illumination.

It took a second for his brain to register what he was seeing.

An arm.

Just an arm, nothing else, lying across the threshold.

Holy fucking shit!

Chuckie drew the CZ, clicked off the safety, and stood stock still, scanning his surroundings, each of his systems alert.

Someone suddenly screamed inside the smaller cabin, and a body, loosely-wrapped in a sheet, came hurtling out through the side window in a spray of glass and wooden gridwork. The body hit the ground, and rolled out of the sheet.

On her hands and knees, Mimsy Borogave looked up at Chuckie with glazed eyes. A darkening bruise spread on the right side of her face. "A woman," Mimsy said weakly, and collapsed.

Chuckie took the stance and put three quick shots through the open window.

FORTY-NINE

Rikka had smashed Brian Hibbs against the ceiling twice when Chuckie opened up with the CZ.

His first shot blew the contents of Hibbs' cranium over Rikka's face and upper torso, momentarily blinding her. The second burned a furrow across the back of her right hand. The third buried itself in a ceiling stringer above Hibbs' body.

Throwing Hibbs in what she hoped was the general direction of the window, Rikka dropped to the floor, wiping gore out of her eyes with her good hand.

She scrambled toward the door, picking up a pair of shoes on the way.

The demoliton guy! He hadn't been in the cabin. Out taking a leak, probably. Now he was *outside* the cabin, with God knew how many bullets left in what had sounded like a forty-five or a nine-millimeter.

Taking careful aim from behind the left door jamb, Rikka took out both porch lights, one shoe for each.

FIFTY

Ignoring the body of Brian Hibbs, draped over the cabin's windowsill, Chuckie backed toward Mimsy's car, half-dragging, half-leading Mimsy. He kept his pistol trained on the open space between the two cabins.

Whether or not Hibbs had been intended as a distraction, whoever or whatever remained inside the smaller cabin had to come out the front door. That, or stay inside, and Chuckie didn't think they would.

He sure as hell wouldn't.

When the two porchlights shattered, he tightened his one-handed grip on the CZ. Here we go, he thought, taking a deep breath.

There! Movement. A blur. He emptied the clip, moving his aim from left to right.

A figure appeared in the moonlight, close to the larger cabin's entrance, staggering once, twice, then vanishing into the cabin.

Chuckie released his held breath.

A hit.

FIFTY-ONE

Her right-side ribs on fire, and her right leg nearly buckling under her, Rikka slipped and crashed down on the bigger cabin's blood-drenched floor, sliding into one of the uprights.

She shook her head to clear it. Damn! She should've taken Virgil up on his offer of a pistol. Pulling herself to her feet against the upright, she felt her broken ribs grate together. At least there wasn't any pain, after the first few seconds.

She looked down. A handspan above her knee, through her ripped pant-leg, torn muscle, ligament, and tendon writhed, knitting back together.

Good, Rikka thought, limping to the door, putting most of her weight on her left leg. Reasonably certain that the shooter would have been closer if he intended to attack her directly, she chanced a quick look around the edge of the door jamb.

They were at the car.

FIFTY-TWO

Keeping his gaze locked on the larger cabin, Chuckie popped out the CZ's empty magazine, stuck it in his pocket, and jacked a fresh clip from his belt into the pistol. He released his held breath a second time.

Woman or not, he'd probably slowed the killer down.

There'd been no return fire, which could only mean that she didn't have a gun. Chuckie couldn't fathom that, but he supposed if you could pull people's arms off, a gun might seem unnecessary.

Until his butt contacted the front of Mimsy's little station wagon, though, Chuckie's gaze didn't waver, and the CZ remained pointing at the door of the big cabin.

Sliding around the front of the car to the passenger side, practically dragging Mimsy with him, he opened the door as quietly as he could and shoved the girl inside. Mimsy's face was a bloody mess, though she probably didn't have more than a few cuts from being thrown through the window. Even minor facial wounds bled like hell.

Once he was behind the wheel, Chuckie continued to watch the cabin while he fumbled the car key into the ignition.

"We're leaving?" Mimsy asked, cleaning her eyes with the hem of the long T-shirt she habitually wore to bed.

"Fucking damn well bet we are," Chuckie replied, firing up the Toyota.

"But the others! We should help them."

"They are fucking *dead*, Mims! I shot that woman, or whatever it is, and that may slow her down, but we are gettin' out of here!"

Mimsy put her right hand on the door latch, started to move it.

Grabbing her wrist, Chuckie said quietly, "You get out, Mims, you're on your own. I'm leaving. Now." He stepped on the gas and spun the car around on the loose gravel and moist dirt.

As they pulled away, Chuckie checked the rearview mirror. He thought he saw something step out of the larger cabin.

He hoped not. He had a very bad feeling about this.

FIFTY-THREE

The pistol shots had sounded cannon-loud, Rikka thought, moving after the Toyota's retreating taillights as rapidly as she could. Even though the nearest neighboring cabins were a quarter-mile distant, it would be only a matter of time before someone investigated

Several of those cabins lay between Rikka and her Cherokee, parked a half-mile away, and she had to make it past them before the inevitable flashlights and floodlights appeared.

Full speed would have gotten her there in under a minute, but she could manage only a lurching trot. Her healed ribs had restored her breathing, but her right leg remained compromised, though gaining strength and function by the second.

Still, she reached the Jeep only a couple of minutes after the Corolla disappeared onto the main road to the lake, and she saw the lights make a definite left. Rikka hauled herself into the driver's seat. Her four-liter engine should make short work of their head start.

A quick glance at herself in the rearview mirror revealed features caked with drying blood and brains. She flexed her lower jaw, dislodging some of it, but she was still a serious mess. Hopefully, no one besides her prey would get a good look at her.

To guarantee that, she'd have to overhaul them before they reached the main highway, and they had a two-mile headstart.

Plus, she still had to figure out how to neutralize the shooter's weapon.

Oh, well. Rikka reached under her seat and pulled out a large bottle of electrolyte mix, guzzling it while working the Cherokee through the gears.

She floored the accelerator, spewing a rooster-tail of gravel. No way were they going to escape while she lived.

Two down and three to go.

FIFTY-FOUR

Mimsy's Corolla proved to be easily the most under-powered piece of shit Chuckie had ever driven. Once they hit the pavement and could actually get moving, the little vehicle would only nudge sixty, not exceed it.

"I thought these things were supposed to be worth a crap," Chuckie said, slapping the steering wheel with one hand, glaring at Mimsy.

Mimsy looked up from dabbing at her facial cuts with her shirttail. She'd pretty much quit bleeding. "I think Daddy bought the environmental protection package," she said, blinking crusted blood out of her eyes. "Is that a problem?"

"Yeah," Chuckie said, keeping his gaze out the front window. He was afraid if he looked at Mimsy, he'd start screaming. Bringing her had been a mistake. He should have just ditched her, used her to distract whatever he'd shot at, given himself a bigger head start. He'd seen the white Cherokee parked alongside the gravel just before they slid onto Highway 46, and his already bad feeling had deepened.

"Why?" Mimsy asked. "We only have to get to Flint, less than ten miles, and phone the police. You said everybody's dead."

Chuckie took several deep breaths. "That's right," he said slowly, "but if I only winged the killer, *she* -- if you're right -- is not going to want to leave witnesses. So, if she can, she's going to come *after* us, which means I will have to *shoot* her. Which could mean that the authorities will want to speak with us on a more than witness basis. I cannot let them know who I am, and -- because I was in the military -- my fingerprints are on file in Washington D.C.."

"Oh," Mimsy replied slowly, "that makes sense. So what are we doing?"

"When we get to Flint, we turn right, drive to the valley, head for Portland. You drop me off at PDX, and I fly away. You go to your folks' house, and play dumb." That last, in Chuckie's opinion, would not be hard.

Better yet, he could snap Mimsy's pretty little neck in long term parking at PDX, leave her body in the Toyota, take the shuttle bus to the terminal, and be extremely gone.

That might be the best course of action, actually.

While he considered that attractive option, Chuckie looked behind them in the mirror. Well back, the canyon wall on the west side of the river lit up briefly. Headlights from somebody in the curves just below the Hotsprings. Shit. No more than a couple of miles behind, and little doubt who it might be.

Distracted by what he saw, Chuckie inadvertently let the Toyota drift across the centerline, and barely missed a rig going in the opposite direction. He caught a glimpse of a large black-and-white SUV with official markings on the door.

A fucking game warden!

Let's just hope he has something more important to do at four o'clock in the morning than us, Chuckie thought, cursing his luck. This was proving to be one of the
shittiest nights of his life.

And when he saw the warden's brake lights flare, he knew it was only going to get worse.

FIFTY-FIVE

If anyone had ever told Carvel Hunnecker that getting whocked in the jaw with a frozen steelhead would turn out to be a good thing, he would have told them they were plumb crazy. As it turned out, Ellen Jean Hollis -- who'd justifiably done the whocking when Carvel grabbed her ass a mite too vigorously -- felt so sorry for him that they were getting along better than he'd thought possible.

In fact, the tall game warden's life was generally going well. People at the State Police office occasionally even remarked how his temperament seemed better than usual this year. He hadn't really rousted anyone the entire season.

Carvel wasn't about to tell them it was all due to the fifteen-pound frozen trout. They'd had enough fun with that already.

His newly-found good nature vanished abruptly, however, when the little punk with surfer-blond hair damn near ran him off the highway. At this hour, in the warden's opinion, the only reason someone would be driving like that involved an act of law-breaking where the guilty party had been nearly caught red-handed.

There could be only one response.

Hunnecker cannon-balled the brakes and backed around to begin pursuit. As his Chevy Blazer worked its way up through its automatic gearbox, the lights atop the rig flashing, he flipped open his comm-line and told his dispatcher what was going down. By the time he'd finished doing that, the Blazer -- moving at close to eighty miles an hour -- was reeling in the little Jap car by leaps and bounds.

In a long straight stretch about six miles out of Flint, Hunnecker pulled alongside of the Toyota, hit his siren, and began easing the smaller vehicle to the side of the road. The driver had a choice of either stopping or driving off the road embankment into the Lautenbach River.

The punk stopped, a wise thing in the warden's estimation. Little surfer shit. Hunnecker parked in front of the Toyota at a forty-five degree angle, boxing it in, spoke briefly with his dispatcher, then picked up his big flashlight and opened his door. As an afterthought, he un-clipped his personal Pancor Jackhammer shotgun from under the Blazer's dash. It might come in handy. You never knew what you were getting into, these days.

The shotgun hanging loosely at his side, the game warden shone his flashlight on the Toyota's occupants as he walked slowly toward the car. A young girl and the blond driver, who looked about fifteen. Hunnecker wondered what they'd been up to.

Well, he thought, as he took a firmer grip on the Jackhammer, he'd soon find out.

FIFTY-SIX

After rolling down his window, Chuckie sat quietly, the CZ in his left hand, resting on his lap. He took several deep breaths, closing his eyes when the game warden's light flashed over him and Mimsy.

Mimsy, holding a hand up to shield her eyes, for once kept her mouth shut.

That was good. Otherwise, Chuckie thought he would have shot her right after he shot the blue-uniformed warden.

Which he did, three times, when the guy was about fifteen feet from him.

The taller man slammed against the right rear corner of his rig. His campaign hat fell to the asphalt, and he slid slowly down the Blazer's side, a surprised expression on his features.

"So long, Dudley," Chuckie muttered, while Mimsy made a shrill whistling sound like an incredibly tiny tea kettle.

"You *shot* him!" she said accusingly.

"*Shut the fuck up*," Chuckie replied, very softly, and back-handed her with his right hand. He put the Toyota in reverse and began to back up to go around the Blazer.

The windshield exploded inward.

FIFTY-SEVEN

The sound of a shotgun -- "blapp, blapp, blapp" -- echoing off the rock walls on the west bank came clearly to Rikka's ears as she sped along the river highway. A few seconds later, she could see the flashing lights of the warden's Chevy, then the Blazer itself. The Toyota sat fifteen feet from the larger rig, lights playing over it like something from a seventies disco.

There were no signs of life around either vehicle.

Rikka pulled slowly past them and parked. She saw the three fist-sized holes in the Toyota's spiderwebbed windshield, saw the warden laid out next to the Blazer, an evil-looking repeater shotgun on the pavement beside him.

Keeping her gaze on the Toyota, Rikka moved around the Chevy in a crouch, and bent over Hunnecker, finding a strong carotid pulse. Three good hits on his torso, none penetrating his flack vest, but fired close enough to bounce him off his rig and knock him unconscious, apparently.

Then how did he fire the shotgun? she wondered. Instinct and self-preservation, she guessed. Still watching the Toyota, Rikka walked around the Blazer to the driver's side and picked up the radio microphone, thumbing it on. "Got an officer down on Highway 46," she said. "Need an EMT unit STAT."

"Who is this?" came the reply.

"A concerned citizen," Rikka answered. "He had on a vest. He isn't wounded, just banged up, but is unconscious at the moment. Probably six or seven miles up the river."

"Identify yourself."

"Sorry. No can do," Rikka said, and hung up. She wiped her fingerprints off the comm-unit and the door handle, and went back to the Toyota. The right side windows were covered in blood, but the driver's side seemed mostly clear.

Cautiously, after winding her shirt around her right hand, she opened the door.

FIFTY-EIGHT

It took a few seconds for Chuckie to realize that someone was talking to him, for the words to penetrate his agony.

"Help me," he said weakly, gasping in pain.

"Nice to see you," someone said. Chuckie recognized the tone, if not the voice. Some of his more sadistic drill sergeants had sounded like that.

Slowly, painfully, he turned his head and saw a dark-skinned woman smiling at him through the Toyota's opened door, her face and T-shirt covered with gore. The smile did not quite reach her eyes, which glittered with something akin to pleasure, but chilled him to the bone.

"You appear to be having some difficulty here," the woman remarked conversationally.

"Help me," Chuckie repeated, focusing on her only with extreme effort. He had trouble breathing.

"You shot me," she replied, as if in explanation, then gestured past him. "Your friend seems to have lost her head, the right side anyway, and you're dying slowly, drowning in your own blood." She made a 'tut-tut' sound. "What a shame. I wanted to be the one to do it, and the game warden got to you first."

"Call someone," Chuckie said.

"Did. For the warden. You won't be alive when the EMTs get here." She grasped Chuckie's lower jaw, twisting his face toward hers. He saw her through a red haze, the colors of the warden's lights bathing her in alternate blue and orange. "Where's the other one that was with you when you killed the Thorsens with your frigging Semtex?"

"He's dead," Chuckie gasped, his breath gurgling.

"Ah," she said, and a smile of true pleasure spread over her features. She released him.

212

"Now will you help me?" Chuckie asked.

"Sure. No problemo. Somewhere in your shotgun experience, some of the more ambitious pellets found your gas tank. There's quite a puddle under your car. Just give me a couple of minutes to get the warden and his rig to safety, and we'll see if the waterproof match container in my pants pocket really *is* waterproof. Okay?"

"No-o-o," Chuckie said, lifting his left hand feebly off the seat.

"Be right back. Just keep dying, all right?"

She disappeared, and Chuckie drifted in and out of consciousness. The Blazer's flashing lights retreated down the road.

At some point, she came back, her face somewhat less blood-smeared.

She held an unlit match in front of Chuckie's face.

"They say that burning alive is the most painful way to die," she remarked. "What do *you* think"

"No-o-o," Chuckie said again, struggling to move and failing. "You wouldn't."

"Give you a taste of hell before you actually get there? Sure I would. I'm not real big on mercy, particularly for the undeserving. I went to a funeral that you caused."

"*Please*," Chuckie implored.

"Sorry. Gotta be gone when the authorities arrive. I killed seven of your little chums, but *you're* the one I wanted most of all." Her laugh was the purest evil.

"*No!*" Chuckie said.

She continued to laugh as she stepped away from the car. He heard the match strike.

FIFTY-NINE

Fire had completely engulfed the Toyota by the time the state police and the EMT van arrived. A hundred feet from the flames, Carvel Hunnecker was awake and semi-lucid. The emergency personnel had him checked over and strapped onto a stretcher within five minutes, while three state police officers sprayed their extinguishers into the fire until the canisters went dry.

"Fire truck'll be here in a few minutes. How's he doing?" one of the staters asked the EMTs, as they prepared to shut the rear doors of the ambulance.

"He'll be okay," the lead EMT said, "except he might be delusional from hitting the side of his rig."

"Concussion?"

"Oh, maybe, or close enough." The EMT laughed. "He thinks a dead woman carried him to safety. Said she was covered with blood."

The cop looked back at the blackened Toyota, jerking a thumb at the heap of deformed metal and burned plastic. "Woman or not, *those* people didn't rescue anybody."

The EMT nodded. "Like I said. Delusional."

"But alive."

"Alive is good," the EMT agreed, grinning as he closed up the ambulance.

SIXTY

Standing on the front porch of the smaller of the Hampson's cabins in the morning sun, Fred Cameron looked around him at the state police vehicles and two big ambulances from the hospital. The EMTs had just brought the second body bag out of the larger cabin. "Some of this is the work of whoever killed the Dilts boys and those Ukrainians, Virgil."

"I know that," Merrill replied, looking down at the shoe lying on the porch. He reached up and touched the ceramic light socket on the porch ceiling, examining the shattered bulb. "You notice the other half of this pair of shoes is on the other porch?"

"No," Cameron said, looking up at the taller man. "Is that supposed to have some sort of significance?"

"Someone was in here when Brian Hibbs was killed. Whoever it was, they were on the floor at some point after Hibbs got his skull emptied. They crawled toward the door."

"The shooter was outside the building?"

"I pried one slug out of a stringer, on the window side, another from the wall opposite. The third got Hibbs. It was on the floor. The staters'll run 'em through forensics. My guess is that our Mister Morberg's nine-millimeter automatic will be the source."

"Nice that Morberg had so much documentation on him," Cameron remarked.

"Unless I miss my guess, Morberg will be the demolitions expert. Savvy enough to always be ready to run. And military, at some point. He had on jump boots."

"Are you going to get around to the shoes on the porch soon?" Cameron asked.

"Sure," Merrill nodded. "Whoever was crawling toward the door used the shoes to break the porchlights."

"Why?"

"Because Morberg was shootin' at 'em."

"Please tell me something that makes sense, Virgil."

"The woman in the car was sleeping in this cabin. So was Hibbs. Whoever killed the Ukrainians and the Dilts brothers went into the other cabin first." The sheriff gestured into the cabin behind them. "Morberg interrupted the festivities in this cabin. He must've been out taking a leak or something. The woman in the burned-out Toyota either jumped or was thrown out the window. She and Morberg drove off -- after he emptied a clip here, the empty magazine found in his pants pocket. I can show you the brody marks over by my car."

"How can you know that Morberg and this woman even *came* from here?" Cameron asked.

"A fair question. There were six people living in the larger cabin, four in this one, judging from the personal effects in the closets and lockers. In here were Hibbs and three others, one of whom was a young woman named Mimosa Marie Borogave. All of her identification and personal belongings appear to be here." Merrill smiled down at Cameron. "How much are you willing to bet, Fred?"

The doctor shook his head. "Sorry, Virgil. You don't bet unless you're certain."

The sheriff continued to smile. "I'm not *quite* certain. There are some unanswered questions. Even if I'm right, we have only six bodies. Where are the other four people? And Morberg had only underwear, socks, toiletries, and a couple of changes of clothes here, including two T-shirts from 'Big Daddy's Flys and Fries.'"

"A fishing gear and fast food place at the Lake," Cameron said, shrugging. "He might have been working there."

"But no Semtex. No detonators." Merrill said thoughtfully, stroking his chin. "I think I'll take a little stroll around the area, give the state boys a hand in their search. My guess is that Morberg will have stashed his work equipment close by, but not so close as to definitely point in this direction."

"You make him sound like a real professional."

"Oh, he was. No doubt about it. But whoever he was firing at spooked him, and he took off. Can't say as I blame him. Pure bad luck that he ran into Carvel Hunnecker and his new shotgun."

Merrill's cell-phone, clipped to his belt, abruptly began to chime. "Damn thing," the sheriff said, looking at the small device in irritation.

He pulled it off his belt, and flipped it open. "Merrill here." He listened for a few moments. "How many?" Another pause. "Thanks, Johnny. Doctor Cameron and I will be right over. I'll radio in another ambulance, meet 'em down at the Lake, and bring 'em on in. About an hour. Yeah, bye."

"That was Johnny Anderson," Merrill said to Cameron, clipping his phone back on his belt. "Three more, up off Ginger Creek. Tree spikers. One beheaded, one cut throat, and one with his neck squeezed to about the diameter of a pencil."

Cameron sighed, his shoulders sagging. "Jesus, Virgil. I'm supposed to be in my office today. Can I bill Ross County for overtime?"

"C'mon, Fred," the sheriff replied, putting his left arm around his friend's shoulders. "Just think of it as more time you get to spend with me."

"Now I'm *really* depressed," the doctor replied.

SIXTY-ONE

In spite of the more than considerable age difference, Rikka Thorsen and the sheriff had a great deal in common, Fred Cameron decided. Different coloration, different features, yet the manner in which their faces reflected their thoughts was so similar. Cameron had seen Rikka for the first time at the Thorsen funeral, and her reaction to the situation and the people around her that day mirrored Virgil's almost exactly. More open, to be sure, but otherwise eerily the same.

Not that it truly mattered, the doctor supposed. It was only interesting. He stuck his key in the thick metal door of the hospital morgue, joggled the door to free up the dead bolt, and unlocked it. "You understand, Virgil, that *you* have every right to be here, but Ms. Thorsen's presence *is* the sort of thing we highly-paid and highly-skilled coroners find somewhat questionable." He smiled at Rikka to take some of the sternness from his words.

She, of course, smiled back, her teeth dazzling against her dark skin.

Youth! Cameron thought. Any way one looked at it, there was no substitute.

"Highly-paid, huh?" Merrill said. "What'd they give you last year? Three bushels of apples?"

"Five," Cameron replied, opening the door and ushering them in. "And some nifty coupons for the Quik-E Mart."

"Not bad," the sheriff said. "I should do so well."

The coroner laughed and re-locked the door behind them.

"Do you two never stop giving each other a bad time?" Rikka asked, looking first at Cameron and Merrill, and then at the row of unoccupied gurneys.

"No," the two men said simultaneously.

218

"Definitely not," Cameron added, gesturing at a smaller glass-fronted door. "The storage room is over here. This'll be pretty much the only chance you'll get to examine the decedents. Most of these kids were from the Portland area, so they'll be trans-shipped tomorrow."

Once they were inside the room, the doctor watched Rikka carefully for a reaction, signs of the uneasiness or repugnance typical of most morgue visitors. Instead, she seemed more alert, her gaze sweeping the double rows of body drawers, her head up. She and Merrill exchanged glances, and she nodded almost imperceptibly.

Odd, thought Cameron, then went into his prepared speech. "All our current guests except one are from last night's excitement, so I'll open each drawer in turn, and you can examine the body." He looked at Rikka. "Will that work?"

"Yes."

"If you start feeling queasy, want me to shut the drawer, or have to leave, just say so." From behind him, he heard Merrill's amused grunt. "Several of these cadavers were dismembered," Cameron continued, "two are badly burned."

"Thank you, Doctor," Rikka said, her voice steady, "I'm sure I'll be fine."

The coroner wasn't so sure, but he went down the double row of drawers, opening them one at a time, and then stepping aside.

He expected Virgil to be fine with it. He expected Rikka to be at least slightly taken aback, but her expression as she studied each corpse remained very clinical and professional. And she did something Cameron had never seen anyone do. Over each body, she slowly inhaled through her nose.

When they were done, Rikka asked, "May I see the other body, please, Doctor?"

"He's not one of the cabin homicides," the coroner replied. "He floated into the lake around mid-morning. He *is* a homicide, however, just not a drowning, which is why he floated. His lungs weren't filled with water. He was dead when he went into the river."

"Any identification?" Merrill asked.

"No, unfortunately," Cameron answered, opening the final occupied drawer.

"He was at the cabins," Rikka said flatly, looking at the partially-clothed body. "And with the group that killed the Thorsens."

"How'd he die?" Merrill put in, looking at Cameron.

"Very thin blade directly into his heart, entry wound from behind. If he'd stayed in the water for a few weeks, it would have been more difficult to identify, but, as pale-skinned as he is, it showed up easily this early."

"Case closed," Merrill said, "as far as the Thorsens are concerned." He looked at Rikka, grinning. "Though I don't suppose we can take your nose into a court of law, can we?"

"Can the dead be brought to trial?" Rikka asked, her brow furrowing.

"Wait a minute!" the coroner said to Rikka, waving his arms. "Are you telling me you can ID people by their smell?"

"Yes," she answered, "provided I've smelled them before. On the day of the murders, I checked out Sharkey's Landing and their route back to their vehicle -- probably the Expedition you two found near that trio up on Ginger Creek -- and got good clear..." She paused and glanced at Merrill, "...smell prints?"

"Good enough," the sheriff said, chuckling.

Cameron looked at Merrill. "Are you going to tell Marvin Bullock *that*?"

The sheriff scratched his head. "Gonna have to. Then I'll tell Hakon and Katie. And you can see we're gonna get our balls in a cleft stick at some point."

"How so?" asked the doctor.

"Simple. *We* know who killed the Thorsens. Marv probably can't hold a press conference and state that we do. That creates a scenario where Marv tells the press that one group of murders is solved, but that the murderers have themselves been slaughtered by person or persons who remain at large. And, even better, we're just darned sure that the Dilts boys and all those Ukranians were killed by the same party."

"I see what you mean," Cameron replied, "but you can hang one death on Morberg -- if the ballistics tests prove that his pistol fired the shot that killed Hibbs -- and of course Morberg fired at Warden Hunnecker, and Morberg and the girl were in turn shot by Hunnecker. So those ten deaths are reduced to seven unexplained."

"Leaving us with a total of twenty-one mystery deaths," Merrill finished for his friend, "plus the Thorsens."

"Will Hakon and Katie accept knowing that those who murdered Sigge, Erika, and their children have been dealt with?" Cameron asked.

"Probably," the sheriff admitted, "but Marv still has to figure out a way to tie our ten environmental commandoes into the Thorsen deaths. Morberg will hopefully be the scapegoat on that. We found his backpack with additional Semtex and detonators. His service record -- and there *will* be one -- should be available to us not later than tomorrow. This still leaves the seven children of a number of very highly-connected wealthy upstate families deader'n doornails."

Cameron nodded. "Scalps will be howled for."

"No shit," Merrill said. "People who were amused or uninterested by the Dilts, and merely confounded by or mildly interested in the Ukrainians, will be really hot to trot on seven environmentally-active altruistic youngsters whacked by an unknown."

"Even though they killed four innocent people?" Rikka asked.

"That'll be left on Morberg's doorstep," the sheriff responded. "Now, I have paperwork I collected from Hibbs' effects in the smaller cabin which would seem to connect these kids to the Planet Prime! organization. Hibbs, the apparent leader, had a very nice electronic organizer with all sorts of helpful information in it. I intend to spend a couple of fruitful hours with it tonight."

"*We* will," Rikka said, squeezing his hand and smiling sweetly at him. Her tone of voice and the intent expression on her face belied her smile, Cameron noticed. Not for the first time, he wondered what her agenda was in all this. He had enough experience with humans and their nature to know she wasn't just tagging along with Virgil for the fun of it. Virgil was not inclined to put down the ball until the final buzzer -- and then some -- and Rikka Thorsen seemed to be of like mind.

Then there was that look of quiet pleasure that had appeared on her face the moment he opened the first body drawer, a look that had grown stronger with each successive drawer until now she positively radiated satisfaction.

Doctor Cameron would gladly give up one of those fictional bushels of apples for a few answers to his questions. But that could still happen, he figured.

This particular continuing saga was quite a ways from being over.

SIXTY-TWO

Though accustomed to being shouted at by his environmental opposites, and the occasional so-called ally, Alexander Carson was not prepared for either Dick Edmiston's loss of control or the tirade that followed.

"Richard," he said, in his best conciliatory tones, holding the earpiece away from the side of his head, "please, please calm down. This is doing neither of us any service."

"*Calm down*! For Christ's sake, Alex! All my people down in North Cedar are *dead*. I just got off the phone with Woodrow Hampson III, Jeremy Hampson's older brother, the CEO of Hampson-Vetter Heavy Industries. His mother is in seclusion, dosed to the gills with Valium. Her 'little lamb' is dead. Woodrow wants answers, and I *don't have any*!"

"Your demolition expert is dead at the hands of the warden he assaulted," Carson replied, still trying to be conciliatory, "and the Borogave girl died in the crossfire, apparently. I read that in *The Oregonian*. What can you tell me?"

Carson heard three deep breaths before Edmiston went on. "I've been in touch with family members, who are either grief-stricken and angry, or just plain angry. Brian Hibbs was shot in the head. My guess is Morberg. Maybe fighting over the girl." Another deep breath. "I don't know. The rest of them, though, were either torn apart, or had their throats slit. Jeremy Hampson's neck was crushed. On the phone, his brother nearly broke up. He had to identify the body yesterday. The authorities either don't know anything, or are sitting on what they do know. Because their families are influential, the newspaper has been referring to them as 'concerned environmentalists,' or 'environmental activists.' That won't last."

"Probably not. *Willamette Week* and the more critical press won't be so kind, I'm afraid, Richard," Carson said, his thick fingers drumming his desk top. A dark cold knot was gathering in his stomach. "I'll make some inquiries, determine what to do, then call you back. If you learn anything additional in the meanwhile, please let me know."

"Okay," Edmiston replied, still sounding shaken.

The two men hung up, and Carson sat looking out his tenth floor office window for several minutes, thinking.

Edmiston hadn't seen the obvious yet. He was too upset. Carson didn't want to, but the conclusion was unavoidable.

Reckon had turned.

Over four million dollars had been spent to create a formidable foe for those who dared harm the environment, and the very valid inclusion of *anyone* who harmed the environment simply hadn't occurred to Carson.

Tree-spikers. People who killed those engaged in sanctioned forest activities. Sims had warned him that Reckon would grow and develop and maturate.

Dear God, wanting to believe the absolute perfection of Sims' bio-weapon, he hadn't seen it.

And the sheriff. Reckon sitting casually on his front porch, chatting with the man's daughter. What did *he* know? Perhaps nothing. Perhaps something. Perhaps *everything*.

Sims, Reckon, the sheriff.

A short list, but every one potentially dangerous to Carson and the people he represented.

He reached into his humidor, brought out a cigar, cut off the tip, lit it with a small gold cigar lighter as he inhaled.

Then he picked up the phone.
Time to move on.

SIXTY-THREE

Those who worked in commodities trading with Robert McDaniel described him as focused and intense. Those who played racquetball against him found him relentless and unmerciful. Those who met him in his secondary employment didn't have an opinion.

They were dead.

McDaniel had finished a pair of racquetball games and just exited the showers at the Multnomah Athletic Club when Alexander Carson called.

At least he was dry and his hair was mostly combed, McDaniel thought, as he sat wrapped in a bath towel, waiting for Carson to get to the point. Carson could do that – get to the point -- but, like most people, the talkative environmental lawyer beat around the bush when he wanted someone killed.

McDaniel had made the referral that resulted in Richard Edmiston hiring Chuckie Morberg -- the acquaintance of one of McDaniel's old service buddies. Now Morberg was dead, along with a bunch of Edmiston's little tree-hugger acolytes. McDaniel had vaguely followed the events in North Cedar in *The Oregonian*, and was of the opinion that whatever was going on down there, people even loonier than Edmiston were involved. And that, admittedly, might be a stretch.

Even loons, McDaniel reminded himself as Carson finally broached his real subject, could have enough money to afford his services. That was important to remember.

Problem was, Carson wanted to haggle, and this process was made more difficult for the lawyer by the fact that Carson and McDaniel had never actually met face-to-face.

"Look, Mr. Carson," McDaniel said finally, holding his cell-phone close to his mouth and keeping his voice down, "when you want three people killed, one of them without violent trace, and a building gutted, it isn't going to happen for chump change. Sorry. Either I see the full funds appearing in my Cayman Islands account not later than the end of the business day tomorrow, or the deal isn't done. Upon the completion of our contract, you'll be notified of my per diem rate for this action, and any additional charges for materials and research. Is that understood?"

Carson gabbled on for another minute or so, McDaniel listening patiently. He'd never actually whacked anyone for Carson or any of his close cronies before, but had arranged a few leg-breakers for Edmiston, all anonymously. No one saw McDaniel at his second job except the occasional subject, and no one knew his face.

When Carson finally wound down, McDaniel said, "Sure, Mr. Carson, just fax all the information on the subjects to this number." He gave the lawyer his home fax number, for one-time-only use, then said goodbye. If any of this turned to shit at Carson's end, and McDaniel could see that it might, should the cops came asking he'd just say he'd been advising Carson on some commodities purchases.

After dressing, McDaniel surveyed himself in the full-length mirror at the end of his locker row. Dove-grey Armani suit with very pale yellow pinstripes over a light blue shirt from Nordstrom, with black Armani loafers. He might be overdoing the Armani thing with the shoes, but the O.J. Simpson trial had flushed his favorite Bruno Maglis out of his wardrobe closet.

As he knotted his blue and yellow Nicole Miller tie, McDaniel considered what clothes to wear in North Cedar. Plaid shirt for certain, with worn Levi's 501s, and definitely throw his ancient Filson jacket in the cab of the old brown Chevy pickup he used for his more rural excursions. Some fishing gear would be appropriate, too, and a license. He could then be just another sportsman, a moderately-tall man in his mid-thirties, with a couple of days growth of dark beard. The only giveaway would be his fifty-dollar haircut, and he doubted anyone would notice that.

There was no good reason to take any of his professional equipment on his first reconnoiter to North Cedar, McDaniel decided. He would drive around, establish the patterns of his subjects' lives, then come back to Portland.

Good thing, he thought, as he picked up his gym bag and headed out of the locker room, that his day job gave him the flexibility to accommodate the occasional opportunity. McDaniel hoped Carson came through with the fee. He found he was looking forward to this one. It sounded interesting.

SIXTY-FOUR

Though still technically 'recuperating,' Ole Thorsen considered himself very close to complete recovery from his eventful trip down off Sharkey's Landing. Another week would find him through with blood thinners, and only a few yellow streaks and splotches here and there remained of bruises which had made the doctors at the hospital shake their heads in disbelief. His shoulders and ribs remained slightly sore, but even that was passing.

Stuck at home, no day went by without a call or two from family members, concerned friends, or acquaintances -- the latter mostly loggers. Every conversation brought the deaths of Sigge, Erika, and their children crashing back into his mind.

Now he approached the jangling phone with trepidation, dreading the pain the well-intentioned call would bring.

Instead, it was Rikka.

"Thank you," Ole said, grinning into the phone.

"For what?" Rikka asked.

"For doing what you said you would."

She laughed. "You think so? My, my. Well, there's still one left, the man behind the curtain. Virgil made some information from an electronic organizer he found at the murder scene available to me. I have a name and a Portland address. Got a pen and paper handy?"

Ole wrote carefully as Rikka gave him the information. They made small talk for another minute or two, then Rikka wished him luck and said goodbye.

His big hands shook as he looked at the piece of paper he held, and a fierce, unalloyed joy surged through him.

It *was* true what the telephone people said.

229

Happiness was just a phone call away.

SIXTY-FIVE

Fifteen miles downriver from Flint, on the edge of the flatlands, Little Norway could easily have been the archetype of any small Scandinavian-settled hamlet in the country. Between fifteen and twenty modest white-painted homes clustered around a century-old Lutheran church, with less than a block total of sidewalks. Opposite the church lay a single gas station, which fronted a small grocery store where the locals could also rent videos, buy bait, and handle their postal chores.

Hakon and Katie Thorsen had been born and raised here, and Ole possessed a lifetime of memories of Yule, Walpurgia, and Harvest festivities in the little village. At the local park, beneath enormous oak trees, he, Sigge, and their cousins would sit huddled in the shadows under the bandstand and listen to the drums and pipes playing overhead. Their small bodies would vibrate to that swirling thunder.

Never again, he thought, as he turned into the driveway of his uncle's smithy, located on the north side of town. Of those carefree, uncomplicated childhood days, only his memories remained.

Those memories are the reasons I am here, Ole realized, passing by the house and seeing the massive smithy looming ahead, surrounded by ash and oak as large as those at the park.

Eight-sided, roofed with red tile over oak beams supported by stone pillars, the smithy resembled a very large yurt, with canvas sides which could be rolled up or down. A smaller, metal roof covered the central vent opening, releasing the smoke and steam from the forge itself.

Ole parked his Ford, took the map case from where it rested on the passenger seat, and climbed out of the truck.

He could count on the fingers of both hands the number of times he had seen his Uncle Ragnar not covered in sweat. Ragnar seemed happiest at his forge, and laughingly called himself "an old salamander," referring to those fire elementals who dwelt in the molten bowels of the earth. Today, naked from the waist up above the glowing coke, Ragnar's grey-flecked golden hair was plastered to his skull, and runnels of sweat made furrows though the dark-blond thicket covering his heavy chest and forearms. Ole nearly winced at the sight of the bare spots on his uncle's pale flat belly, each centered with a fresh, pink, healing scar.

"Olaf," the smith boomed in greeting, his voice even deeper than his large nephew's. He set a pair of heavy steel tongs on the edge of the forge, examined the coals briefly, then embraced Ole. "You seem almost mended," Ragnar said, looking Ole up and down.

Ole nodded, and stood up straighter. At just over six-and-a-half feet tall, Ragnar was several inches shorter than his nephew, but the force of the smith's personality and presence made him seem much larger than he really was. Ole always made every effort to tower over his impressive uncle, though he never felt he truly succeeded.

"Ah, you have brought your plans," Ragnar said, taking Ole's map case and spinning its cap off. "Let's have a look, then." He led the way to a long bench formed from the trunk of a giant oak milled flat on its sides. Slipping the rolled paper from the case, Ragnar spread the plans on the bench surface, securing the edges with small chunks of pig iron.

"I have a name and address in Portland," Ole said. "Virgil found an organizer at the cabins at the Hot Springs."

"Ah," Ragnar said, his teeth flashing white. "Virgil is a good man."

"I got the information from Rikka -- the tall, dark girl you met at the funeral. She was with Virgil."

"I remember her," his uncle said, nodding. His eyes blazed. "I also remember that she is a killer. The stink of death wrapped around her like a shroud. She might as well have had the Wolf's Hook Death-rune burned on her forehead."

"No longer, Uncle. The killers are dead. Sigge and Erika and their children are nearly avenged."

"Have you been to Portland?"

Ole nodded. "Everything checks out."

"Good." Ragnar bent down and studied the plans, occasionally smoothing out some particularly-complicated portion and looking at it more closely. "Only a few changes, I think, and I believe you will need some sort of release mechanism inside the cab. No need to bring it back here with you when the task is accomplished."

"How soon will it be ready?" Ole asked.

His uncle gestured at the lathes and drill presses sitting to one side of the forge, steel-topped tables between them covered with work. "I'm killing busy, more jobs than usual, but some of it's not so pressing. Today is Thursday. I can have your device done and in place by Tuesday, I think, at the latest. Bring the Kenworth over Sunday night." He cocked an eyebrow at Ole. "When will you go back up to Sharkey's Landing for the cut?"

"The week after next," Ole replied.

"Then the timing is perfect." Reaching up, Ragnar slipped a huge metal-handled steel hammer off its peg on the nearest roof pillar. He held it out in front of him at a forty-five degree angle. Ole clasped his hands around the hammer-handle. Both men inclined their heads, closed their eyes, and prayed:

"Odin, far-wanderer, grant me wisdom,
Courage, and victory.
Friend Thor, grant me your strength.
And both be with me."

SIXTY-SIX

A nine-hour day and then being on call should be enough law enforcement for anyone, the sheriff mused, as he jogged along the hillside streets of North Cedar. Still, here he was, prowling around town keeping an eye on things in the guise of a workout. Or vice versa.

The amount of energy he'd had since the start of the summer season kept him moving well above his usual levels of activity, and his workouts tended to be longer and more rigorous.

'Trying to keep up with Rikka,' he called it, though he'd never tell her that.

Feeling good ordinarily wouldn't have nagged at his mind.

even a little bit, but this did. He'd gotten less sleep and more duty than any time in recent years. He and Marv Bullock spoke daily. Only the involvement of the State Police in the 'Lautenbach River Massacre,' as the newspapers referred to it, had prevented things from being even more time-consuming.

But instead of being constantly exhausted and mentally fatigued, he remained surprisingly alert and fresh. The entire month of June had been like that. In fact, if he had to put his finger on it, he'd say it began about the time he and Rikka first slept together.

Which made even less sense.

Merrill glanced at his watch as he started up the long hill on Ridgepole Street. Three blocks uphill, and he'd be at Mendenhall Middle School, named for Augustus Mendenhall, the first mayor of North Cedar, back when the town was mostly bars and mercantiles built beside a couple of sawmills.

Old Augustus would not recognize the town today, that was for damn sure, businesses and homes laying mid-week drowsy in the early summer evening sun. Stretching his legs, getting as much extension as he could, the sheriff accelerated up the sidewalk. He knew on the last block or so his long strides would be shortened to choppy steps as he struggled just to get to the top.

It didn't happen. At the end, Merrill flew over the crest of the hill, still at a full gallop.

He stopped and looked around warily to make certain no one had seen a fifty-nine-year-old codger sprinting as hard and strong as a teenager. Then, hands on hips, he turned and surveyed the hill. No, it wasn't any less steep than before. But his thighs didn't burn, particularly right above the knees, and he wasn't even slightly winded. His breathing had picked up some, and sweat ran into his eyes pretty good, but nothing like usual.

Walking across the grass toward the outdoor basketball courts, Merrill felt the cool evening breeze brush over his exposed skin, felt the light drifting of pollen into his nostrils, separated the smell of freshly-mown lawns from the paler scent of dandelions and clover. What in the ever-lovin' hell was happening here?

Reaching the concrete expanse of the B-ball courts, the sheriff picked up one of the old school balls that the school district always left around the courts. He flipped the ball from hand to hand a few times, dribbled twice, then put up a set shot from twenty feet out.

It dropped cleanly through, nothing but net.

Nice start, he thought, smiling to himself. The shooting eye was the last skill to go, supposedly.

Merrill collected all the balls lying around the courts, placed them in a crescent around the top of the key, then walked the curve, shooting each ball in turn.

Six for six. Not bad. He began shooting jump shots from fifteen feet, then moved out farther, to twenty, then twenty-five.

Everything dropped.

Unusual, for sure, but not unheard of. He hadn't had forty-plus scoring nights in high school without good eye-hand coordination.

When the number of shots without a miss approached fifty, however, the sheriff began to realize that whatever had allowed him to blast untiringly up a three-block hill just might be causing his incredible accuracy.

He stood at the top of the key, eying the basket, holding a ball against his right hip, trying to get a mental handle on just what was going on here. There was a way to prove -- at least to himself -- that something physically odd had happened to him.

Though he'd had good court sense, handled the ball well enough, and possessed an exceptional shooting eye, Merrill's rebounding skills had mostly involved being in the right place at the right time, not in being a great leaper. He'd been able to dunk the ball even in high school, but had worked long and hard to be able to do it. It hadn't been easy. Much of that success had to do with his large hands.

When his daughter Maryanne was taking sports medicine at OSU, she'd talked her father into having punch biopsies of his leg muscles. The results confirmed what the sheriff had long suspected: the Merrill jumping apparatus was powered by a high percentage of slow-twitch muscle fiber, not the more vertically-oriented fast-twitch. He had terrific endurance, a decent first step, and that was the whole story.

Well, the sheriff thought, taking a deep breath, let's just see what the old bod can do this evening.

Three strides, two dribbles, one leap with the ball extended.

His right forearm brushed the rim, an inch or two above his elbow. He flung the ball down through the net.

He landed. Watched the ball bounce away. Stood dumbfounded as the ball rolled to a stop in the grass.

Easy. It had been *easy*.

Merrill looked down at his hands, familiar hands attached to equally-familiar arms. He rotated them, studying his palms. Nothing *looked* unusual or different.

Something surely was.

He put all the balls back in the big steel-and-wire barrel they were kept in, and walked slowly back to his home. The sun had nearly set, partially-obscured by fleecy clouds outlined in gold. A light haze floated along the river, just above the tops of the trees. The sound of the peeler blades came faintly from Schirmer's mill, out of sight beyond the highway.

Everything seemed perfectly normal.

He wasn't.

Showered, dressed in clean sweatclothes, the sheriff sat on the deck off the master bedroom, nursing a tall glass of water. Rikka would be here in a few minutes, right after the library closed. Should he say anything to her? Probably not. This might be some kind of weird-ass tumor or maybe a hormonal disease.

He picked up his cell-phone from beside his chair, dialed Fred Cameron's number.

"Rikka still at the library?" the coroner said, chuckling, when he found out who was calling.

"Very funny," Merrill replied. "As a matter of fact, I'm calling my personal physician for an appointment. How long would it take me to get a full blood work-up done?"

"On you? Come in tomorrow morning -- in a fasting state -- and I'll do a draw. Should have the results by the first of the week." Cameron's voice went from curious to serious. "You got a problem, Virgil?"

"I dunno. Let's just say I'm feeling way too good for the amounts of work and sleep I've been getting lately."

"Any pain, shortness of breath, that sort of thing?"

"Oh, no, nothing like that. I should feel like I've been dragged through a knothole, and I don't."

Cameron chuckled again, sounding relieved. "It's the company you've been keeping, Virgil. You've been rejuvenated. Sort of like guilt by association."

"Whatever you say, Doctor," Merrill answered, grinning into the telephone. "I'll see you at oh-eight-hundred tomorrow."

When he'd hung up, he sat in the gathering dusk until he heard Rikka come in the front door, then called for her to join him.

Cameron's last words kept running through his head.

Rejuvenation by association.

If it were only that simple.

239

SIXTY-SEVEN

For the life of him, Robert McDaniel couldn't understand why Alexander Carson urged him to use caution when he took down Rikka Thorsen. Tall, muscular, and moved like no woman he'd seen recently, she was still just a kid. Kids died easy. They had too much certainty of immortality to be careful of themselves. Thorsen would be no problem.

McDaniel was far more concerned about the sheriff, who looked canny and competent, and always had an extra Glock magazine clipped to his belt. A Vietnam vet, too, and those people frequently tended to be wary about twenty-four-and-a-half hours a day.

His initial impression that this little job would be interesting had been borne out so far. He'd driven into town on Thursday afternoon, after making sure his fee had been wired to his off-shore account, dropped his stuff at the motel, and then just driven around. His brown '75 Chevy pickup fit into the area perfectly. He'd already seen two others just like it.

The odd thing was that Thorsen and the sheriff were together. Carson apparently hadn't known that, and McDaniel wondered *why* he hadn't. He'd also gotten the feeling that Carson wasn't telling everything he *did* know, but that didn't bother McDaniel much. He preferred to scout on his own. A little background info, some on-the-ground study, and he was quite happy. It seemed odd, though, that the sheriff -- pushing sixty -- would appeal to a jockette in her early twenties.

McDaniel had jogged through the little community on Thursday and Friday evenings, had seen Thorsen on her way home from the little mom-

and-pop grocery half-way up through town from the highway. He'd been surprised to see her walk right past her own front gate, go straight to the sheriff's, and let herself in.

He'd even felt a pang of jealousy. Thorsen looked like she had the endurance of an Olympian, and if McDaniel liked one thing in a woman, it was endurance. With that base, and a few training sessions to establish behavioral parameters, a woman could become a good and willing partner. Until McDaniel got bored, leaving only the inevitable begging and pleading at the end.

But that was good, too, the final closure.

Maybe he could work out something like that with Thorsen while he finished her.

A little extra kick.

SIXTY-EIGHT

"Yes, Fred, I know what DHEA and melatonin are," Merrill said, glaring at the coroner in irritation. He'd spent most of the weekend and Monday dealing with the few media people who weren't hounding either the State Police or Marvin Bullock, and, seated in his friend's comfortable office, his mood was not patient. "I'd have to be deaf and blind not to. I also know just how little of those two compounds you and I have in our bodies at our age."

Cameron flashed the sheriff a shit-eating grin. "Not so fast, Virgil. Most people our age -- probably. Me -- certainly. *You*, however, are another kettle of fish, my friend. Every cell in your body is as awash in those chemicals as any teenager."

"What!"

"Yes."

"Don't people vary quite a bit?" Merrill asked. He tried to concentrate on the doctor's face. Fred wore a particularly gaudy and distracting Aloha shirt today.

"Of course, but the trend, when it starts, is always down. It's true we don't have a baseline for you for these compounds -- as we have with your PSA prostate test -- and I doubt *anyone* routinely tests for them. There simply isn't any need. I can tell you, without fear of contradiction, that you are unique in the annals of medicine as I have practiced it. And, while I might be willing to speculate on the cause, it would be only conjecture."

"How's my prostate?" Nearing senior citizen status, and having lost friends to prostate cancer, the sheriff had a more than healthy interest in his prostate.

Cameron leafed through Merrill's chart, peering through his bifocals. "Lower than last time we tested. Your first test, at age fifty, was low. At fifty-five, the same. Now it's even lower."

"Some other kind of tumor?"

"Probably not." The coroner's smile bordered on condescending. "I rattled through the physicians' Internet sites, and nothing produces the kind of overall blood picture you present *except* being extremely fit. And young."

"You're kidding." Relief flooded through Merrill's body.

Cameron shook his head, leaned back in his chair, and clasped his hands behind his head. "It gets better, Virgil. I ran your blood picture off against some results for the Oregon State mens' track team that got posted on the PE school's website. On the basis of oxygen transfer mechanisms, various circulating cellular levels, hormones, and repair debris, you arc in better shape than any of those kids."

He took off his glasses, rubbed them on his hideous shirt, and settled them back on the bridge of his nose. The sheriff couldn't see that they were any cleaner. "So you think this started around the first of June?" Cameron asked.

"Yeah, roughly. Feelin' good doesn't exactly catch your attention, if you get my meaning, and we've been more than busy. The last time I remember being really exhausted was the evening after the Thorsens were killed. 'Course, I'd been up for over thirty hours."

"By my memory -- and local gossip -- that night would be the beginning of your relationship with Ms. Thorsen?"

"Yeah." The sheriff eyed his friend narrowly. "What's she got to do with this?"

"I'm not razzing you, Virgil. A sudden lifestyle change such as that can trigger some body-wide metabolic alterations. Far-fetched, I'll admit, for changes of this magnitude, but I'm grasping at straws here. You'd been uninvolved with anyone since Deb passed away, this young woman comes into your life. You seem uncommonly suited to one another. She is, to my thinking, very devoted to you in a way similar to Deb's, and she is physically quite unusual."

"I can't see your reasoning, Fred."

"I'm not reasoning, exactly. Only speculating. Did something happen the other night to precipitate your phone call?"

Merrill described his workout experience. "Since I hadn't really pushed myself for close to three weeks, I've got no idea if this had been building for a while, or not.
The run up the hill might have just been a good night. And I've always been able to shoot the eyes out of a basket. It was the leaping. I've never been much of a jumper, and all of a sudden, I was." He grimaced. "I don't mind telling you, I got scared."

Cameron nodded. "Well, when all the current excitement dies down, I'd like to do another blood draw. There are a few other fitness indicators we can check."

"Fair enough. But if that doesn't give you any answers, Fred, it stops here. We never know. Nobody else gets told about it. You agree?"

"Sure," the coroner replied, and Merrill could see a certain level of professional frustration in his gaze.

"Now, would you happen to still have that bottle of decent booze in your desk?" the sheriff asked.

"Why, certainly," Cameron laughed. He reached into a drawer and brought out the Black Jack.

"This works," he said.

244

A very nice Mulingar bronze sat on the marble entryway of Maureen Sims' condominium apartment, a horse with its spear-carrying rider standing beside it. Robert McDaniel whistled softly in appreciation, the sound quickly lost in the thick cream-colored carpet and silk wall-hangings.

Though he knew what she looked like, McDaniel hadn't actually seen Sims up close, and she was apparently out for the evening. Her Lexus had been gone from its spot in the basement parking, the first place he'd checked to determine if she was home. In the car's absence, McDaniel had foxed the elevator and gone up to Sims' eighth floor apartment. His assortment of magnetic keys had let him in.

For a scientist, Sims seemed to be mistrusting of electronic scheduling. An Audubon Society nature calendar on her kitchen wall contained numerous penciled-in entries. Tonight's was 'dinner and movie with Ceil.' He glanced at his watch. Nine o'clock. She might not be home for hours.

No matter. He'd settle in and wait, after checking out the rest of the place. He slipped on a pair of latex surgery gloves.

Sims' wardrobe closet blended casual chic -- mostly Ellen Tracy and Donna Karan -- with workout clothes and running gear. Her shoes tended toward Ferragamo and Bally, and she even had the woman's version of his own Armanis.

A class act, McDaniel thought, as he opened and checked the drawers of her built-in dresser. He was not surprised to find a carefully-oiled and bagged Beretta .25 automatic under a stack of T-shirts, and a Gerber clip-knife had been velcroed to the back side of one of her nightstands. Interesting, and he'd bet that there'd be something nasty somewhere in the kitchen, too.

The lady didn't take chances. He approved of that. Whatever. He would see that she ran out of options tonight.

The workstation in her home office sported one hell of an upgraded computer system, currently on, with considerable auxiliary storage and one of the newest DVD drives. Her library matched that info-density, heavy on biology and related biochemistry texts. McDaniel found another Beretta, this one a military ten-millimeter, inside her desk.

When he finished going through the place, McDaniel stood in the kitchen, opened his briefcase, and brought out his SIG-Sauer P225 nine-millimeter and screwed an LEI suppressor into the barrel.

He gave the weapon a final checkover, put his leather briefcase behind the washer in the laundry room, then settled in to wait.

Sims arrived home shortly after midnight, hung a garment in the entryway closet, then poured herself something to drink and walked into the living room. Waiting in the darkness of the bedroom hallway, McDaniel heard no ice cubes, so he guessed she was having a glass of wine before bed. He carefully stuck his head around the corner and saw that she'd gone onto the south-facing balcony, bare-footed, leaning a hip against the railing and looking into the night. Fairly tall, he saw, with short brown hair.

He went into the living room from the kitchen, moving swiftly but silently.

His first shot caught Sims in the right shoulder, and spun her around. The wine glass dropped out of her hand and into the darkness below.

The second and third shots took her in the chest. She flipped backward over the railing. McDaniel had a brief vision of a round face, wide-eyed surprise, and she was gone.

She didn't even cry out.

He walked to the railing, looked down. Eight stories below, he thought he could see one bare foot sticking out from under a Mugho pine, but he wasn't sure.

A party of some sort had been scheduled in the common room, so he couldn't check on the body, no more than twenty feet from the common room windows. McDaniel didn't like that, but figured that nobody could take three good hits from a nine-millimeter, fall nearly eighty feet, and survive.

He'd chance not checking. He went back inside, shutting and locking the door behind him.

Removing the suppressor from the SIG, McDaniel replaced it and the weapon in the briefcase, adding the rubber gloves before closing it. He washed the powder off his hands in the sink, wiping everything dry with a small towel hanging on the stove front.

After a short examination of the living room carpet for footprints, he left the apartment, cleaning the door handle with his suit jacket.

Five minutes later, he was in his BMW and out on the street. He'd met only an older couple, on the elevator, and they had smiled and nodded at the well-dressed young man, who smiled back.

A short visit to Sims' lab, followed by six hours sleep, and McDaniel would be ready to go south to North Cedar.

A good job so far.

SEVENTY

Someone had been in the house. Rikka knew the instant she walked in, late Tuesday afternoon. A man, an aftershave she didn't recognize. Which meant she hadn't smelled it in North Cedar, which meant maybe expensive and maybe out-of-town.

Her mind rapidly running through possibilities, Rikka stood silently just inside her front door, listening.

Nothing.

She made a quick circuit of the house, examining everything. Nothing seemed out-of-place. She went back through, from the opposite direction.

Still nothing.

She checked her computer. She had mail. Her eyes widened when she saw who'd sent it.

Doctor Sims.

'Rikka,' it read. 'If you receive this, something has gone wrong at my end within the past twenty-four hours, and I haven't blocked this message. It may be nothing, may even be that I've forgotten to renew the block, but probably not. I may be dead. You may be in danger. Our mutual benefactor is Alexander Carson, an environmental lawyer. Though I think you or your creation cannot be traced to him or the funds he controls, he may have gotten nervous after the deaths at the Hot Springs, and be seeking to cover his paper trail. Be very careful. I know you have found your own life in North Cedar, as I hoped you would, and I am happy for you. You are probably the closest I will ever get to having a child of my own, Rikka, so take no chances. I would hate to lose you. And remember, even you can be killed. Good luck. Maureen.'

248

Rikka read the message through again, her eyes misting. She *was* something like Sims' child, and Sims truly was like a mother to her.

Alexander Carson. She had seen his picture in the paper, read his words as he expressed his horror over the deaths of 'the young idealistic environmental activists,' and 'the senseless tragedy.' No mention of the Thorsens' pain, or the slow recuperation of Walt Whitaker, but she expected that. For people like Carson, the tide of environmental concern only flowed one direction.

If Sims was dead, and Carson knew exactly where to find Rikka, then her trespasser might have been sent. This might have been a scouting foray. He might be watching the house at this moment. Rikka's scalp crawled. Sims was right, she must be very careful.

Should she tell Virgil? An easy answer. No. She couldn't say, "I'm a created thing, lover, and a stone killer. You've seen my work. My creator may be dead, and someone may be after me. Even though I've killed over twenty people in the past month, I really need your help."

Put that way, her plight sounded even more unappealing. She had to think, and think clearly. No stupid panicking. Carson must know something of Rikka's physical abilities, but he couldn't have known everything, or the person who entered her home would have realized his presence would be discovered. That was a plus, an edge.

Morberg, however, had been a demolitionist for hire, and had come all too close to killing Rikka. Morberg had been a real pro at what he did, according to Virgil, but he wasn't a hit man.

There were other sorts of real pros, though, and they *could* be hired killers.

A sniper, firing from outside the limits of her perceptions, could kill her easily, unless she saw the muzzle flash in the distance. Then she could merely drop to the ground, and the bullet would miss.

Fat frigging chance.

Rikka knew she couldn't count on that, and she couldn't afford to get careless, as she had with Morberg. If he'd been smart enough to come after her, instead of fleeing, she might be dead now.

She had learned from Morberg. Out in her Cherokee, under the driver's seat, lay a Glock 21 like Virgil's, in a holster that hung between her shoulder blades, so it wouldn't interfere with her knives. She'd signed up for a concealed weapons class this coming Saturday, and had already filled out the permit application.

As she considered her situation, Rikka's gaze strayed to the map hanging over her computer, showing the areas she patrolled each night. Even though the Thorsens' murderers had been eliminated, she still ran her patrols, now more for fitness than any other reason. Tonight -- Tuesday on the map -- she'd be up off Bear Ridge, at the western limits of Boundry Road.

Sure, she thought, why not? She'd be safer up there than sitting here at home, waiting for someone to kick the door in. Or up at Virgil's, putting him at risk.

Virgil at risk. That was a hoot. Virgil was the most prepared person she knew.

She'd run from ten until midnight, then walk over to Virgil's. They would make the world go away.

In the meantime, however, just to be on the safe side, Rikka went out to her rig and brought in the Glock.

She forced herself not to look up and down the street on her trip to and from the Jeep.

She still felt exposed.

SEVENTY-ONE

Five seconds after his front door closed behind him, Virgil Merrill heard a hissing pop. Something stung the right side of his neck, and a fist closed around his heart.

He tried to scream and couldn't. In agony, he folded down to the cool surface of the entryway, hands clutching his chest.

"That was beautiful," a young male voice chuckled from somewhere beyond the limits of his pain. "Too bad I didn't bring a video camera, Sheriff, to record your final moments."

Steps sounded dully on the carpet. Curled on his side, Merrill tried to turn his head to see the man, but the red flashes in his vision prevented it. He could only see a few inches. His heart felt like it was going to burst.

Worn and scuffed field boots appeared by his face. He tried to speak, but could only produce a grunting wheeze. "Don't try to talk, Sheriff," the voice said. "Your lungs aren't working very well just now. Coronaries are that way. Breathing becomes less important." He prodded Merrill's ribs with one boot, still chuckling, then hunkered down closer.

A young guy, mid-thirties, expensive haircut, plaid shirt. The sheriff couldn't believe those things still registered. The grip on his heart tightened, his chest contracted, and expelled air blew past his clenched lips.

"It'll only last another five minutes or so, Sheriff, then your ordeal will be ended," he said, pulling the dart out of the sheriff's neck. He laid the barrel of an automatic against Merrill's left cheek, pushing the tissue against his teeth painfully. "A ventricle will rupture, or a valve will let loose, or maybe the

251

pressure will dissect out through the wall of your aorta. An old guy like you, it could be just about anything. I imagine someone'll find you in the morning."

Brown eyes gazed clinically into his blue. "I would have preferred to just blow your ass away, but this has to look natural. Besides, you seem pretty capable, and I couldn't take the chance that you might be able to shoot back once or twice. Sorry about that." He grinned.

The pressure on Merrill's chest had eased a bit. "Why?" he managed to get out, before another wave of pain hit.

"Why did Alexander Carson want you killed? Beats the shit out of me. But I think you were an afterthought. Your girlfriend is the main target. She'll be up on Bear Ridge tonight, and when she gets back to her Cherokee, I'll shoot those nice long legs right out from under her. Then we'll see how much fun I can have before I let her suck on the barrel of my SIG. Up there, it won't matter how noisy and messy things get."

The man stood up, and laughed louder. "You can think about that for the few minutes you've got left. You won't be sticking your dick in that nice, tight, young snatch ever again, Sheriff. Ain't that a frigging shame? But *I* might be. There's a thought, huh? Too fucking bad."

The feet disappeared from Merrill's field of vision. Still chuckling, the man opened the front door and let himself out.

Slowly, painfully, his chest on fire, the sheriff began to inch his way across the floor. Every few feet, he had to stop to rest.

Rikka.

SEVENTY-TWO

After ten-thirty, going on eleven. The old man must be gone by now, McDaniel thought, smiling as he drove his Chevy up the connector road leading to Boundry. Sims dead, her lab torched, the sheriff coronaried. Only the Thorsen kid left.

A very slick op, so far, and Thorsen would be the easiest part. He wondered idly what in hell she did out there in the dark, not that it mattered. And it wasn't all that dark, up here in the middle of nowhere, the mountain skies awash in stars.

He'd be back in the office Thursday at the latest, servicing accounts.

Tonight, maybe he'd get to service Thorsen.

He grinned to himself.

A nice kick.

SEVENTY-THREE

Ten strides ordinarily got Merrill into his kitchen. Digging his fingers clawlike into the carpet, and pushing weakly with his right leg, in between spasms, he managed the distance in forty minutes.

At some point, the pressure in his chest began to ease, and the waves of pain and nausea became less severe and less frequent. Gripping the door jamb, he slowly got to his knees, then paused, panting and sweat-soaked, barely able to lift his head.

His vision had cleared to the point where he could see the kitchen clock. Close to an hour since he'd walked in the door, forty-five at least since the killer had left.

Christ. *Rikka.*

Had she taken her new Glock, he wondered? The killer had some sort of compressed air dart pistol and the SIG. Probably had a night-scoped rifle, too. And he knew somehow where Rikka was, only had to find the Cherokee and settle in to wait. Easy to pick her off, when she came back.

Merrill rested his elbow on the counter, used it as a fulcrum to lever to his feet. He moved sideways to the sink, stuck a glass under the tap, and filled it. Raised it to his lips and drank. Cool and smooth and sweet, it seemed to wash away the remaining pain.

Four glasses later, he felt almost normal. His clothes stuck to him, cold and clammy, and he was still a little light-headed, but he could function.

Whatever the drug had been, it hadn't killed him.

Like Fred said, Merrill was a kid inside. That had to be it, why he wasn't dead. He walked rapidly from the kitchen.

Grabbing an extra box of shells for his Glock, he headed out the door at a dead run.

Or, he reminded himself wryly as he sprang into the Caprice, an *almost* dead run.

To Rikka.

SEVENTY-FOUR

To McDaniel's amazement, there were other people up in the woods at night. All going back into town, though, including a tall guy in a game warden's Blazer.

In his Abu Garcia Reels cap, with a new fishing license in his shirt pocket, McDaniel knew he was safe. As long as no one checked behind his seat, that is, and saw the rifle case, night-vision binoculars, and ordnance bag. Still, even those shouldn't excite anybody in this particular version of the Great Outdoors. It would just mean McDaniel was a real guy.

He passed a group of kids around a fire in a small cul-de-sac. Beer and bullshit, McDaniel thought, recalling his own high school days. Then, a few miles later, at about the point where he thought he might see Thorsen's Cherokee, he caught a glimpse of a shiny black CJ-5 tucked unobtrusively back into the trees. Somebody getting it on, he figured. Close enough to hear his sniper rifle, though, so he'd have to bring Thorsen down with one shot.

Shortly after that, the road angled diagonally up the side of a ridge. At the top, two hundred yards to the west, down a two-track dirt road flanked by thirty-year-old fir, sat Thorsen's white rig, gleaming in the moonlight.

McDaniel pulled onto the two-track, put his old truck in reverse, and backed into the salal until the rear wheels began slipping. He climbed out of the cab, examined the truck's position, then walked backward toward the main road. The Chevy was unnoticeable, a tribute to dingy.

Back at the truck, McDaniel flipped the seat forward, and lifted out the rifle case and his ordnance bag. Ten minutes later he sat with his back against a large old-growth stump, hidden by overhanging branches. His assembled SIG SSG 550 sniping rifle lay across his lap, its EUROVIS-4 night sight in place, and the SIG 225 hung under his left armpit. Litton night-vision binoculars up to his eyes, he scanned the approaches to the Cherokee, all the visible routes up through young trees no taller than shoulder height. Good clear line-of-sight fields of fire.

He adjusted his pants to give his knees free movement, just in case he had to go for a quick second shot, one of the better operating features of this particular rifle.

Ready or not, babe, here I am.

Come to Poppa.

SEVENTY-FIVE

Three miles out of town, the Caprice pushed to its mechanical limits and back-up called in to Bear Ridge, the sheriff realized that he hadn't turned on his headlights.

He thought about that while he tapped the brakes, bringing the patrol car's rear end around to set up for a sharp right-hander.

Some after-effect of his heart attack, he guessed. People coming back from near-death experiences always made reference to lights and tunnels. Maybe it was some sort of lingering visual thing.

No, he thought, his vision wouldn't get *better*. That didn't make sense. This had something to do with whatever had been going on during his workout the other night.

Pushing it to the back of his mind, Merrill gunned the Caprice down a long straight stretch. He had bigger fish to fry. It was well after eleven. Rikka would be back at her rig soon, and, even though the killer didn't know the roads the way the sheriff did, he'd had time enough to be there and waiting.

The patrol car's rear end began to fish-tail some when Merrill slowed for the next corner. He tucked the front end to the left and gradually stepped on the gas, bringing the big Chevy drifting sideways around a left turn.

The steering wheel began to bend in his hands.

He didn't remember that happening before.

Hell with it, and if he didn't need lights, he wasn't going to worry about this, either.

SEVENTY-SIX

When she finally appeared, a few minutes before midnight, Thorsen's speed almost caught McDaniel by surprise. She came out of the bigger timber to the west, over a half-mile away, moving perpendicular to his position in a fast ground-devouring lope.

He picked up the rifle, fitted the sight over his right eye, and watched her.

Thorsen ran along a fifty-foot fallen snag, dancing rapidly between broken-off branches.

Playing, McDaniel guessed. Jesus, she was smooth!

When she leapt from a big stump onto the two-track, and swung around to run directly at him, he curled his right index finger around the trigger.

A hundred-fifty yards.

One-twenty-five.

Perfect.

He began to squeeze.

SEVENTY-SEVEN

Rikka felt a light breeze from the east on her face as she hit the surface of the two-track. Pine and fir resins floated on the gentle wind. She picked up her pace, running easily, drinking in the fresh, clean odors.

The Cherokee sat in the moonlight, just over a hundred yards away.

Home and Virgil in an hour.

Suddenly, Rikka's nose caught another scent.

The *aftershave*!

She threw herself to the right, off the trail.

A muzzle-flash flared a split-second later, in the trees ahead.

Then the sound of the shot, reverberating over the hillsides.

Rikka alternately crawled and tumbled downslope, low to the ground, cursing herself.

He'd seen her map.

He'd been waiting.

She grinned as she dove behind a log.

He'd *missed*.

SEVENTY-EIGHT

Gone!

Dammit!

McDaniel swung the SIG's muzzle over the ridgetop, searching for Thorsen. Nothing moved.

Christ! She'd just *disappeared*.

A motion to the left, out a hundred yards! Something streaked across the road in maybe two jumps, vanished into the young trees. He managed one shot, too late. The scope's field simply wasn't wide enough. He could hear rapid movement on the right slope, still in the distance, but nearer.

Now McDaniel kept the rifle centered on the road. The moment he saw anything move out there, he'd fire right down the middle of the two-track.

She erupted out of the trees on the right, fifty yards away. He fired. Still too late. She was gone again.

This was getting him nowhere. McDaniel stood up, the pistol in his left hand, and the rifle against his right side, snugged in place by his elbow.

Taking a deep breath, he walked down into the road. If he could get her to stand still, even for just a moment, there was enough light to fire accurately.

"Your boyfriend's dead!" he shouted. "I killed him!"

His words echoed away into the darkness. Then silence. He couldn't hear anything except a car or truck engine in the distance, off to the southeast.

'C'mon, c'mon,' McDaniel thought, wanting to finish this. She had to have heard him.

Just when he was about ready to yell again, she walked out of the trees and stood quietly in the two-track. A hundred feet from him. A heavy automatic of some kind hung from her right hand.

"He's *dead*?" she asked, taking a slow step toward him. Then another. Dust rose from each footfall.

"Yeah," McDaniel said, keeping his eyes on her as he set the rifle down at his feet and shifted the pistol to his right hand. "I did him before I came up here."

She took two more steps. "You're certain?"

McDaniel smiled at her. He'd found her button. He was back in control. "Of course." He'd fire when she reached fifty feet away, or if she raised her pistol.

"Then you're dead," she said, her voice flat and emotionless. Despite his own certainty that things had moved his way, McDaniel felt a chill run through his body.

No matter. She was almost close enough. He could see the tears on her face, glistening in the moonlight.

Stupid kid.

Now.

He fired.

SEVENTY-NINE

Three miles from where he thought Rikka'd be parked, Merrill heard the first rifle shot.

He damn near drove off the road, barely saved it five feet from the edge, and threw probably fifty pounds of gravel into the canyon.

Taking a firmer grip on the wheel, he headed more cautiously into the next curve. Putting the patrol car over the side sure wouldn't do Rikka any good.

If anything would, now.

EIGHTY

Thorsen *moved*, flickering to one side, the shot missing her by inches. She kept coming.

Cursing, McDaniel fired again.

He missed again. She snapped in the opposite direction, and never faltered.

Thirty feet away now. Jesus, what the *fuck* was she?

Desperate, McDaniel yelled, "*Sims* is dead, too!" hoping there was some connection between the kid and Sims.

Thorsen paused in mid-step for a moment, her head coming up. He pulled the trigger as fast as he could, three times. She staggered back a step, and relief washed through him.

She *could* be hit!

EIGHTY-ONE

Somewhere between the second and third rifle shots, Merrill could see the ridge he expected Rikka to be parked on. The third shot sounded as he hit the brakes, the patrol car blasting down into a saddle and up the other side.

The sheriff smiled grimly. Whoever this yahoo was, Rikka wasn't making it easy for him. He wouldn't still be using a rifle if he'd nailed her with the first shot.

The Caprice bucked around the last left-hander before the straight run up to the ridgecrest, nearly bottoming in a pair of deep potholes. As soon as he could see to the next corner, three hundred yards in the distance, Merrill floored the heavy car.

In a cloud of dust, gravel schrapnelling out from under its rear wheels, the Caprice rocketed upslope. At the top of the hill, nearly sideways, the sheriff eased off the throttle and let the car's momentum carry it into the entrance of the side road where Rikka should be parked.

He heard three pistol shots as the Caprice's front end came to rest about ten feet from a mid-seventies Chevy pickup parked up the bank. Dust billowed over both vehicles.

The killer's truck, Merrill figured, as he leapt out of his rig, Glock in hand. Through the dust, at the end of the tree-lined corridor, he could see Rikka's Cherokee.

And just past its rear end, he saw the killer, standing in the moonlight, pistol in hand.

The man was looking down, as if watching someone on the ground.

Rikka.

EIGHTY-TWO

One shot was a lunger, right side. A thin trickle of blood, black in the moonlight, ran from Thorsen's mouth as she continued toward McDaniel. A second dark blotch blossomed over her abdomen. And she was still coming, her eyes locked on his, her face still wet with tears, her pistol dangling forgotten from her right hand.

McDaniel considered running. She *had* to go down in a second or two. He didn't want to fire again, unless he had to. He'd made enough noise already.

Just as Thorsen went to her knees, ten feet in front of him, McDaniel heard heavy skidding in the gravel back by the main road. He took the chance of looking away from the wounded girl, and glanced behind him. Dust filled the entrance to the two-track, blowing toward him from the east.

The engine he'd heard in the distance.

They were *here*.

Shit.

EIGHTY-THREE

The killer had turned in his direction by the time the sheriff completely cleared the dust.

"Drop it!" Merrill yelled, sprinting toward the man. He was too far away to fire accurately, and he couldn't see Rikka.

In almost slow-motion, in near-absolute silence, the killer brought his pistol up, training it on the sheriff as he swung around into a straight-up firing stance.

Merrill heard Rikka's voice from behind the man.

"*Liar*." Three shots cracked, nearly lifting the killer off the ground. He tottered on his feet for a few seconds, then slowly collapsed, a puzzled expression on his slackening features.

Dead before he hit the ground, the sheriff figured, but that didn't prevent him from keeping his own Glock pointed at the prone man as he stepped sideways to Rikka.

She lay on her right side in the dust, legs bent under her, her pistol still part-way up. She smiled at him, a smear of blood on her face, more on the front of her shirt. "He said you were dead, Virgil." She let the Glock drop.

He bent down to her, afraid to touch her because of her wounds, but unable not to. "He was almost right. I'm sure he thought I was. Hell, *I* thought I was." He stroked her hair. "I'll get a blanket from the car. How much pain is there?"

She shook her head, still smiling. "I don't feel anything."

Merrill's heart sank. He remembered those words from Viet Nam, all too common from the mortally-wounded. "Oh, Christ," he said, his voice breaking, and felt tears well up in his eyes.

"What's *your* problem?" Rikka asked, raising up on her right elbow, reaching out with her left hand and touching his face. When he hesitated, she said, "Virgil, can you give me a hand up?" waving her left arm at him.

Merrill recalled the first time she'd done this, on his porch. Looking into her brown eyes, he saw she remembered it, too. Then he remembered her wounds. "Just a minute. You need to keep down until we get an EMT rig to take you to a hospital."

"For God's sake!" Rikka said. "Right now, I need fluids." She uncoiled to her feet in one smooth motion.

"Will you please tell me what in hell is going on here?" Merrill asked. "You've been shot!"

Rikka drank thirstily from one of her hip bottles, smiling at him. He realized that her T-shirt was a mess, but not the mess of the truly gut-shot.

"Look around you, Virgil," Rikka said. "What colors do you see?"

"Just the regular ones," he replied. "Greens, brown, yellow, red. Those."

"It's *nighttime*," Rikka said gently. "How do things *smell*?"

It hit him, then, and his world expanded. He could hear the faint sound of his deputies' patrol car, several miles and a couple of ridges away. Nightcalls of birds and beasts drifted on the breeze, along with scents from every level of every little life and death. The dusky iron odor of blood ran strongly through it all. And Rikka.

Both of them smelled the same now, the way the sheets on his bed smelled when Rikka and he'd made love.

"Welcome to the club, Virgil," Rikka said.

He swallowed, his mind struggling to take in what had happened to him. Seeking the familiar, he looked down at the dead hitman. "Well, things seemed to have worked out."

Rikka looked thoughtful, her expression bemused. "Yeah, I guess they did, didn't they? No fault of my own, though."

She didn't speak for nearly thirty seconds, and when she did, her voice was very soft and she didn't look at him. "When he said you were dead, Virgil, I just went all hollow inside." She hugged herself and shivered. "I didn't care if I lived or died, so long as I took him with me. I practically *let* him shoot me." She spat out the final words in disgust.

Then she turned toward him, her cheeks wet with tears, and her arms out. "I've never been happier in my life," she sobbed.

They held each other for a long, perfect, intoxicating minute. Merrill stroked her hair, whispering into it. "He did think I was dead, you know, thought I'd coronary from the drug he shot me with."

"Don't talk," she murmured. "Just hold me. We don't have long. Your people will be here in a few minutes, and you need to get Doctor Cameron."

"Don't remind me," he said, chuckling. "We've about used poor Fred up this last month."

"I've got a cure for that," Rikka replied.

"You *are* catching."

"And you caught me."

"Any way you look at it, yeah, I guess I did." Merrill pulled back slightly, and looked at her, brushing the drying tears off her face. "After all this is taken care of, first thing Monday morning," he said, "you and I are going to be in the Portland office of a gentleman of the law named Alexander Carson."

Her gaze kindled slightly, and he saw a lesser version of the look he'd seen in Ole Thorsen's hospital room. "Why?" she asked.

269

He indicated the body of the late hitman. "Well, whoever this guy is, Carson sent him."

"Really?"

Merrill nodded. "That's what he said. When he thought I was a goner."

Rikka's smile turned predatory, and that dangerous look deepened. "That'll be *nice*," she said, and kissed him.

He doubted Carson would think so.

EIGHTY-FOUR

Robert McDaniel clearly had a fine and ironic sense of humor, thought Alexander Carson, as he examined the business card his receptionist had just brought him. He leaned back in his chair and laughed, a warm, pear-shaped sound suitable for both the courtroom and private gatherings with friends.

Carson was quite fond of his laugh. It suited him and served him well. The card read:

Virgil Merrill
Sheriff
Eastern Ross County

The sheriff, of course, was quite dead, Carson was certain. McDaniel was merely having his little joke. It would be a pleasure to meet McDaniel face-to-face. He punched a button on his intercom and instructed the receptionist to show his visitor in.

Years in the courtroom kept Carson from showing his surprise when confronted with the two people who walked into his office.

Merrill!

The *creature*.

"A pleasure to meet you, Sheriff," Carson said, rising to his feet and extending his hand. Only resting his thighs against his desk stopped the lawyer's knees from buckling. "I've seen you on the news, of course. Terrible things happening in your jurisdiction. Terrible things. So sad." Keeping his expression inquisitive, Carson smiled at Sims' monster, seeing her smooth, dark, vibrant features and expensive maroon silk blouse and tan slacks. And thanking his lucky stars that Sims was dead, that this implacable *thing* could not know of his connection to her.

"My associate, Rikka Thorsen," Merrill said, gesturing at the creature.

"Delighted," Carson replied, gingerly shaking her hand. Reckon's answering smile didn't begin to reach her eyes, and Carson shuddered inwardly. With considerable effort, he managed to go on. "Please, please, be seated. How can I help you today? Would you like some coffee?"

The two sat down. "No, thanks," the sheriff said, in the slow, laconic, *official* voice Carson remembered from the television. "We can only stay a few minutes. Don't want to impose too much on your time. You must be a busy man."

Carson shook his head at his own lack of time. "All too true, I'm afraid."

"Well," Merrill continued, leaning back in his chair and crossing his knees, "a young fellow named Robert McDaniel tried to kill me at my home the other night. Nearly succeeded. Then tried again, or almost tried." He smiled at Thorsen. "Ms. Thorsen intervened -- quite terminally -- so we couldn't question him. He did, however, mention your name at my house, implied that you had paid him. Now, for the life of me, I couldn't think of any reason why a person like yourself -- a highly-respected member of the legal profession -- would want me dead, but I thought you should know about this strange allegation. Seemed only right."

Sims' creature's brown gaze never left Carson's face. A bead of cold sweat ran down his back, between his shoulder blades. He could not look at her. He spread his hands in puzzlement. "I just don't know, Sheriff. The name means nothing to me. Some poor, misguided individual, perhaps."

"A poor, misguided commodities trader, with an impressive military background," Merrill said, and Thorsen began to smile again.

"A professional killer, then?" Carson replied, elevating his right eyebrow a few degrees to indicate his surprise.

"Yupp. Not so very unlike the demolitons expert who was keepin' company with those environmental activists who got themselves tragically murdered the weekend before last. Seems to be a lot of nastily-skilled people turnin' up in our neck of the woods lately." The sheriff smiled. "'Course, *they* keep turnin' up dead, too."

In a setting less constricting than television, Carson saw that the man possessed an element of the actor, James Garner. Somehow that made him more uneasy, as though Merrill knew something. He *did*, of course, but Carson was quite certain that, had the man been positive Carson was involved in an attempted homicide, this meeting would not have been so amicable, and would have involved a formal hearing.

"So, how may I help?" Carson asked the sheriff in the most sincere tones he could manage with Reckon regarding him the way a lion would appraise a zebra.

"You know," Merrill replied, "I'm not just real sure, Mr. Carson. Maybe if you had something like Nixon's list of enemies for me to look at. Someone seems to be out to get you, and I don't really think it was Robert McDaniel. Why don't we just leave it that you'll get in touch with me if anything comes to you?" The sheriff smiled a folksy, rural smile. "Oh, and try to stay healthy."

Carson knew his answering laugh sounded too hearty, but didn't have a better response. He understood perfectly now where Kathleen Merrill had acquired her formidable personality, that this

273

surprisingly youthful-looking man was disarmingly dangerous in a manner in which his daughter never would be.

He also wondered if the sheriff knew just what sat next to him, but quickly decided that question bore no serious scrutiny. No answer could be less than troubling.

"Certainly, Sheriff," Carson said, "and a rousing affirmative on both levels. I will let you know if I think of anything helpful, and shall endeavor to stay healthy."

When they'd departed, however, Carson felt anything but healthy. His only consolation was that Reckon was gone. Even so, her final smile and the almost hungry look in her eyes when she walked through the outer doors had shaken him to the very core of his being. Now, he wanted nothing so much as a snifter filled with brandy.

That would have to wait, however. First, he had a phone call to make.

When the phone picked up at the other end, Carson said, "Hello, Richard? We have a problem."

EIGHTY-FIVE

"Did you really have to look at Carson like you wanted to kill him?" Merrill asked, watching the front of the law office building as Rikka drove up out of the underground parking structure.

"I *did* want to kill him," Rikka replied, angling out into traffic, heading for I-5 South. "He tried to have *you* killed."

The sheriff laughed as he adjusted his seat belt. "True, but that's no reason to scare the poor man half to death. He's probably up there right now, changin' his shorts."

Rikka glanced away from traffic for a second, smiling at him. "He's lucky I didn't give him a terminal wedgie," she said. Unmentioned was the death of Maureen Sims. Virgil didn't know about her, so Rikka couldn't bring it up.

"I only wanted to poke a stick in his anthill, see which way he jumped," the sheriff continued. "He's smart enough to know that if I had anything on him, he'd be in custody. We'll see if he's smart enough to figure out what I'm tryin' to do. Just now, he's probably not thinking too well at all, you scared him so bad."

"You smelled his fear?" Rikka asked, slanting across two lanes, entering the on-ramp for the Baldock Freeway. She cut off an ecru-colored Volvo 740 wagon filled with middle-aged men in bright golf outfits. The driver honked his horn at her, and she swerved at him, glaring. He didn't honk again.

"Oh, yeah. This nose thing of yours is a nice talent," the sheriff said, ignoring Rikka's exchange with the Volvo.

"I swear I didn't know it was transmissible, Virgil. Not that it would have made any difference if I had. I still needed you."

"You saved my life. McDaniel's concoction would have killed me."

"Then we're even."

"I suppose," Merrill said, looking out at the traffic through the Terwilliger Curves, as Rikka swept around a trio of BMWs at seventy miles an hour. "One of these days, you're going to have to tell me all about just what it is that's runnin' around in my body doin' all this fine-tuning. And why Carson seemed to know more about you than I do."

"I don't know how much he knows. We'd never met. But I will tell you what I can when this is over." She frowned. "I don't know that much."

"At what point is this going to be over?"

"When they're all dead," Rikka answered grimly, running up the rear of a Chrysler mini-van that had no business whatsoever in the fast lane.

Merrill watched the van scoot out of their way. "You seem to have a one-track mind with these people."

"As I told you that first night, I'm very direct."

"You drive well, too," the sheriff observed, as Rikka sent a Mercedes diesel scurrying into the middle lane.

"I love you."

"Oh, shit."

EIGHTY-SIX

Even in the late nineties, people in Oregon didn't look twice at any logging truck. Ole Thorsen counted on that invisibility as he worked his way through early evening traffic on McLoughlin Boulevard, Highway 99 East, just north of Oregon City.

The Kenworth, with its logging trailer stoutly chained on its chassis, seemed a bit nose-heavy from Ragnar's device. With a total weight in excess of twelve ton, however, and nearly five hundred turbo-diesel horsepower under its hood, the effect was negligible. The big truck thrummed happily along, heading into east Portland.

In less than an hour, Ole would be in position, at a building site just north of Stark and west of Thirty-ninth.

Then he would wait his chance.

He fingered the small silver hammer hanging from a chain around his neck.

Thor watch over me, he prayed.

EIGHTY-SEVEN

His carefully-ordered world, filled with power and satisfaction, had fallen down around Dick Edmiston's ears in less than two weeks time.

And that overweight fucktard, Alex Carson, was responsible. First his precious eco-avenger had run amok, slaughtering Edmiston's followers, and then the hitman Carson hired to take out the woman had instead been killed himself.

Worse yet, the hitman -- before he died -- had mentioned Carson's name to the local sheriff, and now the sheriff was alerted. Edmiston had a known connection to both the young monkey-wrenchers and to Carson.

The authorities, who'd already questioned Edmiston at some length, would return with harder questions.

Maybe even that damned red-haired sheriff, who'd linked up with Carson's pet monster.

Edmiston carefully folded a second pair of hiking shorts into his L. L. Bean nylon suitcase. No matter how he looked at it, it was time to get out of Dodge for a while.

Even more irritating, on his second trip out to his car, some idiot at the condominiums going up down the street had started up a big diesel generator or some other noisy goddamn thing. Edmiston briefly thought about phoning the authorities -- construction equipment within the city limits had to be shut down well before dark in residential areas. But what the hell. In just over an hour, he'd be safely up at his cabin in Zig-Zag on the flanks of Mount Hood, far away from Portland and its urban racket.

He whistled to himself as he walked down the steps through the stone wall which banked his raised front yard. As he set the suitcase in the trunk and closed the lid, the damned diesel down the street revved a couple of times, and he thought he heard the whine of a turbo.

The condo's street T-ed into his, and every once in a while during icy weather, some klutz would lose control of his car trying to make the corner, jump the curb, and slam into Edmiston's wall.

Jesus, that fucking machine was only getting louder and louder! As he went around his car to the driver's side, Edmiston looked off toward the construction site in disgust. Some people just had no respect for others. He had half a notion to go down there and tell the guy off.

Then, as he opened the car door to get in, the noise grew even stronger, filling the night. He turned to look at the source of the thundering sound. Headlights flashed on, almost blinding him, and he realized that the thing was a *truck* of some kind. He held his arms up, shielding his face.

Ponderous sounds of movement, big tires chirping on pavement.

Rumbling *toward* him.

Faster.

God-

EIGHTY-EIGHT

The newspapers never knew just how to refer to Portland Police Chief of Homicide Karl Elch. Sometimes it was Afro-American, sometimes it was Germano-American, and lately it had been Afro-Germano-American. That last rather appealed to the tall, saturnine Elch. His mother had been an Air Force sergeant's daughter in Germany when she met his father, a *Bundesgrenzschutz Leutnant*, back in the late fifties. Elch had ended up with dark blond curly hair, freckles set in a light mahogany complexion, hazel eyes, a prominent nose and a fine sense of irony. Local political cartoonists had a hey-day with his strong features.

Just now, he found it ironic that several newspaper reporters were barfing their dinners up at one of the more interesting death scenes in Portland this year. He couldn't quite decide, though, whether it was a hit-and-run accident or a homicide.

Whatever it was, all the blood contained in one human body had been involved. That, and what lay between a four-foot-high heavy steel panel and a badly-compressed grey Nissan Sentra.

Apparently the mortal remains of a gentleman named Richard Edmiston, if the Nissan's plate was to be believed. Edmiston's house fronted the street, he wasn't home, and Elch would bet the hiking-booted pulped corpse was Edmiston.

The only thing that held the body's pelvis together were a pair of six-pocket hiking shorts. There seemed to be a blood-soaked bulge in those shorts that probably contained identification. They would find out shortly.

In the meantime, Elch sauntered around the site while his people bustled through their jobs, taking photographs, setting up lighting, and answering and asking questions of curious neighbors. He shook his head. Ten o'clock at night, and there were rubber-necking people all over the place. His one consolation was the absence of television crews. So far.

He squatted down on one knee and examined the huge metal plate, which must weigh a good half-ton. At one edge, next to a large hole which must have been a mounting point on whatever sort of vehicle was involved, Elch saw a small T-shaped welding bead. He took a penlight from his shirt pocket and shone it on the bead.

It looked familiar. Then he remembered his Teutonic father had a tattoo on his left shoulder shaped exactly the same.

Mjolnir. The Hammer of Thor.

Elch smiled at the thought.

How far out could one get?

EIGHTY-NINE

Had Alexander Carson been one to utilize pharmaceuticals, Valium would have been a good answer on this particular day. And yesterday -- Wednesday -- had been even worse. If he hadn't been required to be in state court this morning, he'd be home in his favorite leather chair, with a good book and a glass of something strong.

Things probably wouldn't get better any time soon, either. Karl Elch -- who Carson thought of as mildly adversarial to environmental needs -- had sent two detectives to Carson's office yesterday. The two, a woman and a man, Deakins and Wismer, had been polite and deferential, but hardly shied away from the difficult aspects of Carson's relationship with the gruesomely-deceased Edmiston.

Poor Richard, Carson thought, as he walked down a courthouse hallway. Edmiston and his followers wiped off the face of the earth. There were no doubts in his mind that person or persons unknown had, with malice aforethought, reduced Edmiston to shards of bone and gobbets of flesh wrapped in torn remnants of clothing. He could hardly tell the police that, however. So today, with good reason, Carson admitted to being a bit paranoid.

Sims might be gone, but the monster was still alive, and Carson had no way of knowing how much she knew or had discovered. In addition, many of his friends and colleagues in the courthouse seemed overcome with shyness today, avoiding Carson like a pariah. So, for the time being, he was starting at shadows.

At least he hadn't run across Kathleen Merrill, though she likely was somewhere in the building.

This was, after all, one of the places where she usually worked.

Even as he had that thought, he saw a familiar-looking back walking ahead of him in the hall; a tall, graceful woman, expensively-dressed, carrying a briefcase. Not Merrill, not red-haired. This woman had short, light brown hair, but still looked hauntingly familiar. Then she was gone, around a corner.

Suddenly Carson felt the urge to relieve himself. He ducked into the second floor men's room -- one likely to be uncrowded at mid-morning -- and walked to the far end of the urinal row. Taking care not to splash his highly-polished brown oxfords, he slowly relieved himself, feeling tension drain away as he did so.

Someone came into the lavatory during the process, and Carson heard running water from the line of wash basins. After zipping up, and flushing the urinal, he started toward the door, then stopped when he saw a woman bent over a sink.

The woman from the hallway.

"Excuse me, Ms.," he said, "but this is the Mens."

"I know, Alex," the woman replied, turning to him as she straightened up.

Carson couldn't believe his eyes. His frayed nerves nearly snapped. "Doctor Sims! I thought...I mean, you look ...so different!"

Sims smiled. "You mean so different, as in 'still alive,' right? Well, I am, and I've ensured that we'll have plenty of time to problem-solve this issue." She gestured at the lavatory door, and Carson saw a matte-black device clamped around the handle and the frame, effectively locking the door.

Her smile widened, entirely too reminiscent of Reckon's. She looked leaner than before, more muscular, not at all the angular, slightly stooped figure she'd seemed in her laboratory. And where

283

were her glasses? "So you got nervous, counselor, when Reckon began killing the children of wealth? Decided your tracks *might* be visible, sent someone after me, then my lab, then Reckon. But, of course, you couldn't tell your hireling everything about her, so he didn't take enough precautions, and failed."

"Not at all!" Carson blustered, shaking his head. "I would *never* do anything like that, Doctor." She was smaller than he. He could overpower her, release that lock, get out into the hall, escape.

"Save the bullshit for the courtroom, Alex!" Sims scoffed. "He shot me *three times*! I fell *eight storeys*, and it *hurt like hell*! You *prick*."

Stepping forward, Carson seized Sims' left wrist. He'd *force* her to open the damned door. It was like grabbing an oak limb. She held him off easily, and began to laugh.

"Oh, Alex, you *fool*!" She reached over with her right hand and gripped his forearm.

Fire exploded in his arm, as though a red-hot poker had been wedged between the bones. Falling to his knees on the tile floor, Carson began to keen shrilly, clutching at his crushed, ruined limb.

Sims slapped him twice, loud resounding blows, snapping his head first one way, then the other. "Shut up! For God's sake, you sound like something from 'Deliverance.'" Then she leaned back against the counter and opened her briefcase.

Watching her through his pain, sweat running into his eyes, Carson saw her bring out a knife with a long, wicked-looking blade. Her pale green eyes glittered with pleasure as she looked down at him.

"You didn't think *Reckon* was the *only* one, did you, Alex?" she purred.

NINETY

When the sheriff got home on Thursday evening, the smell of furniture polish permeated the entire house.

Rikka had dusted. She'd been threatening to, even before they'd met the late Robert McDaniel.

Merrill prided himself on being organized and tidy. Throughout the house, he kept everything neatly in its place, folded and tucked, all cupboards closed, and toilets spotless. Rikka, however, had surveyed the place some time back, and declared it "not really clean, just straightened up." He'd bowed to the inevitable, and here it was.

He could hear the shower from the bedroom end of the house, and Kitaro on the CD player.

Smiling to himself, he laid his briefcase and today's *Oregonian* on the dining room table, then went into the kitchen. He briefly examined the large pot simmering on the stove, lifting up the lid and sampling the contents. Vegetables and small chunks of lamb. Rikka food.

He'd reached the bedroom and removed his shoes, uniform pants and shirt, and was pulling on his sweatpants, when Rikka called from the shower.

"Do my back, will you?"

"Sure, if you'll do mine." He walked into the bathroom.

"Deal." Her hand and forearm beckoned over the top of the shower door, through the steam.

Sometime later, clean, dressed, and fed, they sat on teak chaise lounges out on the back deck, sipping beers.

"Have you seen the paper today?" he asked.

"No, haven't had time," Rikka replied. She lay stretched out, her eyes half-open, watching a hawk glide lazily through the thermals high overhead.

"Looks like we've pretty much run out of people to coerce, cajole, and browbeat. First Edmiston, then some energetic soul ambushed your friend Carson in one of the bathrooms at the Multnomah County Courthouse yesterday morning. Cut him into smallish pieces."

Swinging her long legs off the lounge, Rikka spun to face him, elbows resting on her knees. Her brown gaze was very solemn. "Then they're all dead. Maybe this would be a good time to have a talk, Virgil. It might be that I'm not exactly what you think I am."

"Maybe." He turned toward her, lying on his left side. "But I wiped your handprint off that support post in the larger Hampson cabin, after you slid across the floor. If the state forensics lab had run that through the Portland police, they would have found your juvenile record."

Her eyes widened in surprise, then narrowed. "How'd you know?"

"I should've figured it out earlier. Had enough info. Just couldn't quite accept that a woman could be *that* strong, *that* deadly." He grinned. "And your feminine wiles distracted me, even though you kept *saying* you would kill them all. I guess I just couldn't accept it. Carvel Hunnecker pushed it all into place when I talked to the state cops after I got to the cabins. I knew you'd been out that night, and it didn't take me too long to realize that Morberg had somebody after him. Somebody he'd shot at, somebody who broke out the two porch lights with a pair of shoes. When the cops said Hunnecker's Blazer had been a hundred feet from the burning Toyota when they arrived, that an unknown woman had called in the report, and that Hunnecker had told them a dead woman pulled him to safety, it wasn't overly difficult. They disregarded it. I didn't."

The sheriff levered himself upright, and picked up his beer. "I'm in a bit of a quandary here, bein' an officer of the law and all. Suppose you tell me what you know about yourself and your time here in North Cedar."

So she did. At length.

When she'd finished, Merrill regarded her in silence for nearly a minute. Finally he said, "A decent lawyer could make a case for an powerful implanted compulsion, which you definitely have. Also, any number of experts in human physiology would be willing to testify that no one could physically do what you did -- what you *do*. Hell, Fred Cameron told me that much. On that basis alone, it'd be laughed out of court. Any confession you'd made would be disallowed. And everybody involved in making you what you really are is dead."

Rikka shook her head. "McDaniel *told* me Doctor Sims was dead. That's what I repeated to you. And I got an e-mail message on my computer that gave me the impression she *might* be. But she isn't. She sent me another e-mail today. Her research facility was insured, and all her records were backed up on her home computer. She would certainly have to testify against me..."

"As a hostile witness," he put in.

"...but she had to have known what Carson intended. She implanted all the data. The compulsion, or programming, or whatever it is."

Merrill thought about that. "Okay, maybe we could prove your physical abilities -- particularly if there were demonstrations -- but the compulsion defense would still be valid. In the absence of Carson, Sims could merely say that she didn't think you would go *that* far, didn't expect you to *kill* anyone."

"So I'd still get off?"

"Well, there'd have to be a prolonged period of psychological evaluation, but, yeah, I think you would. Not much sense spending taxpayer dollars for that, in my estimation." Merrill grinned at her. "And I never much liked the way the *Maltese Falcon* ended." He shifted his beer to his left hand, put his arm around her and stared off down over the lights of North Cedar. "What's this all mean for us, Rikka? That we live forever?" he said softly. In his mind's eye, he saw Deb's face. If she'd had five more years...but she hadn't, and even if she had, then Rikka Thorsen would never have been able to give him this unintentional gift. They wouldn't have slept together.

"Yes, maybe, if I've got it figured out. We *can* be killed, but I'm living proof it isn't easy."

"Jesus. How much younger am I gonna get, I wonder?"

"Good question. Probably to the appearance of a healthy thirty-something. Just a guess, but your hair's already growing in mostly red."

He ran his right hand over his crewcut, then draped his arm back over her shoulders and sighed. "So, what do we do next?"

Leaning over to him, she kissed his right cheek. "I might suggest we move indoors."

Merrill laughed and stood, pulling her up with him. "Good idea," he said, and returned her kiss.

Laughing, arm-in-arm, they went into the house.

Together.

Acknowledgments

Words: John H. Quiner, Sr. Mary Thaddeus SJM, Michael Contris, Steve Perry, Keith Tittle, and the Lucky Lab Rats Writers' Group.

Faithful Reader: Sandra Hazard

This book is a product of the Oregon timber industry in nearly all ways, the years of working in the mills to pay for school, the education the timber workers gave me whether they realized it or not, and the implosion of the industry in the past few decades. The story of this implosion is not a happy one, thousands of workers out of jobs, families forced to re-locate, family-owned and larger mills dependent upon Federal timber closed, small communities struggling to survive and not able to do even that very well, and the elderly and poor who live in those places, simply stuck. While the timber industry brought some of this travail upon themselves, much of the blame rests on the short-sighted and narrow-minded policies of those who manage our public lands and the elite 'environmental interests' they seem beholden to for reasons having little to do with common sense or the common good. While this book doesn't really debate these issues, some of the minority groups and their stage managers who dictate extremist policies do have those issues redressed in final ways, despite their best or worst intentions. Bags of fun for the aged author.

D.J. Bershaw

www.ingramcontent.com/pod-product-compliance
Lightning Source LLC
Chambersburg PA
CBHW032209190626
46810CB00019B/2327

9 780998 679655